WAKING

THE

WITCH

Books by Rachel Burge

The Twisted Tree
The Crooked Mask

Waking the Witch

WAKING
THE
WITCH

Rachel Burge

HOT
KEY
BOOKS

First published in Great Britain in 2022 by
HOT KEY BOOKS
4th Floor, Victoria House
Bloomsbury Square
London WC1B 4DA
Owned by Bonnier Books
Sveavägen 56, Stockholm, Sweden
www.hotkeybooks.com

A CIP catalogue record for this book is available from the British Library.

ISBN: 978-1-4714-1108-3
Also available as an ebook and in audio

1

This book is typeset using Atomik ePublisher
Printed and bound in Great Britain by Clays Ltd, Elcograf S.p.A.

Hot Key Books is an imprint of Bonnier Books UK
www.bonnierbooks.co.uk

For my mum, Leoni

1

I love it when a butterfly emerges from its chrysalis and unfurls its tiny, shrivelled wings. It's freeing – the idea that whatever your problems, you can transcend them: wake up one day and find that you've changed into a different creature, grown wings and can fly away. Everyone gets excited about the miracle of nature, the power of transformation. At the same time, no one asks what the caterpillar had to sacrifice to achieve those wings. But then everyone loves the Disney version, don't they? We all want to see the ugly grub become a thing of beauty. We all want the fairy tale.

In the real world, orphans go unadopted and little girls who are abandoned by their mothers are raised by wolves, only to be eaten by them. But no one wants to hear that. People aren't interested in the cruel and messy truth, so I don't tell them about me – the same way I don't tell them what really happens to the caterpillar.

It's Friday morning and I'm sitting on the specimen room floor at work, wedged between two cardboard boxes (there's at least one advantage to being small), and hoping my jerk of a boss doesn't find me. Before me is a row of wooden display cases containing various chrysalides, and in my hand is my phone. I glare at it, as if that might somehow shame it into ringing. It doesn't. Eventually the screen dims and somewhere in my heart a light goes out.

Lifting the locket from my neck, I open the tiny, hinged door and take out the slip of folded paper as I've done a thousand times before.

I'm so sorry. I tried to keep you safe, but I see now that I can't. They won't stop until they have you, but I can't let that happen. Be strong, little one, trust no one, and know that

Like me, the scribbled note was abandoned, a half-finished story containing more questions than answers. I stare at the words until they become as blurred and indecipherable as their meaning. Who was my mother keeping me safe from? What was bad enough to make her dump her baby at a motorway service station? I'm named after the cleaner who found me – Ivy. But what name did my mum give me? Where were the rest of my family? I have so many questions, but it always comes down to a single word beating inside me like a second heart. *Why?*

I fold the paper back inside and then tuck the brass locket into my shirt, my fingers briefly tracing the raised butterfly design. I guess it's fitting that I ended up working at a butterfly zoo, but then I've always loved the tiny creatures. The locket is all I have of my mum, so to me butterflies are an emblem of hope, a sign that one day I'll find her.

And now maybe I have.

I've spent years posting on missing person sites asking for

information, and last week someone actually replied. The man said he was looking for his brother when he came across my photo – he has a memory for faces and I looked like a woman he'd met on holiday once. She lived at the lighthouse on Bardsey Island, off the west coast of Wales, and he saw her go to the mainland with her baby and then come back alone. He seemed so certain and the dates checked out, and somehow I just have this feeling.

Getting to Bardsey isn't easy – a bus, two trains and a boat crossing – so I decided to send her a letter with my number. That was seven days ago. From what I've read online the island is tiny and barely populated so it's not going to have the best postal service, but even if she's moved surely *someone* would have received it. I fiddle with the silver stud in my nose and sigh. One thing's for certain, I can't stay in here. My boss will notice I'm missing and I'm the only assistant in work as Tom is late again, which means I have to give this morning's talk.

I crawl out from my hiding place then wrap my arms around a display case which is almost as big as me. There are plenty of smaller ones, but I haven't done three years of martial arts training to take the easy option. With a grunt of exertion, I lift the case and shove the door open with my foot. I love my job – I enjoy seeing the customers' excited faces when a butterfly lands on them and I like teaching them about the different species we have at the centre. I just need to pretend it's an ordinary day at work. You know, forget that my entire life could be about to change with a single phone call.

As I enter the glass butterfly house, I'm greeted by the familiar sound of wet hissing from the vents, a constant tic-tic and fizzling hum of artificial jungle. It's always warm and humid, but the air feels stifling today. Beneath the scent of nectar is a cloying smell of overripe fruit and rotting vegetation and something I can't quite place: a stench of decay that doesn't belong here. It sits on my lungs and makes it hard to breathe.

Tightening my grip on the case, I head to the display area on the far side of the room. October half-term is one of our busiest times and the walkways are full of visitors. They wander amongst the glossy-leaved plants and tropical orange flowers, pausing every now and then to point at a flash of colour flitting about their heads. In other words, not looking where they're going.

'Excuse me, coming through!' I can't see around the case, so I have to shout and hope that people move out of the way.

'You've got your hands full there, Ivy. Can't you get young Tom to help?'

'Hey, Dot. How are you?' I recognise her voice and slow down to let her catch up.

It's mostly families that visit, but in winter we get older people who come for the free heating. Dot is one of my favourites. She wears an immaculate red wig with matching lipstick and hates wearing ugly shoes, but they help with her bunions. She usually brings a romance novel and will read it while eating pick 'n' mix. I once made the mistake of accepting a jelly baby and then had to listen as she spent ten minutes describing a sex scene in alarming detail.

She ambles alongside me and whispers, 'Shame to let a strapping lad like that go to waste. He's a handsome specimen. If I was fifty years younger, I'd rip his clothes off and –'

'Yeah, thanks, Dot. I'll keep it in mind.'

The truth is that Tom would be more than happy to help me, but I don't intend to give him the satisfaction. We're the same age and started working here around the same time, about ten months ago, and we have this rivalry thing going on. Some days I think he only comes into work to wind me up. Besides, I make it a rule never to accept anyone's help.

Dot lays an affectionate hand on my arm. 'You're too proud by half. You want to snap him up before someone else does.'

She hobbles off, presumably heading to her usual bench, and a huff escapes me. Tom's a good laugh, but that's as far as it goes.

When I get to the display table, I set down the case and then wipe my hands on my trousers. Sensing someone behind me I spin around, but there's nobody there. Damn my stupid boss, always loitering and making me feel uncomfortable – it's no wonder I'm paranoid. After checking he's not around, I peek at my phone. Mobiles are strictly forbidden at work so I've set it to silent. I don't want to get fired – I'm already on my second warning – but I have to answer if she calls. Not that I need worry: the screen is blank.

Nearly ten o'clock: time to start. I stand on tiptoes and raise my voice. 'Hello, if I could have your attention, please? The talk will begin soon if anyone would like to join me.' A couple glance over but keep walking. Maybe it's my appearance – pastel pink bobbed hair, blunt micro fringe and nose stud – but people often seem surprised that I work here, even in my uniform. Or maybe seventeen-year-old girls are just easy to overlook.

I make my announcement again, louder this time, and a

bearded man in a dirty anorak shuffles over, followed by a family, then two guys holding hands and a woman and her moody pre-teen daughter who come every few weeks. The woman wears her hair in a scraped-back ponytail and lives in leopard-print jumpsuits, which means I spend more time than I should wondering how she pees. We've chatted a few times, and now she waves and gives me a friendly smile. The girl sees me and rolls her eyes, seemingly convinced that Wye Valley Butterfly Zoo is lame and nothing I can say will change her mind.

I feel her pain – the border between England and Wales is blessed with amazing views (if you like hills and sheep) but isn't exactly known for its entertainment options, and the poor thing must have heard my talk a dozen times. Her mum tries to hug her, but the girl shoves her off and takes out her phone. The casual indifference of the gesture cuts a hole in my chest and jealousy reaches in and squeezes my heart, quickly followed by resentment. Between them, they have a mighty strong grip.

Get it together, Ivy. Focus on work.

I avert my eyes, uncomfortable with my own feelings, and bring my attention to the dozen people who've gathered to hear my talk. The man in the anorak stares at me, his facial muscles rigid as if they've been frozen into place. I wait for him to say something, or at least blink, but he doesn't. We get some odd characters at the centre; dealing with them is part of the job. Even so, I can't help feeling a little unnerved. He strokes his beard, repeating the movement robotically, and I wonder if he has a nervous tic or anxiety. I smile reassuringly at him, then thank the group for their patience and scan the walkways for latecomers.

A family enters through the hanging plastic strips that cover the entrance and something occurs to me. I included both my work and home addresses in the letter, so my mum might turn up here.

No. It's so far to come; surely she'd ring me first. I don't care how hard it is to get to Bardsey. If she doesn't call by the end of the day, I'll phone in sick and go to the island tomorrow. I *have* to know if it's her.

A loud gasp brings me back to reality. People are pointing and staring at a spot above my head.

'What the hell are *they*?' asks jumpsuit woman. I glance up and fluttering over me are three huge grey moths – *acherontia atropos*, to be precise. These ones are adults of the species, each with a twelve-centimetre wingspan.

'They're death's head hawkmoths,' I tell my audience. 'They get their name from the skull-shaped pattern that adorns their thorax.'

The sight of them makes me shiver, despite the heat. Not because they're an omen of death, but because there's something unnatural about the way they circle over me. Butterflies and moths usually fly haphazardly, going one way and then another, not around and around in a neat pattern. But this is like watching a few frames of film on repeat.

A high-pitched, pulsating screech fills the air and I raise my voice. 'They make that noise to scare away predators. It's particular to the species; not many moths do that.'

A few people in the crowd nod and look relieved, and then

the creatures flit towards a fern and the sound disappears as quickly as it started. Unable to pull my gaze away, I watch their strange flight with a growing sense of unease. I've never seen *anything* here fly like that.

2

Needing to get the group's attention, I clap my hands and turn up the wattage on my smile.

'Well, that was quite a display. Hello, everyone, my name is Ivy Jenkins and I'm an assistant here at the centre. As you may know, the female butterfly lays its eggs on plants, and these hatch into larvae called caterpillars. These voracious eaters spend their days consuming as much vegetation as they can and will shed their skin several times as they get bigger.' I point at the case. 'Once fully grown, the caterpillar forms a chrysalis.'

The man in the anorak hasn't looked away once. He stares at me with bulbous eyes but doesn't seem to actually see me. It's like his eyeballs have stopped working. A prickle of dread creeps over my skin and I hurry on with my talk. I'm halfway through explaining the process of metamorphosis when the moody girl interrupts. 'Ew, can't we just look at butterflies? I mean, that's why it's called a butterfly zoo, right?'

Pretending I haven't heard, I continue. 'They may look like cute little sleeping bags, but these chrysalides are actually made from the caterpillar's own skin. It sheds it one final time and remains inside while the metamorphosis takes place.' The group peers at the branch and I smile sweetly at the girl and whisper. 'You might think the caterpillar is resting inside, but it's actually busy dying. The enzymes it used to digest its food are now used to break down its body. It devours itself and from the leftover juices, the butterfly is born.'

The girl's face pales and a flush of satisfaction runs through me. The science is way more complicated than that, and the last bit is *not* in the approved script, but then why shouldn't she know the truth? Nature is like life – cruel to some. Refusing to look at Anorak Man, I ask if there are any questions and a small boy tugs my sleeve. 'Does it hurt?' he asks.

I start to answer, when one of the chrysalides sways and pulsates as the tiny creature inside wriggles and moves about. Who's to say the caterpillar didn't panic as it shed its skin and formed a prison from its own body? Maybe it had been aware of another being inside it trying to take control; perhaps it didn't want to die so that a new version of itself could be born. A while ago I mentioned this to a group of schoolkids and their heavily pregnant teacher complained afterwards, saying I'd upset them. Yet as far as I could tell, she was the only one who had cried. People are strange.

I smile at the boy and try to sound reassuring. 'No, of course not. Don't worry. They're just grub-like little things. They can't tell what's happening to them.'

The man in the anorak grunts and my body tenses, but then I notice his eyes are no longer staring and he's stopped touching his beard. His face is relaxed and he seems normal.

'I think you'll find that's putting the process rather simply, and they aren't grubs. They're larvae,' he says.

I feel my face redden but keep my smile in place, even when the girl shoots me a smug look as if she's caught me out. 'I didn't call them grubs. I said they were grub-*like*.' Remembering the customer is always right, I add, 'But thank you for pointing it out, sir. Both caterpillars and grubs are insect larvae, but they come from different families.'

A figure walks through the hanging strips of plastic and my heart sinks. My boss *would* have to turn up when I have a difficult customer. As usual, he's wearing shorts that are a size too small for him. I don't have anything against the vertically challenged – I'm one of them – but his tiny shorts only accentuate the fact that his hairy legs are disproportionately small for his body. To make it worse, he walks at twice the normal speed, like a mechanical toy that's been wound up too tight. Right now his face is bright red, telling me he's one angry outburst away from firing someone or having a heart attack. Possibly both.

Thankfully, Anorak Man doesn't push the grub issue so I carry on speaking. 'We have more than fifty species of butterflies and moths here at the centre. You'll have noticed that they have lots of different patterns on their wings. Butterflies have many predators, and their wings help to keep them alive. Some act as camouflage, making it harder for them to be seen. Others have brightly coloured wings that are designed to make them look poisonous and trick predators into leaving them alone.'

I glance up and see another figure walk through the door. This one is tall and well built and wearing shorts that fit. Tom. He flicks his floppy brown fringe from his eyes, a rueful smile on his face, and lopes along like he's just won a prize he can't be arsed to collect. Tom is Mr Neeson's nephew, which means he's safe from getting fired, unlike the rest of us, and he often saunters in late. With his crumpled uniform, he looks like he's just rolled out of bed. And he probably has. Tom is a gamer and often boasts about his latest weaponry haul to the other staff, so I imagine he stays up at night killing people. We all need a hobby, I guess.

As he walks by, he crosses his eyes and sticks out his tongue and I suppress a smile. Tom's favourite pastime at work is trying to put me off whenever I'm giving a talk to the public. Yesterday he left a plastic cockroach on top of the display case, which I calmly placed in my pocket before any of the visitors noticed. I'm surprised he didn't think to put one in my lunchbox, which he *still* hasn't given back after our little game of hiding things last week.

I got him back by filling his half-empty water bottle with salt. He took a gulp while giving a talk and nearly spat it out over everyone. The shock on his face made me laugh so hard I had to hide behind a banana-leaf palm and take calming breaths. Maybe Tom sent the guy in the anorak to freak me out? No. He's not that devious, or that smart.

Turning my attention to my audience, I invite people to ask any final questions. How many species do you have at the centre (more than fifty, you clearly weren't listening); can we buy a pet butterfly from the gift shop (no, you cannot); where are the toilets (just before the exit on the left). The group thank me and start to wander away, apart from Anorak Man.

'What qualifications do you have?'

I get this sometimes, and it's always men that ask. I step

back, determined to keep my cool yet feeling a little wary now it's just the two of us. I've no idea what triggered his odd behaviour before, and I don't want it to start again. 'I'm taking Biology and Life Science at A-level and I've got a place at the University of Worcester to study Ecology and Environmental Science next year. I make a point to learn about all the species we have here.'

He huffs as if unimpressed then glances at something behind me. I turn and see Tom, or rather his collarbone. Standing over a foot taller than me, he lowers his head and whispers, 'You look like you need rescuing, Shorty,' before straightening up and addressing the man. 'Is there something I can help you with, sir? I work with Ivy at the centre.'

I smile through gritted teeth and introduce him. 'This is Tom. He has zero interest or qualifications in zoology, but I'm sure he'll do a much better job of answering your questions as he has a penis.' I mutter the last part under my breath, but evidently not quietly enough as Tom's lips begin to quiver. Tom has a very distinctive laugh. It starts with a twitch of his lips and then builds to a full-on giggle that makes his face turn pink and his shoulders shake. It's the kind of laugh that keeps coming back. You think he's got it under control, but it starts again a few seconds later. I've seen him dive inside a giant fern, tears streaming down his face, trying to contain it. It's a ludicrous laugh really, but also weirdly compelling. When you've seen him giggle like that once, you want to see if he'll do it again.

I glare at him, remembering why I'm annoyed. What was he thinking, interrupting me like that? I don't need rescuing, and

I certainly don't appreciate him offering to 'help' a customer I'm already dealing with. Thankfully the man doesn't seem to have heard my remark and looks confused when Tom stifles a giggle. 'Ivy's right. She's far more qualified.' Barely able to contain his laughter, he strides off to find someplace private where he can explode.

I watch him go, annoyed at myself. Why didn't I just let Tom answer the man's questions? Now I'm stuck with him. Taking a deep breath, I turn to face him, but his broad back is already disappearing off down the walkway.

I blow out a sigh, but my relief doesn't last long. A hand squeezes my waist, startling me. My boss is right behind me. As always, it's reassuring to know he values and respects me highly, as he does all his female employees.

'I'm watching you, young lady.'

Don't I know it. I swear the man has tiny crosshairs stamped on the back of his eyes.

'I hope you're *behaving* yourself.'

I smile weakly. 'Of course, Mr Neeson.'

His eyes shine as he looks me up and down, taking an audit of my body. 'Hmm, that shirt is a little tight.' He says it with a faint smirk and I glance down at my uniform, which is loose-fitting and buttoned up to the neck. He starts to say something else, but I point to Dot on her bench. She has her head in a book and is sucking the legs off an unsuspecting jelly baby. 'The lady over there wanted my assistance earlier, so . . .'

He steps closer and I move back, bumping into the table. The last time he pushed up against me in the staffroom I *accidentally* tipped hot coffee over him, but he obviously hasn't got the message. I've dealt with worse than him before. Teenage girls are like butterflies: we have a lot of predators.

'Can you smell something?' I ask.

He grins and sniffs the collar of his polo shirt. 'Picking up my pheromones, are you?'

I turn my head away. 'I don't know – it smells rotten, like a dead animal.'

He frowns as if he can detect the weird smell in here too.

'Might be rats,' I say helpfully. 'It's the time of year when they come inside.'

His face turns redder. 'Why, have you seen one?' He spots Tom and hurries after him, his legs working overtime, presumably about to send him on a rat-finding mission. I smile at the thought, and then I get another waft. Whatever the horrible smell is, it's getting stronger.

My phone vibrates in my pocket, making my heart leap. I fumble with it and it drops to the floor. I should go somewhere private, but there isn't time. Cursing, I snatch it up and swipe to accept the call.

'Hello?'

A timid voice answers in a Welsh accent. 'Is that Ivy?'

I try to answer, but the words are too big for my throat and it takes me a moment to speak. 'Yes. Is that, are you my mo—?'

'Listen, there isn't much time. You're in danger.' She speaks in an urgent whisper then snatches a breath, her voice trembling. 'They can take control of anyone or anything, people you know or strangers. You won't know who they are, but they're coming for you.'

'What? Who are –?'

15

The man in the anorak has paused at the far end of the path, his head twisting to look over his shoulder at me and then forward again. He stares with lifeless eyes, his nostrils flared and his fleshy cheeks pale and clammy. He keeps on turning his head, repeating the motion as if he's stuck in a bizarre time glitch.

The woman gabbles down the phone. 'You shouldn't have put your work and home address in the letter. They're always watching me. Now I know where you are, they will too. Go somewhere else, anywhere, but whatever you do, stay away from the island. Their powers are strongest at the lighthouse. I'm sorry, but you have to run. Please, Ivy – run!'

She repeats the warning and I lower the phone, my heart pounding. Anorak Man starts walking, his eyes bloodshot and his forehead beading with sweat. He's coming straight for me.

3

I swallow hard, my mouth dry. Even if I run, I can't reach the exit or even the staffroom without going past him. Maybe I should shout for help. But then what am I going to tell people – I didn't like the way a customer looked at me without blinking? A family with young children appear at the end of the walkway, but no one pays the man any attention. But why would they? He's not moving his head back and forth now.

No one is out to get you, Ivy. Take it easy.

Forcing my shoulders to relax, I remind myself that I'm at work surrounded by people – perfectly safe. The guy's been acting oddly all morning. He obviously has some kind of problem, but that doesn't mean he wants to hurt me. He's probably just going to ask me a question or bore me with some random fact about grubs.

He's moving quickly, just twenty paces away. I slide my phone into my pocket and flash him my best customer-service smile.

'Hi, can I help you?'

He doesn't answer – just keeps heading towards me, his face fixed in a grimace. It has to be a coincidence. My mother couldn't have known about him.

My mother.

I should be jumping for joy that I've found her, but I don't know how to feel. The things she said were so strange. And then I remember the note. *I tried to keep you safe, but I see now that I can't.* I always presumed she was protecting me from someone in my family, or maybe she was unwell. Whether the threat was real or imagined, surely that's all in the past now.

Ten paces away. I try to read his expression, but there's no anger there. There's no emotion at all. His gaze is vacant; it's as if he's looking *through* me.

Six paces.

Why isn't he slowing down?

Three.

He lunges for me and my stomach clenches with sickening realisation. He's going for my throat. It happens so fast I barely have time to think. I block his hand with my right arm, the movement automatic, and then steady my weight on my back leg. He reaches for me again and this time I'm ready for him. He's big, maybe twice my weight, but I'm fast. I grab his wrist and twist sharply, tripping him with my front leg and using his weight to propel him forward. He lands on his knees with a thud, sprawling face down on the floor.

A toddler cries out in alarm and I glance up to see her mum grab her and shield her face. The woman looks at me, her eyes wide with shock, and I stare back. We're trained in first aid and what to do in case of fire and missing children, but the staff handbook didn't cover this. Before I can think what to say, my boss hurries over. He takes one look at the man at my feet and glares at me like I'm a poacher who's brought down a majestic beast.

'Ivy, unhand that man!'

Anorak Man whimpers. Realising I should probably let go, I release my grip and watch as he cradles his arm to his body. More visitors appear and the man blinks up at them, seemingly as confused as everyone else.

'Why would you . . . how dare you!' he blusters.

He looks embarrassed and more than a little outraged, but otherwise normal. And yet just a moment ago . . . If I hadn't witnessed it myself, I wouldn't believe it was the same person.

Mr Neeson heaves the guy to his feet, both men sweating and grunting from the exertion, and I watch in disbelief as my boss fusses over him. 'I'm so sorry, sir. Here, let me help you.' He *actually* apologises to him. Injustice throbs in my throat, but I know how this could go and there's no way I'm being dismissed as the hysterical girl in all this.

I speak loudly, my voice steady. 'Mr Neeson, this man attacked me.'

Anorak Man's cheeks wobble with indignant alarm. 'I did no such thing. There's been a mistake.'

My boss surveys the herd of bewildered mums then narrows his eyes at me. Surely he can't imagine this is my fault.

'Do you know this man?' he asks.

'No.'

'Why would he attack you?'

'I don't know.'

Mr Neeson addresses the onlookers. 'Did anyone see what happened?' A few people murmur but most watch in silence. I point to the mum who was staring wide-eyed at me just now, but she shakes her head.

'I only saw him on the ground. I didn't see what happened before that, sorry.'

Suddenly everyone is talking. My boss gestures for quiet, but several of the women raise their voices, outraged he's questioning my version of events. A pretty woman with an afro puts her arm around my shoulders and then the lady in the jumpsuit does the same on the other side. I smile at them and my heart softens with gratitude.

While my boss calms the crowd, I gently extricate myself from the women and take out my phone. I'm hoping my mum might have messaged or left a voicemail, but there's nothing. Mr Neeson grabs my wrist and hisses through clenched teeth, 'Put that thing away and tell me what the hell's going on here.'

Dot's voice warbles out. 'Someone needs to call the police! If you won't let the poor girl do it, then I will.' She winks at me then rummages in her handbag and I feel a surge of affection for her. Dot doesn't own a mobile; it came up during one of our chats once. She buried hers in the garden after the *Daily Mail* said they make your hair fall out.

Mr Neeson drops my wrist with a forced laugh that's as tight as his shorts. 'Oh, I don't think there's any need for that. I'm sure we can sort this out, can't we Ivy?' He glares as if daring me to say otherwise and I keep quiet, enjoying his discomfort. Having the police here isn't good for business, but it might not be good for me either. I don't want the man to be taken away; I need to find out why he tried to attack me. I nod and my boss lets out a breath. 'Good girl,' he says, rewarding me with a smug smile that makes me want to drop-kick him into next week.

A few seconds later he jumps up and waves his arm, seeming to spot someone along the path. 'Ah, just the man! Could you take this gentleman to the staffroom, please?'

Tom pushes his way through the crowd and my heart drops a notch. He's the last person I want to see right now. I brace myself for his look of glee and inevitable ridicule, but he takes in the scene with a worried frown.

'You OK, Ivy? What happened?'

I shake my head. I don't know how to explain any of this – to my boss, Tom, or even myself.

Mr Neeson snaps, 'Come along, Tom,' but he doesn't. He looks at me as if I'm the only person in the world. 'Someone said you'd been attacked?'

'I'm fine. He went for me, but I threw him.'

'You threw him?'

'I do karate. I'm OK, really. I just . . .' I glance at the dozens of people watching me and suddenly I want to get away. 'It's not me who needs to be answering questions. It's *him*.'

Tom follows my gaze and his brow wrinkles in surprise. But before he can say anything, my boss puts a protective arm around Anorak Man, evidently deciding to take him to the staffroom himself. 'Come on, I'll make us a nice cup of tea and we can sort this out.'

As he's steered away, Anorak Man throws me a look over his shoulder. 'I'm within my rights to press charges, you know,' he grumbles.

Mr Neeson chokes back a cough, his eyes watering like a toad that's swallowed a larger-than-expected fly. 'Everything's under control,' he calls to the spectators. 'Please enjoy your

21

day out.' Lowering his voice, he glares at me. 'You – stay here, understand?'

'Yes, Mr Neeson.'

I understand perfectly well. But am I going to stay put while the grown-ups talk? No, I am not. Once he's gone, I hug Dot and thank her and the others for their concern, then make my way to the staffroom. There has to be a reason why the man went for me. Maybe he's had episodes like this before; he might have some kind of condition. The woman's words – my *mother's* words – ring in my head, but I can't believe something made him try to hurt me.

As I walk to the staffroom, a trio of death's head hawkmoths flit around me. They're flying normally now, yet their movements were so strange earlier. No one seemed to notice, just like they didn't see the man attack me.

Tom catches me up. 'So, Karate Kid, you kept that quiet.' He walks by my side, mock-karate-chopping the air, and I roll my eyes. For a moment I thought he was actually concerned for me, but I should have known better. 'Hey, don't worry,' he whispers. 'You don't have to explain. I know exactly what happened back there and I don't blame you.'

I search his face, confusion and hope swirling inside me, and he grins. 'You can only keep up the fake smiles and customer service bullshit for so long. You had to snap one day.'

My shoulders drop and I let out a sigh. I know we're not exactly friends but I hoped he might be supportive. That's what you get for putting your faith in people: disappointment. I pick up my pace and he follows me, each of his long strides easily matching two of my own.

'I'm busy right now, Tom. Can I ignore you some other time?'

He laughs and flicks his fringe from his eyes. 'So are you going to tell me what happened or not?' I keep walking and he touches my arm, his voice serious. 'That weirdo didn't actually hurt you, did he?'

'No.'

'Good. I would offer to beat him up, but it seems you've got it covered. I'm amazed you managed to throw a guy that size, but hey, kudos to you. I like a woman who can take care of herself.'

The phrase triggers something in me and I stop and scowl at him. I want to tell him that I didn't learn martial arts the way that some girls take up yoga or gymnastics. For the past few years I've taken the bus into town after school and paid for lessons using the allowance my various foster families gave me, and then the wages from this job. I did it to keep myself safe. I *take care of myself* because I have to, because there's no one else to do it.

'Quit it with the Jackie Chan stare, would you? You're making me feel uncomfortable in the workplace.'

On any other day, I would ignore his feeble attempts at humour and remind myself that he doesn't know anything about me. He doesn't know that I've grown up in care – like the people at school and my martial arts class don't know, because I don't tell them. He doesn't have any idea of the things I've been through, what I've seen other kids in the system go through. Any other day, I would hold my head high and walk away – but not today.

'Get lost, Tom.'

A hurt look flashes into his eyes, but I don't have it in me to feel bad. I march along the walkway, brushing aside overhanging palms and the questions of overly inquisitive visitors as I go, then round the corner to the staffroom.

Mr Neeson sees me coming and darts inside. A few moments later he reappears in the doorway, partially blocking my view of Anorak Man, who is seated at the table behind him.

He holds out my coat and bag. 'You're fired.'

'What?'

'You know very well that using a mobile phone at work is a sackable offence. You're already on a written warning and if you check paragraph five of your employment contract, it states quite clearly that –'

'Some man attacks me, and I get fired for using my phone?'

Tom pushes in front of me. 'You can't sack someone after *one* written warning.'

My boss sniffs. 'You're forgetting the other little incident.'

I groan, realising what he's talking about. A few months ago I squeezed myself into a cupboard in the staffroom, intending to scare Tom by passing him the ketchup when he opened the door. Only it wasn't him who opened it. Mr Neeson was halfway through eating a jumbo sausage roll and was so shocked when I handed him the bottle of sauce that he started to choke. I regret bruising his ribs – but in my defence, I acted quickly and he was in no danger of dying, despite what he put in the disciplinary letter.

I mutter 'the choking thing' to Tom and he shakes his head.

'You gave her a written warning for that? It was an accident! Come on, you've got to be kidding, Uncle Mike.' He's never called him that before, and from the look on my boss's face I have the feeling he won't be doing it again.

Mr Neeson adjusts his shorts, his voice rising an octave. 'Well, I for one had hoped you'd learned a valuable lesson that day. These little pranks of yours have consequences. You need to take things more seriously. *Both* of you.'

Tom puts his hand on my shoulder, refusing to back down. 'Sack Ivy and I quit too.'

Mr Neeson laughs. 'We both know you'll be back by the end of the week. But fine, I accept your resignation.'

My shoulders drop and I stare at the floor. This job is one of the best things I have going for me. I've worked through most of the school holidays and nearly every weekend, and I've never once been late or taken a day off sick. I love seeing the wonder on children's faces when a butterfly lands on them. I like feeling I'm good at something, that I have knowledge worth sharing with people. I can get another job – I'm smart and I work hard – but I don't want to go anywhere else. I want to take care of the butterflies and moths and learn about the different species. My feelings must be written on my face, as Tom voices what I can't bring myself to say.

'Ivy is brilliant at this job and you know it. Please don't do this.'

Mr Neeson glances back at Anorak Man and clicks the door shut behind him. 'I don't have a choice. He's threatening to press charges.'

'But he attacked *me*.'

'So you say, but there are no witnesses.'

'What does he say happened then? Let me talk to him.' I try to push past and my boss draws himself up to his full height, all five foot five inches, which is still enough to tower over me. 'Please, Mr Neeson, I need to know why he –'

'No, Ivy. I'm not letting you in there. He says he came over to ask you a question. He touched your arm to get your attention and you overreacted.'

'That's not what happened.'

'No?' Mr Neeson gives me a knowing look. 'You teenage girls are all the same. A man only has to look at a bit of skirt these days and she's filing a complaint. Why anyone would teach karate moves to schoolgirls is beyond me.'

'Excuse me?'

He opens his mouth and I snatch my coat and bag from him, stamping hard on his foot as I do. Whatever offensive rubbish he was about to come out with is replaced by a yelp.

'You know what? Stick your stupid job.'

4

I barge through the exit doors and stomp into the car park. After the tropical heat of the glasshouse, the cold autumnal wind is like a slap to my face. It's not just rage making my cheeks burn, but shame. I've put up with my sleazy boss for months, and for what? So he could sack me at the first opportunity. I should have spoken up or done something before now.

'Hey, Ivy, wait!'

Tom calls out behind me and I spin around. 'What?'

He looks at me with an odd expression on his face – a mixture of expectation, bewilderment and hurt. I wait for him to say something else but he doesn't. He just stands there with his hands on his hips, his hair ruffled and blown by the wind.

'You're going? No goodbye or . . .'

So that's what this is about. He wants me to thank him, even though we both know it was an empty gesture. There's no way he could hold down a job anywhere else.

'*Thank you*. Is that better?'

'What? No.'

A gust of wind blows rain into my face and I drop my bag to pull on my coat when I hear a splash. My rucksack is lying in a dirty brown puddle, the once-cream canvas rapidly turning the same colour as the day I'm having.

Way to go, universe.

My shoulders slump and I think about retrieving the bag when Tom bounds over. He lifts it up, now dripping wet, and presents it to me with an exaggerated bow. 'My lady.'

I snatch it from him and his eyes fill with reproach. Why am I being so horrible? None of this is his fault, and he didn't have to take my side just now.

'I'm sorry, Tom. I'm just having a bad day.'

'Want to get a coffee and tell me about it?'

I shake my head and look away. I wouldn't know how to explain about my mum and everything, even if I tried. 'It was kind of you to stick up for me, but you may as well go back inside.'

He frowns at the glass exit doors. 'No. Uncle Mike's crossed a line this time. I've seen the way he leers at you and the girls in the café and gift shop. The guy's a creep. I'm embarrassed to be related to the cockwomble.'

We've moaned about Mr Neeson plenty of times – all the staff here do – but I've never heard Tom sound so resolutely angry before. Or use the word cockwomble. It makes me wonder how he'd react if he knew what our boss is really like; how it isn't just his eyes that wander.

Tom balls up his fists. 'If he wasn't my uncle, I'd . . .'

'You'd what?'

'Well, I'd do something.'

I open my mouth to tell him how reassuring that sounds, when he grips my shoulder. 'You want to know what I'd do if anyone tried to hurt you?' He searches my face and then whispers, 'I'd hold your coat for you while you beat them up.'

'Very funny.'

He kicks at the gravel. 'Seriously, though, Ivy, I'm done with this place. Besides, there's no point coming into work if you're not here to annoy.'

'Well, you *do* have a talent for it. And you of all people can't afford to waste talent.'

'Hey, I've got skills. I'm good at . . . um.' He scratches his head. 'Damn it, I nearly had something.' He sees my smile and grins. 'So what will you do now?'

I shrug, but I know exactly what I'm going to do. I'm going to wait for Anorak Man to come out. There must be a reason why he attacked me. And if he really believes nothing happened, I have to know if he's blacked out or forgotten things before. And while I'm waiting for him to appear, I'm going to phone my mother. I have to make sense of all this somehow.

The sky darkens and the rain begins to pelt down, pattering on the roof of the glasshouse like stones and gushing down the windows in great rivulets. I used to love working here when the weather was bad. There was something about being in the warm surrounded by jungle plants and butterflies while it rained outside. It made me feel cosy.

I yank up my hood and a ball of sadness rises to my throat. This place isn't just a job. It's been a home to me, the visitors my family. I bite the inside of my cheek, the pain preferable to the sting of tears behind my eyes. How could I have let this happen? I'm so careful to steel myself each time I move foster family, knowing the placement might not last long. For once, I allowed myself to feel that I belong.

Tom shakes the rain from his hair. 'Ah, there's nothing like a refreshing shower after a hard day's work.' He isn't wearing a coat and must be freezing in his work shorts and shirt. 'Come on,' he says, pulling his car keys from his pocket. 'I'll give you a lift home.'

Home. The word is a rusty nail and my mind is forever catching on it. I call it that, but it's not really. As nice as my foster parents are, it's just another place to sleep.

'Thanks, but I'll get the bus.'

He raises his eyebrows and nods towards the dilapidated bus shelter across the street. 'Is that the mythical bus which comes twice a day if you're lucky?'

'Three times, if you know the right incantations to mutter.'

He shrugs. 'OK then. I guess this is goodbye.'

'Bye, Tom.'

He turns and jogs to his car, shielding his head with his arm and leaping over puddles as he goes. Maybe I should have told him that I'm going to miss working with him. I shake the thought from my head. I know better than to get attached to people – it's safer to push down my feelings where they can't hurt me, and move on.

I watch Tom open the door of his mud-splattered Volvo and then turn my attention to the exit behind me. Surely Anorak Man can't be much longer. Realising he may not want to speak to me, I move a few paces to the side of the glass doors. If I'm lucky he won't see me when he comes out and I can spring an ambush.

Tom's voice calls over the noise of the rain. 'You live in Coleford, don't you?'

'Honestly, it's fine.'

I huddle into my coat and turn my body to avoid the worst of the downpour, and he shouts again. 'You're waiting for him, aren't you, the guy in the anorak? I don't think that's a good idea. I mean, phone the police, yes, but –'

'I can handle it, Tom.'

My irritation must sound in my voice as he recoils with a gesture that says he wouldn't dare argue with me. He disappears into his car and a moment later the window lowers and he leans out. 'Think I might stick around for a bit. Come sit with me?'

I sigh, wishing he'd just go. It's going to be hard enough to get Anorak Man to talk to me without any distractions – but at the same time, it's nice that Tom cares enough to make sure I'm OK, and it would be good to escape the rain. I check the sky, hoping it might call off its deluge, but the stubborn clouds show no sign of relenting. Maybe I could wait in his car for a bit. I'm still thinking about how to reply when a black BMW drives by with Mr Neeson behind the steering wheel and Anorak Man next to him.

Goddamn it, cockwomble.

They must have left via the back of the building, where management park. I hurry towards them and Mr Neeson peers through the windscreen at me in alarm. He puts his foot down and I cut a diagonal and charge towards the exit junction. I'll block them from leaving if I have to. The BMW reverses sharply, drenching me in a wave of cold puddle water, and I watch helplessly as it turns and speeds out of the car park.

'What the hell, Ivy?' Tom runs over and I want to tell him to get back in his car and follow them. But even as the idea comes to me, I know it's no use. They'll be at the main road by now, and there's no way to tell which direction they'll go.

He opens the passenger door of his car, but I step back and shake my head. 'No, you don't understand. I need to know why he attacked me. I need to . . .' I take out my phone, my fingers fumbling in the wet. If I can't talk to the man, then my mother has to explain instead. I wipe the raindrops from the screen and press the button to return the call. Number withheld.

No. No. No. This can't be happening.

Tom flaps his arms. 'Christ, Ivy, what does it matter? He probably doesn't even *have* a reason. Maybe he just didn't like the smell of your perfume.'

I stare at my phone in disbelief. I have to meet my mum. I don't care what she said about staying away from the island.

'Please, Ivy! Would you just get in?' Tom glares at me in exasperation, rain dripping from the end of his nose, and I have a feeling it's not the first time he's asked.

I climb into the passenger seat and awkwardly draw up my knees. There are so many computer programming books there's barely any room for my feet. He gets in beside me and flings some of them into the back, which is already piled high with boxes and bin bags. We sit without speaking, our breath fogging the windscreen. Eventually he turns and looks at me like he's expecting an explanation. When I don't say anything, he fastens his seatbelt and sighs.

32

'So we could sit here in awkward silence, or – and it's a *crazy* idea, I know – you could let me take you home.'

I shift in the seat, my clothes squelching beneath me. The sensible thing would be to go home so I can change and pack a bag, but my foster parents will be there. I don't like lying to them – they're both great guys and it's been ages since I've lived anywhere for more than a year – but they don't know I've been searching for my mum and I can't risk them trying to stop me.

Tom rubs his hands together. 'Awkward silence it is then.'

'Can you take me to the train station, please?'

He looks confused but nods. 'Of course.'

'Thanks.'

Accepting a favour from him makes me feel uncomfortable, but I don't have a choice. I fasten my seatbelt, feeling a little better as a plan forms in my head. From what I remember, I need to get two trains and then a boat to Bardsey Island. I'll text my foster parents before I'm due home from work, so they don't worry. I've no idea what I'm going to say, but I'll think of something. Sadness tugs at my heart as Tom drives out of the car park, but I keep my eyes fixed ahead. Better to never look back.

Once we get onto the main road, I look up train times on my phone. The next one goes in thirty minutes. We should make it, as long as there are no holdups. I relax back in my seat – until I see the ticket price. It's twice as much as I was expecting. How can . . . ? And then I realise. I was looking at advance tickets before, not ones on the same day. I have enough in my account to cover the fare, and hopefully the bus ride, but that's it. There's a few quid in my wallet, but knowing National Rip-off Rail prices I'll end up with a packet of stale custard creams for lunch.

As I might have guessed, the roads are a nightmare: queues of traffic at temporary stop signs, stubborn cyclists pedalling up the hill in packs of three, and a learner driver in a Nissan Micra determined to crawl along at twenty miles an hour in a forty zone.

When we eventually pull into the station, I open the door before the car's even stopped.

'Cheers for the lift.'

'No worries.'

I get out and charge up the dozen steps to the ticket office.

'Hey, Ivy!'

I turn and Tom is standing on the street, holding my bag. 'You might need this.'

I run down and he throws my bag. Only it doesn't reach me. It lands face down in the gutter – over a drain. I open it and look inside. Everything is there, apart from one thing.

'My wallet!'

He walks over and laughs. 'You're not telling me . . . ?'

I peer into the drain but there's no sign of it. All I can see is darkness. Grabbing the drain cover, I pull with all my might but it doesn't budge. This can't be happening. Tom says something, but I don't hear him. I stare in disbelief, unable to accept that my wallet has gone.

Fighting the urge to punch him, I stand up and shout, 'Why did you have to throw it?'

'Hey, I'm sorry, OK? It was an accident.'

I glare at him, rain pouring down my face. 'I can't get the train now.'

'Where's your bank? I'll take you into town.'

'What's the point? They won't let me withdraw cash without any ID. Everything I had just went down the drain.'

Tom leads me back to the car and I climb inside in a daze. A few seconds later, he slides in next to me. 'So how much do you need?' he asks.

I slump in my seat. 'Eighty-two pounds.'

He gives a low whistle. 'Where are you going, Paris by Eurostar?'

'It doesn't matter now.'

'I wish I could help, but I've only got forty quid on me and they've cut me off again.' Before I can wonder what he means, he adds, 'But you know what? I have a full tank of petrol and my boss has just given me the day off.'

'I can't ask you, Tom, it's too far.'

He takes out his phone. 'Postcode.'

He says it like a surgeon demanding a scalpel and I watch him, not daring to hope.

'I need to get to a town called Aberdaron.'

He taps at the screen and grins. 'Found it.' And then the smile slides right off his face. 'Jesus, Ivy. That's on the west coast of Wales. According to this, it'll take four hours.'

He carries on talking but I'm only half listening. I gaze at the window, my eyes following a solitary raindrop as it glides helplessly down the glass.

'We need the A49. It looks fairly straightforward, but I'll need you to navigate once we get closer.'

'What?'

'I said I'll need you to navi—'

I turn to him in disbelief. 'Really? You'll take me?'

'Of course.'

He smiles and I feel my face flush. 'Thanks.' And then I remember I need money for the boat fare. 'Is it OK if I borrow twenty quid? I'll give it you back.'

'Sure.'

'And I'll pay you for the petrol once I get my card sorted.'

'If you like, but there's no rush for it.' He twists his body towards me, then puts his hand on my seat and leans in.

I flinch from him, feeling a sudden stab of déjà vu, and he frowns in surprise. What must he think of me? He was reaching for something in the back, not leaning in to kiss me. His face pales and I bite my lip, annoyed at myself for making things awkward. Neither of us speaks and each second that passes feels more painful than the last.

Worried I've offended him, I find myself saying, 'I know there's nothing like that between us. I mean, you're great and everything, but . . .'

'We're just mates, Ivy,' he says quickly. 'I wasn't –'

'I know. Sorry, ignore me. I'm just . . .'

'Having a bad day?'

I rub my head, relieved when he gives me a cautious smile. If I'm honest, I don't know why I reacted like that. When he leaned towards me, I had the strongest feeling that he'd tried to kiss me before – and yet Tom's never once made a move on me, and I wouldn't want him to. Just because we have a laugh doesn't mean I have feelings for him. He's only giving me a lift because he feels bad about losing my wallet, and he isn't like that anyway; he wouldn't expect something in return for helping me.

He reaches behind him and grabs a bin bag, then rummages inside and throws me a grey sweatshirt and shorts, before pulling out a towel and more clothes.

'Eyes, please.'

I don't respond and he clamps his hands over his chest with a mock-shocked face.

'Oh, right. Sorry.' I close my eyes, grateful he's doing his best to lighten the mood. A long minute passes, punctuated by much fidgeting and huffing. Eventually he announces, 'All done. Your turn.'

I check out of the window – a couple of old ladies are battling a dysfunctional umbrella with a will of its own, but otherwise there's no one. While Tom covers his eyes, I undo my seatbelt and struggle out of my wet coat and shirt. I put on the top then remove my damp shoes and socks and change into the shorts. Both are ridiculously big but I don't care how I look; it feels good to be comfortable and dry.

Tom starts the engine and drives in silence, his eyes fixed on the road. Every now and then, though, I catch him glancing over at me.

'You OK?' He fiddles with the heater. 'Warm enough?'

'I'm fine, thanks.'

'Do you want to talk about what happened before? That guy attacking you, you must be feeling a bit . . .'

He doesn't finish the sentence and I don't help him. After a moment, he switches on the radio and Taylor Swift blasts out, informing us of her intention to shake it off.

'Actually, I'm a bit tired.'

'Of course, sorry.'

He shuts off the music and I reposition my head against the window and try to get comfortable. I was up late last night reading about Bardsey again; maybe a nap will help.

I wonder if the place is as inhospitable as it looks in the photos. Most of the search results were about its rugged scenery and wildlife, or its history. The island has been a site of holy pilgrimage since the fifth century and there are meant to be thousands of saints buried there. Some claim it's the site of Avalon, where King Arthur was taken after he died, and there was something about Merlin being trapped in a cave or glass tower. I came across so many peculiar stories that I began to feel unsettled and had to stop reading.

Tom taps rhythmically on the steering wheel and does a little shimmy with his shoulders, presumably singing in his head and making up the moves as he goes with Tay-Tay. I wish I could shake it off too, but I can't. Today has left me feeling so unsettled; maybe talking it over with Tom would help me to make sense of it all?

I press my cheek to the cold window, my pulse beating in time with the windscreen wipers. No. I've confided in people before, like the social worker who said she had my best interests at heart, and I'm not going to make the same mistake. As a child, I used to fantasise that my mum would burst through the doors of whichever care home I was living in at the time. She'd say there had been a terrible mistake and take me away to live with her and my many sisters, who

I would love and share all of my secrets with. Over the years, I got used to being alone, the way you do when you have no choice. And then I met Katie . . . I take a deep breath, refusing to think about what happened. The truth is that I haven't had a proper friend since her, and I don't think I ever will again.

The rain is coming down harder now. Tom leans forward and frowns at the road, the wipers squeaking in protest as they speed back and forth. I watch him, unused to seeing him so intensely focused, and then my gaze drifts back to the landscape outside. A patchwork of fields, rolling hills and woodland flashes by in a blur of green and brown, their vivid autumn colours dulled by the rain. With the swish-swipe of the windscreen wipers and the slosh of the road, it isn't long before tiredness gets the better of me. I close my eyes and feel myself begin to drift when I hear a voice on the edge of my consciousness. Tom whispers, 'Maybe when you wake up, you'll tell me why I'm taking you to the arse-end of nowhere.'

Sleep wraps around me and pulls me under and I let myself be taken. I'm held within a vast darkness, cocooned in silence for the longest time – and then I'm somewhere else, called to a place veiled in white mist.

The swirling strands of vapour pull apart to reveal a gleaming tower. It stands defiant against a storm-ravaged sky, lashed by wind and lightning: impenetrable, unknowable, terrible. Something unspeakable is waiting for me within its walls, something strange and sinister and not of this world.

The wooden door creaks open as I draw near. Before me is a flight of narrow stone steps leading upwards. I climb them, my legs heavy with dread, and enter a circular room with lots of windows. I can't see much at first, but then I make them out: nine grey shapes, each as big as a person, lying in a circle on the cement floor. I step forward and something hard crunches under my feet. The ground is littered with black feathers.

I approach the nearest grey shape and crouch down. Each one is a human-sized chrysalis. The outside husk lies open; whatever was inside has flown away. I walk around the circle and come to one that's still intact. Beneath the rough papery casing is a network of softly glowing, pulsating arteries – an organic, beating thing of sinew and flesh. Inside is the shadowy face of a woman, her eyes shut.

Chanting fills the room. At first it's an ominous whisper muttered over and over, and then it grows louder, rising up in a vortex of sound until it becomes one with the howl of the wind.

Eko eko azarak. Eko eko zomelak. Eko eko azarak.

I don't understand the words but I feel their power. The chant repeats over and over, invading every corner of my mind.

I have to wake her. Wake her . . . I have to wake before it's too late.

I open my eyes with a start, the remnants of the dream clinging to me like cobwebs.

'You OK? You were making some strange noises.'

Tom's voice snaps me back to the present and I straighten up and wipe my face.

'Yeah, it was just a dream.' Only it didn't feel like that. It felt like a memory of somewhere I've visited often. 'How long was I asleep for?'

'Over an hour.' He glances at me and grins. 'I didn't know you talked in your sleep.'

'How would you? *I've* never slept on the job.'

'True.' He laughs.

I massage my temples, wanting to remember the details of the dream yet feeling apprehensive at the same time. I know I heard chanting, but I can't recall the words. Could I have spoken them? I eye him warily, aware that this might be another one of his wind-ups.

'So go on. What did I say?'

'It was weird. You kept muttering the same thing over and over.'

'Yes, but what did I actually say?' It comes out sharper than I intended and I fiddle with my nose stud, suddenly self-conscious. I don't know why it matters to me, but it does.

He shoots me a quizzical look. 'I dunno, Ivy. It was gibberish. It sounded like echo echo, azzer something.'

'*Eko eko azarak. Eko eko zomelak.*' The words fly out of my mouth unbidden.

'Yeah, that's it. What does it mean?'

'I don't know. Nothing.'

The phrase repeats over and over in my mind. The words sound like they're made up and yet I know them. Not just from the dream. I know the cadence of the chant in the same way I know the curves and hollows of my body; the rhythm as natural to me as breathing, the words as familiar as my own name.

You're not who you think you are.

41

The thought comes from nowhere and I touch my temples, feeling unsettled.

A sign for services appears and Tom yawns and rolls his shoulders. 'Thank God, I'm starving.' He turns off the main road and I rub my arms, trying to shake off the sense that the chant means something. I can't have heard it before. It just feels that way because of the dream. Like Tom said, the words were gibberish – meaningless.

5

The rain has slowed to a drizzle as we pull into the parking area. Tom finds me some socks, sniffing several pairs until seemingly satisfied, and I put them on, preferring not to inspect them myself. I pull a face as I shove on my damp work shoes and Tom reaches into a bag and produces a pair of white trainers. They're gigantic – three times the size of my feet. He waves them up and down, making them do a little dance on the air.

'Come on!' he laughs. 'It would be funny to see you walk in them.'

'Hmm. I look ridiculous enough without the need for clown shoes.'

As I exit the car, I realise the scale of the challenge facing me. The shorts are so big that I'll need to hold them up as I walk, or they'll fall around my ankles. Even when I tighten the drawstring and fold over the waistband, they still reach past my knees. Why does Tom have to be *so* tall? With the huge baggy sweatshirt, I look like I've been shrunk in the wash.

Tom presses his lips together, his face flushing pink, and I can't blame him for wanting to laugh. I loosen my grip on the waistband, letting it drop even lower. 'Something you find funny?' I ask. He has that look about him. Any second now he'll erupt into giggles. He shakes his head a little too vigorously and walks off, leaving me to gather my dignity up with the shorts and waddle after him.

The main building resembles a warehouse – long and squat and painted dark grey, with a dozen concrete steps and a ramp to one side, leading to a parade of glass-fronted shops. Above the entrance hangs a colourful banner, advertising the exciting retail options inside (a supermarket, café, post office and garden centre) and declares the place to be a *thriving and vibrant shopping experience*. The car park is practically deserted and the only people I see are two teenage boys slumped on a bench and an old lady with long white hair muttering to herself as she sorts through a trolley full of bin bags. Whoever came up with that slogan has clearly never left rural mid-Wales.

Tom spots the entrance to the café and takes the steps four at a time (why do tall people always have to show off?), leaving me behind as usual. One of the boys sees me coming and elbows his mate on the bench. Ignoring them, I hold on to the crotch of the shorts with one hand and get my swag on Billie Eilish-style – to hell with the drop risk.

'Hey, sexy, I wanna play with you. Can I get your phone number?'

I stop and turn my head. They're wearing school blazers and look about fourteen, fifteen at most. 'Sure. Is it mainly Saturdays you need? Only weekdays can be tricky.' The boy stares at me, a mixture of surprise and panic on his face. Presumably he's used the line before, yet curiously has never had a taker. 'My number . . . you need a babysitter, yeah?'

He mutters under his breath while his mate snorts with laughter, and I hoist up my shorts and keep walking. I expect Tom to be in the café by now, but he's stopped to give money to the old lady with the trolley. Her skin is lined with wrinkles, but she has the brightest blue eyes which twinkle when she realises we're together. I know the look – it's the one Dot used to give me whenever she saw me with Tom. It says 'you've got a good one there'. Poor Dot. She comes across as strong and feisty but I can tell she's lonely. I hope whoever Mr Neeson employs next takes the time to chat with her.

I go over and something moves in the trolley. Amongst the bags of clothes is a little white dog curled up in a basket. I pat him and he nuzzles his head into my hand and licks my fingers. His thin body is trembling, perhaps from the cold or old age.

'Do either of you need anything?' I ask. 'A hot drink or . . . ?'

She smiles and speaks with a soft Welsh lilt. 'No, thank you, my lovely. I think your friend is waiting for you.' She gestures towards Tom, who has taken off and is now holding the café door open.

I stroke the dog again and say goodbye to her, hoping they'll be OK, and Tom checks an imaginary watch. 'I know you've only got little legs but hurry up, would you? I'm wasting away here.' I walk over and jab him in the side as I pass under his outstretched arm.

'Ow! What is it with you and bruising guys' ribs?'

I give him a look and he makes a show of rubbing his side. 'I wouldn't mind, but I bruise like a peach.'

'You wouldn't be complaining if you were choking.'

Tom closes the door behind us and muses. 'True. If I had a

sausage roll stuck in my windpipe I wouldn't be saying anything at all.'

The room is warm but basic: a dozen or so wooden tables with chairs and fluorescent strip lighting overhead. There are no tablecloths, curtains or pictures, just a blackboard menu behind the counter, covered with tiny white writing. Apart from a tired-looking couple with three young boys, the place is empty.

I squint at the menu. 'Well, I think Mr Neeson was right – I learned a valuable lesson that day.'

'Don't hide in cupboards and jump out at your boss?'

I laugh, remembering the shocked look on Mr Neeson's face. 'I think it was me handing him the ketchup that did it.'

Tom nods. 'Dangerous things, condiments.'

The lady behind the counter takes our order (two burgers and fries with Coke and a chocolate muffin for Tom) and I have no choice but to let him pay. I grab a few sachets of not-so-dangerous-looking ketchup, while Tom chooses a table by the window with an impressive view of the rain-soaked car park.

He pulls out a chair for me and I roll my eyes. I don't know if it's his upbringing, but he's ridiculously gentlemanly. Another reason Dot loves him. I have a theory he only does it to annoy me. I sit down and another thought enters my head. Maybe the reason I feel irritated has nothing to do with wanting to be treated as an equal. Maybe it's because Tom has a way of making me feel cared for, and I don't know what to do with that.

The family across the room is making lots of noise, the parents struggling to keep the kids entertained, and I smile when the woman tips her baby upside down and sniffs its bottom. She shrugs at the dad, though judging from the smell wafting over, the child definitely needs a nappy change. A moment later, the waitress appears with their food and apologises for the wait. The dad tells her not to worry, but their eldest toddler is more critical of the service. He throws his chicken nuggets on the floor and wails.

Tom flinches and turns away in his seat. He's never shown an interest in the kids who visit the centre, whereas I loved taking the school groups, but I didn't know he was *that* offended by them. He puckers his mouth and I laugh. 'I'm guessing you don't ever want children.'

His eyes flash. 'Please tell me you don't say that kind of thing when you're on a date, Shorty.' I give him my best withering look and he leans across the table and whispers. 'It's not that I don't like them, I just don't trust them. They're here to replace us.'

One of the toddlers stands up in his seat, his podgy hands shaking the back of the chair, and scowls over at us. His mum grabs his arm and hisses. 'Stop that, or your dad will take you outside.' Evidently untroubled by the threat, the boy repeatedly stamps his feet. His mum yanks him down and he clambers to the floor and charges at us in a ball of fury. Before he can reach our table, his dad snatches him up and carries him kicking and screaming out of the café.

Tom shoots me a told-you-so look and we watch through the window as the boy's dad tries to calm him down. It appears to be working – until the boy turns and sees me. He throws himself at the window, banging his fists on the glass, and I nearly jump out of my seat. For a moment, the look on his face reminded me of Anorak Man. I shake my head and laugh at myself for getting the jitters over a toddler.

The boy's mum calls over. 'I'm so sorry. I don't know what's got into him.'

Tom replies cheerfully, 'Don't worry. Ivy *loves* kids,' then turns back to me and mutters, 'She's planning on having a dysfunctional family of her own one day.' I kick him under the table and he glances out of the window and stiffens. I wonder if the toddler is back to mount another attack, but then I see the teenage boys from before heading across the car park. They wander past his car and Tom visibly relaxes.

'Need to keep an eye on my stuff,' he explains.

Suddenly it occurs to me – all the bags in his car. I was so wrapped up in my own thoughts before, and now I feel bad for not asking. 'Are you moving house?'

'Something like that.'

Before he can say more, the waitress arrives with our order. Tom's eyes light up and he does the thing he always does when he's about to eat: he rubs his thighs and wriggles his shoulders. It's the slightest movement, but one you can't un-see once you notice it.

I tear open a sachet of ketchup and Tom snatches it from me.

'Oi, get your own.'

He swipes it over his burger and grins. 'I bet you're an only child.'

He's asked me about my home life before, but I usually manage to find a butterfly that needs inspecting or a visitor with an urgent question they didn't know they had. Right

48

now I want to talk about my family, or lack of one, even less than usual.

Like always, Tom dispenses with a knife and fork and eats with his fingers. I try not to let my eyes pass comment as he grabs a handful of fries and chows down. He picks up another chip and dips it in ketchup before jabbing it at me.

'I'm right, aren't I? It's obvious you don't have siblings. You're terrible at sharing and refuse to accept anyone's help. I'm all for fiercely independent women – you're looking at Beyoncé's biggest fan – but you can take things too far, you know.'

I flinch at his words. Growing up in care taught me to do things for myself and I don't see how it's possible to be too self-reliant. Unsure how to respond, I take a bite of my burger. I know Tom's from a big family, but not how old he is compared to his siblings. As I swallow, the answer comes to me. 'I bet you're the youngest.' He raises his eyebrows, telling me I'm right. 'It's obvious, really. You're lazy because everyone babies you, and it explains your reliance on humour to get attention.'

He laughs. 'I feel so seen. Yes, I have four older sisters. But I'm not the baby of the family, more the runt of the litter.' An edge of bitterness creeps into his voice and I want to ask more, but I resist the urge. The sooner we get off the topic of families, the better. We eat in silence for a while and then he asks, 'So I know you're an only child and you live in Coleford. Did you grow up there? Are you visiting relatives in Wales, or . . . ?'

I shove my plate away, the food half finished. 'Can we talk about something else?'

He drops his burger. 'You know, I can't figure you out. I feel like I'm getting to know you and then you put up this wall and –'

49

'I put up walls?'

'Like a human breeze block.'

He sits forward in his seat, his face flushed and his eyes bright. I'm not sure where this is going, but I sense it's nowhere good.

'Whenever I ask about your family you change the subject. You never come out for drinks with the guys from work and you insist on getting the bus, even though I could take you home or you could get a lift with the girls in the café. Then today you go all Jackie Chan on me. You don't get skills like that from watching YouTube, yet you've never mentioned you do martial arts. It's like you don't want people to get to know you.'

I wait, wondering if he's finished, but apparently he's just getting started. 'Take this morning with the guy in the anorak. Fair enough, you don't want to talk about what happened, but you haven't even said why I'm taking you to Wales.' A huff escapes me and he adds quickly, 'I'm happy to take you, whether you tell me or not. It's just –'

'It's just *what*?'

He gives me a pained look and I can't decide if it's exasperation or hope on his face. 'I'm just trying to be a friend to you, Ivy. We all need someone to talk to, even me. I might walk around at work like everything's fine, but deep down inside . . .' I lean across the table and he sniffs and hangs his head. 'Deep down inside my shoe, my sock is sliding off.'

I tut and he grins. 'Sorry, sometimes I don't know when to stop. Seriously, though, I'm not a bad listener if you did want to talk about anything.'

I know he's doing me a huge favour by driving me all this way, and I guess it's only natural for him to wonder why I didn't go home to get changed or pack a bag. I open my mouth, unsure what to say but feeling I have to tell him something.

'There are things you don't know about me.'

'Erm, yes, we've established that.'

'I mean *big* things.'

'Like?'

I don't answer and he crosses his arms. 'There are things you don't know about me either.'

'It's not a competition, Tom.'

He laughs. 'Look, we all have secrets. We all have *stuff*. Human beings have this thing called conversation. One person asks a question and the other person answers. It's a highly effective means of social bonding. You should try it some time.'

I still don't say anything.

'Come on, Ivy. Just tell me. What harm can it do?'

When I don't reply, he lays both his hands on the table and looks me in the eyes. 'The stuff in my car . . . I'm not moving house. I had an argument with my parents a few months ago and left home. I've been sofa surfing ever since. It was fun at first, but now my mates are sick of me and some nights I sleep in my car.'

He exhales loudly and keeps talking. 'I've spent the past six months designing a new game with a group of people in the States. We want to launch it but that takes money, and my parents refuse to help. They're happy to pay for me to go to uni and study programming, but they won't give me the cash for what I really want to do. If I'm honest, I'm close to giving up. The time difference means we need to have meetings in the middle of the night, and I'm tired of always being knackered. Even if I get the financial backing somehow, there's still a chance it will fail and my parents will be right and I'll have been wasting my energy.'

I knew he was into gaming, but I didn't realise he wanted to launch one as a business venture. Maybe he's not as lazy and lacking in ambition as I thought.

'And you're telling me this because?'

'I haven't told anyone else. I mean, my mates know about the sofa surfing – I'm six foot four so pretty hard to miss when you're eating your Crunchy Nut Cornflakes in the morning – but I haven't told them I sleep in my car some nights. It's not always easy to share stuff about yourself. I thought it might help if I told you something about me.'

I take a sip of Coke, my stomach fizzing. I know he's expecting me to say something, but it's been so long since I've told anyone about searching for my mum. Tom gives me a reassuring smile and I remind myself that he isn't a social worker; he isn't going to try and stop me meeting her.

'If you really want to know, I was abandoned as a baby. I've grown up in care homes and foster placements, most of them in Gloucestershire, and I've spent years searching for my mother on missing-person and long-lost-relative sites. Then last week . . .' I rub an invisible smudge on my glass, my knee bouncing under the table.

'Last week?'

I sigh, realising he's only going to keep asking questions if I don't answer. 'Last week I got a lead. A man replied to my post and told me about a woman he'd met while he was visiting an island off the coast of Wales. She lived in the lighthouse cottage there, and he remembered her because she seemed upset and he was worried about her. She went to the mainland with her baby and came back the next day alone. He said my photo looked just like her.'

Tom doesn't say anything, so I continue. 'He stayed on Bardsey Island seventeen years ago, the same week I was abandoned. I looked online but couldn't find a landline for the lighthouse cottage, so I sent a letter with my number and this morning she called me – my mother. That's who I'm going to see.'

I lean back feeling shaky and raw, as if telling him has peeled away layers of my skin.

Tom blinks at me. 'Wow.'

'Wow?'

'Sorry. That's a lot to take in. It can't have been easy for you.'

My throat tightens and I rub my head, hoping he doesn't ask me anything else. Thankfully, he seems to realise I've shared enough for one day as he squeezes my arm and whispers, 'I'm glad you told me.' Changing the subject, he leans back and announces loudly. 'Now you'll have to excuse me, but I need a moment with my muffin.'

He lifts up the muffin, his shoulders doing a tiny wriggle, and looks at it adoringly. Before he can take a bite, I grab a chunk and shove it in my mouth.

He holds it out to me. 'I'm sorry. Would you like some?'

I shake my head, pleased we're back to messing about.

He demolishes the rest in a few quick bites and mutters, 'Oh my days, that was good,' then stretches his arms wide before checking his phone. 'You said your mum lives on an island. Does that mean you need to catch a ferry?'

My smile drops off my face. How can I have been so stupid? I haven't booked the boat crossing, and from what I read online there's only one guy who does it. What if he's not going today or I've missed him? I take out my phone and search for the website.

'You OK?'

I answer without looking up. 'Yeah, I just realised I should probably book the boat.' I find the page and click to call the number, but there's no answer.

'I can't get through.'

Tom shrugs. 'You can try again on the way.'

He stands up and hands me his car keys. 'I need the toilet. See you out there?'

'Sure.'

He walks away and shouts over his shoulder. 'If I'm not back in two minutes . . .'

I raise my eyebrows. 'Then what?'

'Then just wait longer.' He grins.

I open the café door and shiver as the cold hits me. The blustery wind carries the threat of rain and something else – a foul smell. I thought one of the kids needed changing, but maybe there's a problem with the drains. I head for the steps, doing my best to hold up the shorts and not inhale, when the old lady from earlier hurries towards me.

She's pushing her trolley, her long white hair flying in the wind. 'The shadows,' she cries. 'They're trying to get inside.'

She points a shaking finger at the ground and I see it too. Beneath the empty bench is a patch of shadow. It moves along

54

the walkway towards us, swirling around on itself like a tiny tornado. I tell myself it's just dirt caught up in the wind, but something about it doesn't look right. I blink, not trusting my eyes, as it comes towards us, expanding and getting darker. It moves faster, whirling over the ground – and then it creeps up over the woman's trolley and is gone.

Suddenly, the dog stands up in its basket and shakes itself as if it's wet. Again and again its body twists and turns. It's like watching a few frames of film on repeat . . . like the moths, and Anorak Man stroking his beard and turning his head back and forth. Realisation washes over me like a slimy film and I step back, feeling nauseous.

The woman begs the dog to stop, tears streaming down her cheeks, but it keeps shaking. Just when I think it will never end, the poor thing whimpers and collapses. A moment later, the shadow slides across the woman's face and I gasp as her expression changes – the bewilderment and fear in her eyes replaced by a blank stare. Her bony knuckles tighten on the handle of the trolley and then relax. She repeats the movement, her hand clenching and unclenching.

Run. I need to run.

I turn and race away and she follows me, her trolley bumping and banging down the steps. My lungs ache as I charge across the car park but I don't stop to catch my breath. I get to the car and shove the key in the lock. As I snatch open the door, I glance over my shoulder. She's twenty paces away, moving fast, her face a mask of fury.

Tom appears alongside her and I shout. 'Quick, get in!'

'What?' He runs past the lady and goes to the driver's side.

I jump in and then reach over and open his door. He slides in next to me, just as the trolley slams into my side of the car.

'What the hell's happening?'

I throw the keys at him. 'Drive!'

The woman backs up a few paces and then shoves away the trolley. She stands motionless, her eyes bloodshot and her long hair flying wildly all about her, then charges at the car. I stifle a scream as her forehead smacks into the glass, leaving a smear of blood.

'Tom!'

He starts the engine and she backs up and comes at me again, but this time she doesn't make contact with the window. Tom accelerates hard and we screech out of the car park.

6

We've been driving for more than two hours and the silence grows heavier with each passing mile, taking on a weight and shape of its own until it feels like there's another person in the car with us. At first we couldn't stop talking. We went over and over what happened – Tom trying to persuade me that being attacked by two strangers on the same day is an unlikely coincidence but still within the realms of possibility. After I said there *was* no rational explanation, he gave me a worried look and went quiet.

But then Tom doesn't know the things my mum told me. He didn't see the shadows or the dog shaking itself. Several times I decide to tell him everything, but I can't bring myself to do it. He'll think I've lost my mind, and how could I blame him? Right now, it feels as if my mother is the only one who can give me answers.

I try the boatman's number for the tenth time, but there's still no answer.

According to the map on the website, we're only a few miles from the harbour. I point up ahead. 'You need to take the next right. Aberdaron's that way.'

Tom continues our previous conversation as if the past two hours never happened. 'You do realise that lots of homeless people have alcohol problems. The woman could've had a bottle of vodka in her trolley for all we know.'

'She didn't smell like she'd been drinking.'

'You said she talked about seeing shadows?'

My voice comes out small and unsure. 'She said they were trying to get inside.'

'Well, that must tell you something.' He holds my gaze as if determined to get a response, and I look straight ahead.

A tractor appears before us and my heart leaps to my throat. 'Tom!'

He brakes hard, cursing under his breath. 'Look, I know it's strange after the guy in the anorak, but she clearly wasn't in her right mind.'

'And the toddler in the café?'

He checks his mirrors to overtake and then huffs when a bend appears in the road, blocking his view. I'm not sure whether he's worried about us being late, or is keen to see the back of me, but I can feel the stress rolling off him in waves.

'Sorry, what was that about the kid in the café?' he asks.

I know I should stop talking, but I can't. 'You saw the way he ran at me and how he banged his fists on the window. It was like he wanted to hurt me.'

Tom laughs but it's a hollow sound. 'OK, so you're actually starting to worry me now.' He overtakes the tractor and blows out a sigh. 'I know being attacked by that woman must be upsetting, especially after this morning, but don't you think you're taking it all a bit personally? The kid was having a hissy fit because he didn't like his chicken nuggets; it's what kids do. And he ran at both of us.'

I remember what my mother said. *They can take control of anyone or anything, people you know or strangers.* I thought the boy was having a tantrum when he kept kicking the back of his chair, but what if the repetitive behaviour was caused by something else? So many things have happened today that can't be explained. The way I see it, there are only two possibilities. Either my mum is right, or I'm losing my grip on reality.

I flip down the windscreen visor and peer at my face in the rectangular mirror. There are dark circles under my eyes and my short fringe looks messy, my blonde roots showing through the pastel pink dye. Whenever I got upset as a child, I would stare at my reflection and silently order myself not to cry. The other kids laughed and said I was ugly: my eyes too wide set and my cheeks too round to be pretty. I don't know if all children are cruel, or if having nothing makes you want to take a chunk out of someone else's happiness, but I didn't care if I was pretty or not. I only cared that I had myself. Those same wide-set eyes stare back at me now, assuring me that I know when I'm sleeping and when I'm awake. I know the difference between illusion and reality. I just have to trust myself. I'll cope, like I always do.

Feeling a little better, I close the visor and glance out of the window. At first there are just fields, and then a sign for Aberdaron appears. The village only has a few dozen houses and we pass through it almost as soon as we arrive. Realising I can't put it off much longer, I text my foster parents. I tell them that a girl from work has broken up with her boyfriend and wants me to stay for a few days. I don't like deceiving them, but I can't face a big conversation, or worse, them coming out here. As expected, I get a text back within minutes, telling me to take care and keep in touch. Apart from going to my martial arts group, I never meet up with anyone outside of school or work. If there's one thing they're always encouraging me to do – aside from talking about my feelings – it's to make friends.

After a mile or so the road begins to climb steeply and I check the directions again. 'There. We're meant to turn there.' I point at the turning and Tom swerves just in time, taking us onto a rough dirt track. On the right is a line of skeletal black trees and on the left is a drop to a water-filled ditch. Looking out, I see that the wheels of the car are dangerously close to the edge. We slow to a crawl and I press my thighs into the seat as we bump across deep ruts and potholes. The track twists downwards and gets even narrower. I flinch as branches scrape along the side of the car, twigs snapping like broken bones. Tom bites his lip, his knuckles white on the steering wheel, and I feel bad about his car getting even more damaged.

Eventually the road widens and becomes flatter. We take a sharp corner and without warning the sea appears: huge grey waves surging between jagged black rocks, spray hissing and spitting high into the air. Bardsey Island sits in the distance and looks exactly like it did in the photos. Even though it's misty, there's no mistaking its outline. With a rounded mountain on one side and flat land on the other, it looks like a giant humpback whale skulking off the coast.

Excited, I sit up in my seat and search for a ferry. The only vessel is a yellow catamaran, thirty or forty feet long, positioned at the bottom of the long concrete slope before us. Two men wearing overalls and work boots are loading barrels into the back of it. A couple of dirty Land Rovers and a small orange tractor are parked nearby. This has to be it.

Tom pulls up and puts on his jacket. He gets out and goes to my side of the car, then squats down. I'm used to him opening doors for me, but this is a new one. I lower the window a crack and cold air whistles inside, assaulting my nostrils with the smell of the sea.

'What are you doing, laying your coat over the ground for me?'

'Not quite.'

I get out and the blustery wind pulls me in every direction, tugging at my sweatshirt and shorts, as if I don't have enough trouble keeping them up. I wipe the sea spray from my face, then turn and see what he's looking at. There's a huge dent in the side of the car door and the paintwork is badly chipped. The trolley did more damage than I thought.

'I'm really sorry, Tom. I'll pay for it to be fixed as soon as I get a new job.'

'Don't be silly, it wasn't your fault.' He stands up and rubs his arms. 'Jeez. It's cold enough to freeze the balls off a snowman.' He opens the boot of the car and takes out my coat and holds it open for me with an apologetic smile. 'The heater's dried it a bit, but it's still damp.'

Deciding it's better than nothing, I slip one arm inside and then the other. As I do, I feel my shorts drop. I grab the waistband with one hand then turn around and attempt to do up the coat with the other. Tom reaches to help with the

61

zip just as I yank up my shorts, resulting in me headbutting his collar bone.

'Careful there, Shorty,' he laughs. 'You know I bruise easy.'

'Yeah, you might have mentioned it.'

He returns my smile and a feeling of warmth radiates through me. 'Thanks, Tom. Thanks for everything.' He's been so nice – not just driving me here but sharing things about his life so I would find it easier to talk about my mum. His kindness means more to me than he can know. He pulls the zip up to my neck, standing so close I can feel his breath on my forehead, and then pats my shoulders as if he doesn't know what to do with his hands.

'Oh, I nearly forgot.' He reaches into his pocket and hands me two ten-pound notes. 'The money you wanted. Are you sure it's enough?'

'Thanks.' I take the cash and sadness wells up inside me at the thought of saying goodbye. The strength of the feeling surprises me and I take a quick breath.

He tilts his head, his brown eyes soft with concern. 'Are you going to be OK?'

Feeling uncomfortable, I bite my lip and give a tiny nod, relieved when one of the men by the boat sees us and raises his arm. As he jogs up the slope, my body tenses. I don't know if the shadow I saw before was a trick of the light, but *something* made those people attack me. What if it happens again while I'm at sea? Anorak Man was unsteady on his feet, but I don't fancy my chances on a boat.

This man is tall and broad-shouldered, with wavy brown hair and a moustache so big and bushy I'm not sure whether to be impressed or suspicious of what it might be hiding. He speaks in a strong Welsh accent. 'Can I help you?'

'Hi, yes. Are you running trips to Bardsey Island?'

'Today?' He laughs incredulously. 'I'm sorry, but you've had a wasted journey. The tourist season's finished for the year. The holiday cottages are closed now and most of the islanders have left for winter.'

I feel the blood drain from my face. 'But I need to visit someone . . . family. She lives in the lighthouse cottage.'

'Sarah?'

My mother's name is Sarah. He says it like he's tossing away loose change, yet it's worth everything to me.

'Yes. Is she still on the island?'

'Oh aye, she's the only one that stays in winter. She hasn't said anything about a visitor, mind.' He looks me up and down. 'I'm guessing you're one of Gwen's girls. Sarah's niece?'

'Yes,' I lie, happy to let him believe anything if it means he'll take me. Tom shoots me an uncertain look and I wrap my arms around myself. I have an aunt – my mother at least had some family, she wasn't all alone in the world. Does Gwen know her sister abandoned me? Where is she now?

The boatman glances out to sea. 'I don't know how long it's been since you last saw your aunt, but Sarah isn't the type to have visitors. She's . . .'

'I know all about her. It's fine. Please, it's important I see her.'

He sighs and strokes his moustache. 'As it happens, I'm heading to the island now. I'm returning tomorrow, but I don't know when I'll be going again. It might be a week or more until I can bring you back.'

My shoulders sag with relief. 'Thank you.'

'I'm David and that's my cousin,' he says, pointing to his companion who's now heading towards the tractor. We watch the man haul himself into the seat, then drive it forward and position it at the front of the boat. David raises his arm in signal then turns to Tom. 'Are you going to get your bags then?'

'Actually, it's just me going,' I say.

The boatman strokes the fuzzy caterpillar attached to his upper lip and sniffs. 'You're not going together?'

I shake my head and he huffs. 'I'm afraid that changes things. The island isn't a place for a young 'un to be travelling alone.'

'I'm seventeen.'

'That may be so, but I'm not taking you by yourself.'

My hands clench. 'Why, because I'm a girl?'

Tom steps forward. 'Ivy can take care of herself, honestly.'

David heaves a sigh and slaps Tom on the back. 'Son, you need to understand that the island isn't like other places. There's no roads, no electricity, no running water. The mobile signal is non-existent and there's no help available if your friend here gets into trouble. Conditions can change like that.' He clicks his fingers for emphasis. 'One summer, I took some tourists across for the day and a storm came in. They were stranded there for three weeks. So you see, I'm not about to leave *anyone* over there by themselves.'

'But I won't be alone. I'll be with Sarah.'

David's face tightens as if that's what concerns him. 'It's like this. I take both of you or neither. Why don't you have a little chat about it and decide.'

The boatman walks away and I stare out to sea, my stomach heaving with the waves. The island is right there. I can't believe I've got this far and might have to turn back.

'Tom, I don't think he's going to change his mind.'

He rubs the back of his neck. 'Before you ask, I'm sorry but I can't. We're launching the game soon and I need to catch up with the team. Not to mention the fact I need to sort out a new job and find a place to stay. And then there's my stuff. I can't risk leaving it.'

I glance at his car. 'I can't see many people coming down this way – the track's pretty deserted.' I hate asking him for help, or anyone else for that matter, but I don't have a choice. 'I know it's a lot to ask, but it would really mean a lot to me.'

When he doesn't say anything, I hang my head, unable to keep the disappointment from my voice. 'I'll tell David we're leaving.' I turn and walk after the boatman, my hopes sinking with each step I take.

'Wait, it's OK. I'll come.'

I release a breath – which I'm very aware that I've been holding, and spin around. 'Thanks, I owe you. But only if you're sure?'

'Yeah, I can stay for one night and come back with him tomorrow. I don't know what he's so worried about anyway. Your mum wouldn't have invited you if it was dangerous.'

A gull wheels in circles overhead, its harsh cry mocking me. My mum practically ordered me to stay away from the island. She was right about people attacking me, so maybe I *shouldn't* go? I've no idea whose 'powers are strongest at the lighthouse', and after my dream about the woman in the chrysalis, I'm not sure I want to find out.

Tom must see the anxiety on my face, as he adds, 'Don't worry – I won't get in your way. I'm used to kipping on the sofa. You'll barely notice I'm there.'

'Time's up! Are you coming or not?'

Tom calls back to the boatman. 'We're coming. Hang on, I'll just get our things!'

He lopes off towards the car and I chase after him. I've no idea how my mum will react when she sees me; I can't let him do this without warning him.

I grab his arm. 'Tom, there's something I need to tell you. My mum didn't invite me here, she told me to stay away. She said some weird stuff on the phone and, well, I'm not sure how pleased she'll be to see me.'

His face drops. 'Oh.'

'If you don't want to come, I'll understand.'

He leans into the open boot of the car and I watch as he shoves clothes into a rucksack, trying to read the movements of his body. He puts my wet clothes into a bin liner then hands them to me, along with my work bag.

'No, it's fine. I mean, if it's what you want?'

I nod and he grabs a sleeping bag then locks the car. 'OK then.'

We trudge to the shore in silence, picking our way over the rocks and keeping our heads low to avoid the worst of the sea spray. Seagulls fly high above us. Buffeted by the wind, they squabble and pick at one another in mid-flight, their cruel squawks filling the air. Yanking up my shorts, I glance at Tom's face. He probably thought he was going to some joyous family reunion. I bet he regrets offering to come with me now. But

66

whatever thoughts are circling in his head, his expression gives nothing away. I don't like keeping things from him, yet how can I tell him the truth – not just about what my mum said, but about everything?

7

The boat is sitting on a low metal frame, which is attached to the tractor. Behind it, the pebbly shoreline is covered with mounds of stinking brown seaweed, the sulphurous odour so strong I can taste it in the back of my throat. It reminds me of the horrible smell in the butterfly house and then outside the café, and I feel my stomach clench.

As we reach the end of the slope, I check the boatman for any signs of odd behaviour, but he seems normal – apart from huffing impatiently.

'Come on. That's it, this way now.' He gestures towards a metal ladder at the rear of the boat and we climb the six steps and go aboard. At the front is a covered cab and along the sides are two narrow benches, their yellow paintwork rusted and peeling. It's much smaller than it looked from a distance; I'm guessing it could carry a dozen passengers at most.

David follows us up the ladder and I offer to pay, but he refuses to take any money.

'You put that away. Family's different.'

'OK, if you're sure. Thank you.'

An odd look flashes across his face: pity mixed with anxiety. He turns away and then produces two lifejackets, watching as we put them on and then tugging at each of us in turn to check they're secure. Seemingly satisfied, he goes to the front of the boat and ducks his head into the cabin. A moment later, he leans out and shouts something in Welsh. On his signal, the tractor pushes us down into the water. Once the boat is afloat, the engines grumble into life and the tractor reverses up the slipway, taking the trailer with it.

I hold on to the metal rail and peer over the edge. Waves slap and slop against the side of the boat, sea foam surging and dispersing amidst the swirling seaweed, the long brown tendrils wavering like the hair of drowned women. Tom sits on the bench opposite me and stares at his feet.

'Are you OK?' I ask.

He glances up and frowns. 'Sorry, I'm not good with boats.'

'It isn't far. We should be there soon.'

He manages a weak smile, then drops his head once David steers the boat around and motors us out to sea. The thrum of the engines vibrates through my body, filling my ears with its drone until I can barely hear the gulls and the relentless wind is reduced to a thin whistle.

While Tom hunkers into himself, I turn my face upward and breathe in the salty air. The water is brisker away from the land, the choppy green-grey waves churning and heaving, their colours darkening to murkier greens and black. Staring into their depths fills me with melancholy and I pull my gaze away and watch the trails of white bubbling in our wake. As the shoreline dwindles, I'm gripped by the sense that my life will never be the same again. That somehow, I can never go back.

The boat picks up speed, waves hitting us on every side and sending spray exploding over the deck. Glancing at Tom, I wonder whether to tell him about the things my mum said and everything that's been happening. He grips the seat, his knuckles white, and then bends forward and covers his mouth. Maybe now isn't the time.

A shadow falls over us and I look up and see a bird, flying three or four metres above the boat. It's almost impossibly big – a prehistoric-looking thing that reminds me of a Pterodactyl. Several more appear alongside it and a shiver of excitement runs through me. I hold up my arm and my heart lifts, wishing I could reach out and touch them, wishing I could fly with them. The feeling surprises me and I laugh at myself. I'm like one of the little kids at the butterfly centre, enraptured by the magic of nature.

David shouts from the cab. 'Tom, isn't it? Come and look at this!'

Tom groans, his face sickly pale. I can't see him going anywhere until we're back on dry land. Watching my footing on the slippery deck, I walk over and he mutters, 'Gonna vom', then turns and deposits his lunch into the sea.

I pat his back, wishing I could help. 'Hang in there.'

He wipes his mouth and looks so embarrassed I feel bad for him. I reach inside my bag and hand him a bottle of water.

'You know what's good for seasickness?' I ask.

He takes the water and smiles weakly. 'Sitting under a tree?'

I laugh. 'Keeping your eyes on the horizon, it can help to re—'

He shoves me aside and I jump back as he vomits into the

waves again. If there's one thing worse than throwing your guts up, it's doing it with an audience.

Deciding to see what David wants, I lift up my shorts and head to the covered cab. The relentless rocking of the waves is worse now I'm standing, and it isn't long until sweat prickles on the back of my neck and I start to feel queasy. I walk a few steps and the boat lists to one side. Taking a deep breath, I get my balance and shuffle forward when it moves in the opposite direction, making me lurch sideways.

Eventually I stagger into the open cab and find David sitting at the steering wheel, peering at something through the dirty window. He sees me and looks surprised.

'Tom's feeling sick,' I explain.

'Oh. I was going to show him this.'

My legs are freezing cold and hopelessly weak. Not trusting them to hold me up, I drop onto the seat next to David. He points outside. One of the huge black birds is perched on the bow of the boat, facing out to sea. It turns to the side and its proud black chest shimmers with bronze scales that flash green and purple.

'What is it, a cormorant?' I ask.

David raises his eyebrows and nods, seemingly impressed. 'Sea-ravens are what we call them. The Irish call them the *cailleach dhubh* – the black hag. Sinister-looking things if you ask me. I've seen plenty in my time, but never had one land on the boat before.'

The creature repositions its feet and spreads its massive black wings, hanging them open to dry like a broken umbrella. It makes a juddering, throaty sound almost as if it's talking – then it turns to look straight at me and cackles.

I flinch but the bird has already gone – taken up into the clouds with a single, mighty flap of its wings. The boatman ducks his head and we watch through the window as more dark shapes appear in the sky.

'That's five, six. No, wait . . . eight of them. Well I'll be.'

'What's that?' I ask.

He strokes his moustache and sniffs. 'There's an old superstition that says the birds are witches. If you see nine of them in the sky at once, death is sure to follow.'

'How cheerful.'

He laughs. 'The island is full of stories. I don't imagine King Arthur or Merlin is over there either, despite what some folks would have you believe.'

I think back to the research I did, remembering how some people think the place is Avalon. In the stories, King Arthur was taken by boat to an island shrouded in mist. Bardsey is the nearest island to where he fell in battle on the mainland, and there was something to do with Avalon meaning 'Isle of Apples' and Bardsey having its own species of apple tree. It all sounds a bit convenient; a way to bring in the tourists. But there were other things I read too.

'Is it true about the saints?' I ask.

David nods. 'Aye, that's right. Twenty thousand holy confessors and martyrs are buried on the island. Dig anywhere and you'll find bones. Religious men have been making pilgrimages to the place since the fifth century; hundreds still do every summer. The land is said to be so holy that anyone who dies there goes to heaven. I can't say if it's true, though there have been plenty of ghost sightings over the years. I just know the place is special.'

I nod and make a mental note not to go digging. He peers at the sky through the window, and I count eight of the birds, flying so low I can see their long thin legs. It's easy to imagine a group of witches above us, their wings fluttering like tattered black cloaks.

David shrinks into his jacket and mutters, 'There's no getting away from it, people have seen some odd things. Your aunt, for one.'

My heart beats a little faster. 'Sarah?'

His body tenses on the seat next to me. 'When did you last speak to her?' he asks.

I fiddle with my nose stud, not wanting to say the wrong thing. 'A while ago. Why?'

'I'm afraid she's . . . well, she's more preoccupied of late.'

I nod, pretending to understand. 'Is it the same thing as before?'

'Aye. I don't think living alone helps, but she refuses to leave the island – reckons she needs to keep them at bay.' He clearly thinks I know what he means by 'them', and I don't want him to realise I know nothing about her.

He peers at the sky again then narrows his eyes at me. 'You look just like her, you know. I saw the family resemblance straight off.'

I glance away, excited to know it's not just the man who replied to my post who thinks we look alike.

He huffs and adds, 'I don't like to think of her alone there in winter. It's not right, being the only one on the island without a living soul for company.'

I glance at the misty outline of the island, which is growing bigger by the minute, and a pulse of alarm beats in my throat. I knew Bardsey had a small population but I didn't realise we would literally be the only ones there apart from my mother.

'Is there no one else on the island at all?'

'There are ten families who live there in summer and the holiday cottages are always booked up, thanks to the tourists. But everyone leaves in winter, even the animals.'

'You said you were bringing them across tomorrow. Do you mean people's pets?'

He laughs. 'No, the farm animals. There's a larger boat we use to take over livestock. We bring the whole lot of them to the mainland before winter sets in.'

'Because of the cold?'

He gives me a strange look. 'That too.'

'Can't anyone stay to look after them? It seems a lot of effort to move them all.'

He shrugs. 'The island trust hired a family to act as caretakers a few years back. They came over from the mainland and were meant to maintain the holiday cottages and look after the place in winter. They made a BBC documentary about it. The family didn't last two minutes. Their little lad slipped on the rocks their first day here and got his leg badly cut up. The island likes company in summer, but come winter . . . No, you couldn't pay me to stay.'

Something dark and vast slides across the surface of my thoughts like the shadow of a cormorant flying overhead, and I decide that I don't want to hear any more of his stories.

I grab the edge of the seat and get to my feet. 'I should check on Tom.'

David doesn't respond, seemingly too busy staring out of the window and counting non-existent witches. I leave the cabin and take a few steps when he calls out. 'Ah, there she is – Bardsey Island, or to the Welsh that live here, Ynys Enlli.'

Grabbing the rail, I spin around and gasp. Ominous cliffs appear out of the mist, towering over me. I crane my neck upwards. Hundreds of seabirds are nesting on the jagged black crags, the rocks beneath streaked white by feathers and mess. Dozens more fly in dizzying circles high above me, tiny specks of white whirling like snowflakes. The air is alive with their cries. Somehow it feels like a warning.

8

We approach the island from behind the mountain, moving parallel to the cliffs and keeping our distance from the rocks that protrude from the sea like broken teeth. Forced through narrow inlets, the water explodes in great towering arcs of sea spray, shooting and spurting in cascading showers. My heart thuds with each boom and crash of the waves, the noise so loud I can feel it in my body.

The sea is choppier now, the water heaving and rolling, and the boat feels tiny and insignificant as it pitches up and down. Tom clings on to the rail and what's left of his stomach contents and I feel bad for leaving him. I take a few lurching steps towards him, then we round the headland and I get my first proper view of Bardsey.

The sight stops my breath. The rounded mountain that dominates one side of the island gives way to land that is almost completely flat. About a dozen stone houses sit at the base of the mountain, leading in a line towards the cliffs. Beyond are fields with a scattering of farmhouses, stretching a mile or so to where the lighthouse stands. Even from this distance the red-and-white striped tower looks imposing.

I wipe my eyes, my face sore from the wind, and scan the smaller buildings that surround the base of the tower. I can't make out the details from here, but one of them has to be the lighthouse cottage where my mother lives. It's strange to think of her living in such a desolate place, so cut off from the rest of the world. I can't imagine what it's like to be here alone with only the crash of waves and wildlife for company.

As the boat motors towards a distant bay, I gaze ahead at the view, wanting to absorb every detail. Clouds race across the windswept sky, creating a shifting patchwork of shadow on the fields below and spotlighting the lighthouse in a shaft of silvery sunlight. The scene is so familiar it makes my chest ache. I feel as if I've been here before, even though I know it's impossible for me to have a memory of the island. My mother abandoned me when I was a tiny baby; I was too young to remember living here, or anything else. And yet I *know* this place. The strength of my conviction makes my skin prickle. I don't feel like smiling but a grin spreads across my face anyway.

Finally, I am home.

The words bubble up in my mind and though the voice is my own, the thought doesn't seem like mine. It feels like it belongs to someone else.

Unnerved, I turn my back on the island and head towards Tom, who's bent over with one hand covering his mouth and the other gripping the rail.

'We're almost there now.'

He looks up and his face is deathly white, the tips of his ears bright pink. Relief flashes into his eyes and then the boat hits another wave and he buries his head in his hands. I sit and touch his shoulder. A few days ago, the thought of stroking his back would have filled me with awkwardness, but he looks so poorly and I owe him so much. It's not just that he's driven me all this way, or that I feel guilty he's only here because of me. Tom is the first person I've opened up to in a long time, and it's nice to have someone who feels like a friend.

An outcrop of granite lies ahead of us, its surface covered with waving seaweed. Looking closer, I realise the rippling movement is actually blubber – dozens of seals are slapping their weighty bellies against the rocks and nudging each other. I notice several pups amongst the hefty adults, their pale fur easy to spot against the mass of mottled browns and black. The animals seem untroubled by our presence, but as we get closer the sound of the boat's engine makes some of the adults grunt and lumber away, their large bodies moving with surprising agility as they slip into the water.

There are more creatures than I first thought: maybe even a hundred of them basking on rocks and dipping playfully in and out of the waves. Round wet heads pop up from beneath the surface all around us, their sleek faces watching me with curious, soft black eyes. I've never been this close to seals before, or seen so many in one place.

After a few minutes, the engine lowers a gear and the boat heads into the bay. I notice a grey shape on the beach, smoother and softer looking than the rocks that surround it. Beneath the foam and seaweed is a pup. I watch, concerned that it's so far from the rest of the group, when the surf flips it over. Its body is cut open, revealing a gaping red hole, its black eyes staring lifelessly. I turn away and remind myself that death is a part of nature, but it's always worse when a baby dies. I guess the desire to protect the young is hardwired into everyone whether you have children or not – or at least it's supposed to be.

The boat slows, bumping gently along a line of black tyres attached to the harbour wall, before coming to a stop. I squeeze Tom's arm. 'You can come out now. We're here.' He takes a while to respond and I'm relieved when he straightens up and looks around.

'Thank Christ for that,' he murmurs. 'I never want to see another boat ever again.'

David exits the cab and raises his hand in acknowledgement, then climbs down the ladder and jogs across the walkway towards a wooden boathouse. We watch as he gets into a specially adapted tractor, similar to the one that pushed us into the water on the mainland, and drives towards us. Once in position on the trailer, the tractor hauls the boat out of the water and up onto the island.

Standing at the bottom of the ladder, David calls for us to hand him our things. Tom steps forward and immediately sways to one side, glaring at his feet like he's woken from a night of heavy drinking to find his shoelaces have been tied together.

David chuckles. 'How are you holding up there?'

'Tom's not good with boats,' I say, giving him a wry smile.

'Oh, I wouldn't say that,' Tom replies. 'It was very refreshing. I'm already looking forward to the return crossing.' He runs a hand through his fringe then pats the side of the boat a little too enthusiastically. Something tells me he'd chop it up for firewood if he could.

I hand David our bags and he laughs. 'Just as well. We were

lucky with the weather today but the forecast isn't looking so good. It might get a bit rough next time.'

Tom flashes me a look that says he doesn't want to find out what a 'rough' crossing is like, and I know how he feels. Yanking up my shorts, I go down the ladder first, taking it slowly. We might be on land now but my legs don't seem to know that. Tom follows me and stumbles down the metal steps, his arms flailing as his knees buckle beneath him.

I cover my mouth and try not to laugh, but thankfully he sees the funny side. As we walk behind the boatman, Tom staggers into me and throws his arm around my shoulder. 'Why do I feel like we should be going to an all-night kebab shop?' he whispers.

'Is this what you're like after a pint?'

'I'm more of a tequila man.' He laughs.

'Very exotic. Is that the one with the worm inside the bottle?'

He rubs his stomach. 'Actually, tequila is the devil's work. I had a bad experience with the stuff once. Let's not talk about it.'

I smile and he takes his arm from my shoulder, letting me go first up the narrow path. Ahead of us are almost a dozen cottages of various sizes, sitting in a line at the base of the mountain. The climb is steep, the ground rutted with stones and overgrown with knee-high spiky grass, and it isn't long until both of us are breathing hard.

David stops before an imposing stone farmhouse with a crumbling wall at the front. 'I'm staying here tonight, in case you need me.' The same look as before flashes across his face – anxiety mixed with pity. He opens his mouth as if to say something, then seemingly changes his mind and walks to a muddy two-seater quad bike with a trailer on the back. While he puts our things inside, Tom and I glance around at the barns and outbuildings.

Even though there's no one here, I have the sense that someone is aware of our presence. I scan the ground, worried I might see a swirl of shadow, but there's nothing. No horrible smell either, just the briny scent of the sea. The back of my neck prickles and I glance at the farmhouse, half-expecting to see a figure looking at us, but there's no one.

Tom frowns. 'Bit of a lonely place to live, isn't it?'

A sheep bleats in the distance and I'm reminded that there won't even be any farm animals when David takes them across tomorrow. Surely they can survive here just as well as on the mainland? And then I remember that the animals aren't the problem, it's finding someone to stay and look after them. I still don't understand how an island can supposedly tolerate company in summer but not winter. I thought farmers were practical people, but they must be as superstitious as everyone else here.

'So are all of these houses empty?' I ask David.

He climbs onto the seat of the quad bike. 'Aye. Like I said, the families who live on the island have already cleared out for winter. They won't be back until spring.'

I look down the hill towards the bay and over the windswept fields with their smattering of isolated farmhouses. The boatman follows my gaze and sighs. 'The holiday cottages are shut up now and the old flint schoolhouse was closed in the fifties. It's the same with a lot of islands. The population dwindles and before you know it, a whole community's lost.' He clears his throat and I realise he's waiting for us. 'Best get moving while there's still light. It's not the most comfortable ride, but the lighthouse isn't far.'

Tom's face falls but he dutifully climbs into the trailer and then rearranges the bags so we have something to lean against. There's barely any space and he has to bend his knees to fit his legs inside. I find a small gap and tuck myself into it, doing my best not to look smug.

David turns in his seat. 'You kids comfortable back there?'

I nod and Tom elbows me. 'Yeah, apart from Shorty here taking up all the room.'

It doesn't seem too bad, until David starts the engine and the trailer begins rattling along the stone-rutted track. My stomach lurches with each bump and jolt and I feel guilty for putting Tom through the boat crossing and now this. Even so, I will us to go faster. I've waited so long to meet my mum that I don't want to wait a moment longer.

We pass a big white house and a stone chapel, then more cottages and a much older structure.

'What's that?' shouts Tom.

David glances to his right. 'What's left of the old abbey – a medieval monastery from the fifth century.'

The crumbling stone ruin overlooks a plot of gravestones, which stick up from the long grass at odd angles. Several are Celtic in design, as tall as men with a round circle enclosing an even-sided cross on top. I think of the twenty thousand saints who are buried here and how the earth must be jam-packed with bodies. It feels wrong for the dead to outnumber the living. If they were to rise up, there would be an army of them.

David takes us past the last few remaining properties then turns off the dirt track and bumps across open fields. The wind is crueller now we're more exposed and I wipe my eyes as we pick up speed. From up here, the expanse of slate-grey sea looks even more hostile – monstrous white-crested waves racing ceaselessly to the shore, waging war on the land.

The dark blue sky is streaked with clouds, the light already fading. Peering hard, I shift position in the trailer and lean sideways to get a better view of the lighthouse. It sits at the far edge of the island on a thin strip of land that juts into the water, the square tower four times the height of the dwellings that surround it. Beyond the buildings, wavering grass slopes down to a beach on either side, the land so narrow it would only take a few minutes to walk to the nearest shore. Beset by the raging sea, the lighthouse appears lonely and haunted, yet fiercely proud too – defiant even.

Tom is frowning at the view, his hair messy and ruffled by the wind. I'm wondering what he makes of being here when he notices me looking. 'How are you feeling?' he asks.

I manage a tight smile. So many emotions are swirling inside me right now, I couldn't put my feelings into words if I tried.

When I don't say anything, he asks, 'So what's the plan? We get your mum to persuade David you can stay here with her, and I go back with him tomorrow?'

'Yes, thanks.' I smile properly this time, grateful for his company. With the strangeness of everything that's been happening, it's a comfort to be with someone I know.

Only one more field to cross and we'll be there. I clutch the locket around my neck, my palms sweaty despite the cold. As the lighthouse looms bigger, so do my fears. What if my mum refuses to speak to me? What if she sends us away?

The quad bike stops at the bottom of a long dirt track that leads to the lighthouse and Tom and I share a glance. Surely he isn't going to make us walk the rest of the way? David gets off the bike and approaches the rear of the trailer.

'Here we are. Like I said, I'll be back in a week for a last check of the place, weather permitting. So you'll need to come with me then, or you'll be here until spring.'

Tom flashes me a look then climbs out of the trailer. 'You're going back tomorrow, right?'

The boatman nods. 'Aye, that's right. I'm taking the last of the farm animals across. I'll be leaving at two. If you come looking for me after that, I shan't be there.' He points along the track towards a group of white buildings. 'Sarah lives there – the one with the sloping roof, adjoining the tower. It's the second green door you want, the one at the end.'

Tom grabs our things and turns to David. 'Aren't you coming up with us?'

'No, I'll get off. I've already delivered Sarah's supplies for winter and I don't want to turn up unexpected.' He straightens his back and I get the sense he's steeling himself to leave us. 'She's never had visitors before; you must be very special to her. Give her my best, won't you?'

I smile politely, surprised by his sudden formality. 'Well, thanks for everything. It was kind of you to bring us.' I raise my hand in farewell then yank up my shorts and march along the path.

The quad bike starts up and Tom stands and watches it drive away.

'You coming?' I call.

He hurries to catch up with me. 'It seems a bit weird, dropping us here. I mean, what if your mum's out?'

'I hardly think she's popped to Tesco, do you?'

'No, but I thought the plan was for her to talk to David, and persuade him to let you stay on your own.'

I shrug, not knowing whether she's going to let me stay the night, never mind both of us. 'Don't worry. I'm sure David will take you back with him tomorrow.'

Tom nods, but his eyes are full of uncertainty. I'm not sure whether he's worried about being stranded on the island, or how my mother will react when she has unexpected visitors. Either way, I'm glad I warned him that she doesn't want me here.

We make our way along the track without speaking, the wail of the wind and the crashing waves the only sounds. A faint early-evening moon hangs high in the sky, its silvery face shrouded by cloud. I glance at it and shiver. If my mum doesn't let us stay, we'll have a long walk back to the farmhouse – in the dark.

A red light appears, bathing the gravel before us, and we lift our chins and look up. The glow is coming from the top of the lighthouse.

Tom mutters. 'I thought lighthouses had a white light?'

'Me too.'

The light doesn't sweep across the land. It remains fixed, stretching for miles in all directions, spilling over the earth like blood. The tower seemed so majestic from a distance, but close up it looks different – a tyrannical, monstrous thing.

We pass several disused-looking properties and Tom stops to peer inside the window of a circular stone building with a flat roof, its white-painted walls badly peeling. I look inside and see a bed in the centre of the room, surrounded by bits of broken furniture.

Next to it is the lighthouse. Adjoining the square tower is a low connecting building, no more than six feet long, with a dark green door in the middle. At the other end is a cottage with a row of square windows on the ground floor and two large dormer ones in the slate roof. We walk to the end of the cottage and find another green door.

Tom smiles at me encouragingly. 'Ready?'

I nod and raise my hand to knock, when it swings open.

A petite woman stands in the doorway, her face framed by long blonde hair. I stare at her, struck by how similar we are – we have the same wide-set eyes, rounded cheeks and thin lips. Apart from our hair and a few lines on her face, we look almost identical. Hope blooms in my chest. I've found her. After years of searching, I've finally found her – my mum.

For a moment, she doesn't move or speak. She just stands there, blinking at me. I walk forward, desperately hoping for a sign that she's pleased to see me, when I notice something glint in her hand: the silver blade of a carving knife. My stomach tightens and I pause, suddenly wary. Unsure what to say, I reach into my coat and lift the butterfly locket from my neck. Her eyes fill with tears and she rushes forward and hugs me.

She speaks in a soft Welsh accent, her voice a breathy whisper. 'It's you. It's really you, my darling Carys.'

'My name's Ivy now,' I say quietly.

'Of course, sorry. You said in your letter.' She holds me a moment longer, then draws back, her forehead creasing as she glances down the track. Gripping my shoulders, she stares into my eyes. 'You shouldn't have come here. I told you it's not safe.'

9

She grabs my arm and pulls me into the house, then gestures for Tom to enter. We stand in the hallway and watch as she leans out of the door and checks in both directions. 'Were you followed?' she asks. There's an animal-like nervousness to her – it's not just her wild eyes and unbrushed hair. Every muscle of her body seems tense, her energy ragged like a creature that's lived on fear too long.

I glance at Tom, unsure what she means. 'The boatman brought us, but he left.'

'The shadows – have they found you?'

Bile rises to my throat. Part of me had been hoping the shadow I saw was an optical illusion, but it must have been real. How else would she know to ask about them?

She locks the door, sliding across several heavy iron bolts, and then tucks the knife into the waistband of her skirt. 'You've seen them, haven't you?' I nod and she holds my shoulders, her eyes flashing. 'Think. Have you seen any on the island?'

I shake my head and she lets out a breath then turns her attention to Tom. He looks ridiculously tall under the low ceiling, and more than a little rattled. I can't imagine what he must be thinking.

'This is my friend, Tom.'

He smiles warily. 'Hello. I hope you don't mind me coming along.'

'Has he been infected?' she asks.

Tom coughs. 'Excuse me?'

'Have the shadows entered him? Is he showing any signs?'

I'm desperate to ask her what the shadows are, but I can't with Tom here. I try to sound reassuring, concerned that she might make him leave. 'No. He's fine.'

Tom laughs like he's been left out of a bizarre joke and someone will explain it at any moment. When I don't say anything, he frowns at my mum then at me, his expression darkening.

'Follow me, quickly now.' She turns and hurries down the dimly lit passageway and I start to follow her, when Tom grabs my arm.

'I don't know what's going on here, Ivy, but we should leave.'

'If you want to go, you can. I'm sorry, but I have to stay.'

He watches my mother's retreating back and cringes. 'Your mum clearly needs help. Please come to the farmhouse with me. Let's talk to the boatman and maybe he can –'

'I told you, I'm not going.'

He clenches his jaw. 'But I *can't* leave you here on your own. Not while she's waving a knife around.'

'So stay.'

He glances at the door and back to me, and I shrug to show I don't mind either way. But I do. I want him to stay, I just can't bring myself to say it. He rubs his forehead and sighs as if he's about to do something he knows is stupid. 'OK. I'll stay, but I want you to come back to the mainland with me tomorrow. Whatever's going on here, it doesn't feel right.'

I nod and he looks past me and raises his eyebrows. My mum has stopped at the end of the hallway and is crouched on the floor. She holds out the knife and stands up, drawing a rectangle in the air. I walk over and notice a line of white powder on the floor.

'Salt for protection,' she explains. 'Step over and I will close the opening after you.'

Tom's eyes widen and I touch his arm, willing him to go along with it. I do as she says and a sudden draught of icy air swirls about my legs. Feeling unnerved, I watch as Tom follows me, but if he notices the inexplicable change in temperature he doesn't say anything. My mother steps over the salt and then turns and crouches down again, mumbling indistinct words as she traces an invisible door in the opposite direction.

'The line marks the edge of protection. Whatever happens, do not cross it and never, under any circumstances, enter the lighthouse. You must do exactly as I say or I can't promise you'll be safe.'

I nod as if I understand, and she walks to the end of the passageway and opens a door to reveal an old-fashioned kitchen. A sturdy-looking dresser flanks the right side of the room, its shelves cluttered with glass jars and bottles. On the left are two windows and a cracked ceramic sink, and in the centre is a table with eight chairs. A range cooker sits at the far end, bunches of dried herbs hanging above it, attached to a rail suspended from the ceiling.

The slate floor and exposed stone walls make the place feel old, and the only light comes from paraffin lamps dotted about the room. Mixed with the red glow from the lighthouse, their flickering light makes everything appear strangely unreal. A fusty dampness permeates the air and there's another odour – the bitter, pungent smell of burning herbs. Smoke billows from a brass dish on the dresser and I spot another on the floor, the pale wraiths of vapour swirling around the empty chairs like ghosts.

My mum picks up a lamp from the table and its flame leaps up, casting dark shadows about the room. As she raises it to my face, I'm struck again by how similar we are. It's like looking into a mirror, only the grey eyes that stare into mine don't reassure me that everything will be OK. They are full of pain.

She tucks my hair behind my ears and whispers, 'I can't tell you how much I've longed to meet you.' Her eyes glisten with tears and emotion closes my throat. There's so much I want to ask her, so much I want to know, but I'm afraid to speak in case I cry. She strokes my cheek and I think she's going to say something else, but then she glances at Tom, as if remembering we have an audience. Sighing, she turns and grabs two lamps from the dresser, then slides a box of matches into her skirt pocket. 'I'll show you where you can sleep. It's not much, sorry.'

We cross the room and follow her into a different gloomy corridor. 'The bathroom,' she says, pointing to a closed door on our right. She walks towards a narrow staircase and takes the first step, then whips around as if she has heard something. At the far end of the passageway is a door with several large planks of wood hammered across it. Whoever boarded it up did a rough job, or they were in a hurry.

'What's with the door?' asks Tom.

My mother's eyes shine in the lamplight. 'It's blocked up for good reason. Stay away from it – no matter what you hear on the other side.'

Tom mumbles, 'Of course, should have known.'

I give him a look, but I can hardly blame him. This *is* all starting to feel very weird. My mum continues up the stairs and I glance back at the door, wondering what could be behind it to make a noise. Rats? The connecting building looked short from the outside, nothing more than a passageway leading to the lighthouse tower, so it's not like there can be a whole other room there. Peering at it, I notice that dozens of symbols have been painted on the door. On the ground is another line of salt, but protection from what?

We follow her up the stairs, the wood creaking and groaning under our feet as if the house doesn't want us here. At the top are three closed doors. She points to one and says, 'That's my room,' then passes another closed door and pushes open the last one.

A large dormer window dominates the attic space, bathing it in the eerie red glow from the lighthouse. There are two single metal beds, one on either side of the window, both with stained mattresses. Between them is a bedside table that looks at least fifty years old. To the right of the room is a battered wardrobe and chest of drawers and along the opposite wall is a sagging bookcase, its shelves crammed with books. Piles of them have been stacked vertically on top, reaching all the way to the sloping ceiling.

She places the lamps on the chest of drawers, along with the matches she pulls from her skirt, then goes to the wardrobe. The door creaks in complaint as she opens it, releasing an unpleasant waft of mothballs. She takes out some bedlinen and drops a pile onto each bed.

'The other room is used for storage and doesn't have any beds. I hope you're OK to share?'

'It's fine. Thank you.' I smile tightly and glance around.

Maybe it comes from moving around so much, but I've always been able to pick up on the emotions of a place. As soon as I walked into a foster placement, I knew if the kids before me had been happy or not; an intuition that proved helpful more than once. Standing here now, the damp-spotted walls and fusty smell don't bother me – I've stayed in worse places – but something feels off. A sour sadness hangs in the air, along with a feverish kind of fear, as if whoever slept here had terrible nightmares.

Tom makes towards the other bed, banging his head on the sloping ceiling. He rubs it and mutters something I can't quite catch, but was unlikely to be 'duck'. He throws his stuff down then goes to the window. 'Is it me, or is the light even redder up here?' he asks.

My mother steps forward and looks outside, her voice quiet. 'The light used to be white but they changed it some years ago. Migratory seabirds had a habit of flying into the tower. Thousands of them would die in a single night, their bodies littered over the headland. I remember helping my father pick up the carcasses as a little girl. Scientists couldn't understand why it was happening. They thought the rotating white optic affected the birds' navigation somehow, so they changed it to a fixed LED lamp.'

'And did it work?' I ask.

'Not really. But then it wasn't the light attracting them to begin with.'

Tom coughs awkwardly and changes the subject. 'And those other buildings, what are they?'

'The white circular building used to be the engine room to the lighthouse, but it's run by solar energy now. The other cottage is disused, no one's lived there for years, and the rest is used for storage.'

I take my phone from my pocket and place it on the bedside table, then empty my work clothes onto the mattress, followed by the contents of my rucksack: hairbrush, some chewing gum and a box of tampons.

My mum glances at my damp clothes, a look of pity on her face. 'Is that all you have?'

'I left in a rush.'

She points to the wardrobe. 'You should find something in there that fits.'

'OK. Thanks.'

She goes to the dresser and fiddles with the dials of the paraffin lamps, making the flames jump. 'There's no electricity, so you'll need these.' She picks up one of the lamps and hesitates. 'You must be hungry. I've got something in the oven. I'm sure I can make it stretch.' Her gaze softens and I have the impression she doesn't want to leave my side, even for a moment. 'If you want to come down now, I can make you a hot drink?'

'Sure.'

Tom rubs his cheek. 'If it's OK, I'll get washed up and join you in a bit.'

My mum nods and gives me a hopeful smile. 'See you in the kitchen.'

Once she closes the door, Tom flops onto the bed by the bookcase. He sweeps his fringe from his eyes and I know he's going to ask me questions I can't answer.

'How much do you know about your m—'

I speak at the same time. 'Thanks for giving us some time alone.'

He shrugs. 'No worries. I'm sure I'll find something to keep me entertained.' He surveys the bookshelves next to him and pulls out a hardback and turns it over. '*A Shadowbook of Spells.*' He frowns as he reads out more titles. '*Celtic Lore and Spellcraft of the Dark Goddess, Protection Against Black Magick.* Yup, sounds like my kind of thing.'

He turns on the bed to face me. 'I know it's not my place to say anything, but you can see why I'm not comfortable staying here, can't you?' I nod and he muses, 'I thought it was weird how the boatman didn't want you to come here on your own, but it makes sense now.' He takes a moment then adds, 'You know how your mum was going on about shadows?'

'Yes?' I answer, hoping he might have seen something before. If he's seen them too, then maybe he can help me make sense of things.

'Didn't you say the old lady talked about shadows trying to get inside her?'

I nod and he looks relieved. 'Well, that explains it. You probably misheard what she said because of the weird ideas your mum's been putting in your head. You said you've only spoken to her on the phone. I mean, how much do you know about her really?'

'She didn't mention anything about shadows on the phone.'

'I thought she told you some weird stuff?'

I draw in a sharp breath. 'She did, but . . .'

He must be able to sense my frustration, as he softens his voice. 'I'm just worried you don't know anything about her.' He looks at me expectantly then frowns. 'You're not saying much. I mean, her behaviour isn't exactly normal, is it?'

I know what he's thinking, but however strange my mother seems I know she's not delusional. I've seen the shadows too. Even if I tell him, he's not going to believe me – I'm not sure *I* would believe me.

He sighs as if sensing I'm not going to answer. 'Right, I'm going to get washed up.'

I watch as he takes off his coat, then grabs his bag and stands up, forgetting the low ceiling. 'Ow! I don't think this house likes me very much.' I laugh and he comes over and rests his forearm on my head like he used to at work sometimes. 'Don't be mean, you know I bruise easy. Good luck with your mum, yeah?'

'Thanks.'

Once he goes out of the door, I open the wardrobe and search through the rail of clothes. I take out a long woollen skirt and black jumper, and then find some thick tights and socks in a drawer. It's a relief to put on something that fits, even if it does reek of mothballs. Pushing up the sleeves of the shapeless jumper, I realise I'm dressed identically to my mum.

I pick up the lamp and turn to go when I notice something move at the window. A dark shape swoops past, too big for a bird, and then I remember the cormorants I saw on the boat. I walk over and look out, but I can't see any of the fearsome black seabirds.

The lighthouse stands at the end of the building, dominating the cottage. Its pale walls take on an ethereal glow in the dying light, the bands of red paint the colour of dried blood. A white metal platform runs around the glass lantern at the top. Just the thought of being up there makes me feel vulnerable. Something about its red light feels invasive, penetrating even. Why do I feel like it's watching me?

I close the curtains, relieved to shut out the unnatural crimson glow, and then turn my back to the window. The room is so much darker than it was before. I raise the lamp and the flame shudders, making strange shapes leap along the walls. The light isn't strong enough to reach into the corners of the room and I peer into a dense patch of grey that lingers beneath the sloping ceiling. I don't know why, but I have the feeling I'm not alone.

The thought sends a shiver through me and I head to the door. As I step onto the landing, the floor creaks, making me jump. And then I hear Tom singing in the bathroom downstairs, though who exactly he's inviting to *put a ring on it* is unclear. I smile and blow out a breath, determined to get it together. I bet Beyoncé isn't afraid of the dark.

I make my way down the stairs, the wood betraying my every step, then pause and listen for Tom's voice. All I hear is the wind and the crash of waves. I tell myself to turn and go to the kitchen, but I don't. My head swivels towards the boarded-up door.

Holding up the lamp, I walk to the end of the passageway and study the symbols I saw earlier. They flicker and dance in the lamplight: squiggles, dots and shapes, their outlines thick and blurry as if someone used their finger to paint them. And yet they seem too purposeful to have been done by a child. I press my palm to the wood and something in me bristles with indignation, almost as if a door has been slammed in my face. Heat prickles across my chest and my other hand grips the lamp so hard my fingernails bite into my flesh.

You're not who you think you are.

The thought comes from nowhere and I shake it from my head. Looking closer at the markings, I realise they aren't black, as I first thought, but dark red. I touch one of them, surprised to find the surface flaking away, when I hear a whisper. I recoil and it comes again, more insistent this time. Fear sluices through me. The words are low and hard to make out, but it sounds like a woman.

'What are you doing?'

I spin around, my heart banging in my chest, and find my mum staring at me. I hold her gaze and try to sound casual. 'Nothing. I was just looking at the symbols on the door.'

She glances behind me then gestures to the kitchen. 'It's cold out here. Why don't you come and get warmed up?'

I nod and wait for her to walk back down the passageway, then press my ear to the door. This time there is only the low moan of the wind outside.

10

I follow her into the kitchen and sit down while she busies herself at the stove.

'Is milk OK?' she asks.

'Milk's fine, thank you.'

She takes a pan off the stove and pours the liquid into two mugs, then hands one to me. I push the thick, wrinkled skin with my finger then take a sip, enjoying the sweetness. While I drink, my mother takes a casserole dish from the oven and a waft of onions and meat fills the room. She stirs the pot, then slides it back inside and turns to face me.

'So how long have you known Tom?'

I tighten my fingers around the mug. 'Nearly a year; we work together at the butterfly centre.' A stab of regret pierces my heart as I remember that I don't work there any more. She raises her eyebrows and I add, 'We're just friends. We're not . . .' She looks at me blankly and I wonder if she's asking about him for another reason.

'I meant what I said before. He hasn't been *infected*.' The word feels ugly and misshapen on my tongue and I gulp some milk, scalding my mouth.

She drops into the chair opposite me and leans across the table. 'But you have seen the shadows. You've seen what they can do?'

'I think so. A man attacked me at work this morning, and then a woman on the way here. They had this look on their faces. They were staring at me, but it was like they were looking through me. I think the shadows got into the woman's dog too. It kept shaking itself.'

She glances nervously about the room and nods knowingly, her expression tense. 'Yes, they can sometimes enter an animal while looking for a human host. With some people it takes longer for the shadows to get inside, but they always find a way.' She squeezes my arm so hard it hurts. 'It doesn't matter how strong the person is, or how much they love you. You can't trust anyone. Not Tom, not me . . .'

I pull away from her and she hangs her head. 'I don't want to frighten you, but the shadows are still in me and I don't know if or when . . .' She takes a deep breath. 'If the worst happens, you must do whatever it takes to survive.'

Panic grips me. 'What are they? What do they want?'

'I don't have all the answers. I can only tell you what I've seen.' She exhales and suddenly looks older, her brow furrowed with lines. 'You have to understand that the island is different; it has a special kind of energy. People have been drawn here since the fifth century, but the saints were mistaken. They thought the place was holy.' She gives a bitter laugh. 'The tourists who come in summer don't know the truth, but the islanders do. They know what happens, but they keep it secret.'

'Keep what secret?'

'Witches.' She glares in the direction of the hallway, her face full of hatred. 'Some call them faeries, but they're not. They're evil, vile creatures.'

My mouth feels dry and I swallow thickly. I don't know what I believe any more, but witches? Surely she can't think such things exist.

Her voice lowers to a whisper. 'I don't understand how or why. All I know is that they come in winter and take the form of birds. They swoop over the island, tormenting the cattle and sheep.'

My scalp prickles with realisation. 'So that's why they move the farm animals.'

She nods. 'The islanders know it's not safe to be here in winter.'

I remember the voice behind the boarded-up door and goosebumps cover my arms. Even though I find it hard to believe what she's telling me, I find myself asking, 'So why don't you leave too?'

'The witches come through the lighthouse and my spells and enchantments are the only thing holding them back.' She must notice my incredulous expression as she lets out a sigh. 'I didn't believe in witches either – not until I saw them with my own eyes. I've done everything I can to keep them out. I've read every book on the subject, tried every protection spell I can find. I don't claim to understand it – how muttering words and scattering salt and burning herbs works – but it does.'

'Why's it up to you to stop them? Why not just move away?'

'I had to make sure they weren't able to leave the island and find you.'

'*Find* me?'

A muscle twitches on her forehead and she rubs at it rhythmically. 'I saw eight of them crowded around your cot on the night you were born, ugly bent-over creatures with huge black wings and long, tangled hair. One of them turned to me and her eyes were cloudy white, her face covered with veins.'

I stare at her in shock. 'What?'

'I grabbed you and ran from the room. My father heard me scream and came running and that's when I saw it – the shadow. It slid over the wall and then passed across his face. One moment he was comforting me and the next he tried to . . .' Her voice breaks and she shakes her head. 'I had to leave to keep you safe.'

'You left me at a motorway service station.'

She swallows a sob. 'I never wanted to give you up, you have to believe me. I thought that if we got to the mainland we could start a new life together. I didn't realise the shadows had entered me until it was too late. I could feel them *inside* me, controlling me. I was afraid they'd make me hurt you.'

I sit back in my chair, my mind reeling. What she's telling me is impossible and yet there has to be *some* explanation for what's been happening. The wind moans and howls around the cottage, and my hand goes to my locket, remembering the note she left me. *I tried to keep you safe, but I see now that I can't.* I always thought she'd come from an abusive family, or was suffering from postnatal depression and was imagining things. I tried not to, but a tiny part of me resented her, believing she could have sought help if she'd wanted to. But if what she's telling me is true, I can't completely blame her for what she did. At the same time, a familiar hurt twists inside me and I have to ask.

'And you never tried to find me? I mean, over the years?'

She reaches across the table and takes my hand. 'Not a day has gone by when I haven't thought about you. I've missed you so much.' She starts to say something, then rubs her head as if she's changed her mind. 'When I read your letter, I sensed the shadows stirring in me again. It was the same feeling I had all those years ago. I realised that once I knew where you were, they would too. That's why I phoned to warn you.'

I glance around the smoky room with its eerie red glow, wishing I understood. Aside from the fact they don't exist, why would witches want to hurt me?

'What about other family – your parents, my father?' I ask.

'Mam died when I was small and my dad passed a few weeks after you were born; his heart gave out.' She sniffs sadly and adds, 'My sister Gwen took off to the mainland soon after. We haven't spoken since. As for your father, I barely knew him. He was here on holiday and we had a fling. I don't know his surname or where he lives.'

I nod, feeling disappointed. It would've been nice to have had a big family, but maybe there's a way I can track down Gwen and her daughters. I'd like to meet them at least.

'What about you?' she asks.

I stare into my empty mug and she says in a quiet voice, 'You hear about couples who can't have children and want a baby. I hope you were adopted by a nice family?'

I raise my gaze, trying not to get angry and refusing to feel sorry for myself when I know so many other kids have it much harder than me. 'No, I wasn't adopted. I've lived in care homes and with different foster families. Some of them were OK.'

Her face falls and I feel bad for telling her. She stares into space and rubs her forehead again. There's something odd about the way her finger moves back and forth, the motion jerky and pronounced.

'Are you OK?'

She doesn't respond.

'Mum?'

She lifts her chin and stares at me with empty eyes.

I leap to my feet, my heart racing.

She looks straight through me, her expression rigid. And then she shakes her head and the muscles of her face relax. 'Sorry, I lost my train of thought.' She glances at the stove. 'Dinner will be ready soon. Do you want to call Tom down?'

11

My legs feel unsteady as I walk along the passageway and call up the stairs. The voice that comes from my mouth is weak and raspy and doesn't sound like me at all. I shout for Tom again, louder this time, and a moment later he appears on the landing.

He bounds down with a grin. 'I take it dinner's ready. What is it?'

'I don't know – some kind of casserole, I think.'

'How did it go?'

I shrug and head to the kitchen. *I think my mother is under the control of witches and may try to kill me.* The thought is so absurd it almost makes me want to laugh, and yet what's the alternative? *My mum is suffering from paranoid delusions and it must be hereditary as I've been seeing things too.*

We sit at the table and she plates up the food with a smile. I watch her face for some sign of strangeness, but there's nothing. Maybe to her it felt like she had simply lost her train of thought, but I *know* that look. I've seen the staring eyes and rigid expression before. If the shadows are still inside her, how long will it be before it happens again? How long until she attacks me?

My head throbs trying to make sense of things, but it's nothing compared to the ache in my chest. I want so much to have an ally in the world, someone to belong to. I'm tired of always having to move on to the next 'family' that isn't mine. I want to get to know her and build some kind of relationship, but how can I if I don't believe her?

Tom lowers his fork, his table manners exemplary for once, and asks something about the local wildlife. Listening to their conversation, I realise they've been talking for a while. 'Wicked, hateful birds they are,' says my mum. She starts to say something else about the cormorants on the island and anger rears up inside me, the emotion so sudden it seems to come from nowhere. My face flushes and I throw down my cutlery, my food half eaten.

She looks at me in surprise, then quickly turns her attention to Tom. 'Would you like some more?'

He rubs his thighs, his shoulders doing a little wriggle. 'I'd love some, thank you.'

While her back is turned, he looks at me questioningly and I smile to show I'm OK. But I'm not. Why am I so upset? It's not like I know or care anything about cormorants. Aside from the fact the feeling makes no sense, I've always been good at controlling my emotions. I've had to be – kids with a temper don't get to stay with the best foster families for long. Even when I stamped on Mr Neeson's foot, I felt in control. I did it after months of self-restraint; if anything I should have done it sooner.

Tom stretches his arms. 'That was delicious, thank you. I'll do the washing-up.' He stands up and reaches for my plate and my mother tuts at him.

'No, you will not.'

He sits back down and for a moment no one moves or speaks. The sound of crashing waves fills the room, so loud it feels as if the sea is pounding against the walls outside, while the wind screams around the cottage. Why does it sound like women wailing? Suddenly the red light and swirling smoke is overwhelming and I can't breathe. I need to get out of here. My chair screeches against the floor as I stand up.

'Sorry, but I have a headache.'

My mother's face crumples, but then she straightens her shoulders and forces a smile. 'You've come a long way. You must be tired.'

Tom jumps to his feet. 'Don't worry. I'll make sure Ivy is OK.'

He takes two lamps from the dresser and I follow him along the passageway and start to climb the stairs, when my mother comes up behind me. She clutches my arm and whispers, 'The house is protected so you should be safe as long as you stay inside. But in case.'

I look at the knife in her hand, but don't take it.

'Please, Ivy. I couldn't bear it if . . .' She lets out a breath, her eyes shining with tears. 'I didn't say anything before, but I did look for you once. I took a boat to the mainland, but the authorities wouldn't tell me anything. I even went back to the same motorway service station. I sat there for hours, unable to stop crying, and a lady came over to me. I told her how I'd given you up, and she suggested I visit the nearby children's home. I walked around outside, hoping I might recognise you, and then I saw a girl wearing a butterfly locket.'

'You saw me?'

She nods. 'You would have been thirteen. You were with another girl, both of you wearing tiny plaits in your hair. I started to approach you, but then I sensed the shadows stirring inside me. It broke my heart, being so close to you and not being able to say hello.'

I fight back a tear, wishing we could have spent just a few minutes together. The girl she saw me with must have been Katie – we used to spend hours together, chatting and doing each other's hair. Katie was taken into care when she was ten as her mother had a drink problem. Growing up wasn't easy for her, but I was envious that she at least knew her mum. She had a face and a name to hold on to. She wasn't completely adrift in the world.

The fact that my mum tried to find me makes me feel a little better, but thinking of myself in the care home brings a fresh stab of pain. It would have meant the world to me to know she cared.

'Why didn't you tell me this before?'

'I don't know. I suppose I feel guilty that I didn't stay and talk to you. I was afraid the shadows would make me hurt you. If I'd been stronger, then maybe . . .'

I touch her hand, not wanting her to torment herself, and she holds out the knife. 'Please, Ivy. I want you to be safe. It's all that matters.'

I take it from her and she kisses me on the head. 'We'll talk more in the morning.'

Unsure what to say, I hug her then turn and run up the stairs.

Tom holds open the bedroom door for me and I go inside and throw the knife on top of the dresser.

'Expecting trouble?' he asks.

I turn away, hoping he doesn't see the distress in my face. Any minute now, he'll ask about my mum, but I can't face the prospect of a meaningful conversation. My body feels restless, my muscles tight with pent-up energy, and I pace the room in an effort to contain the emotions fighting inside me. Trying to keep a lid on my feelings is suffocating and suddenly I don't want to think about my mum, or being here, or anything else.

'It must be a lot to process, meeting your mum for the first time.'

Ignoring him, I kneel before the dresser and open a drawer. I'm sure I saw a nightdress in here earlier. After a few seconds of rummaging, I pull out a thin white gown that looks like something a Victorian ghost might wear. Suddenly I wish I was at home with my foster parents, eating takeaway pizza in my fleecy pyjamas and watching TV.

Tom blows into his hands, apparently thinking the same thing. 'I'd sell my soul for central heating right now. I can't believe I have a duvet in the car and didn't bring it.'

'Don't. I wish I'd stopped at a chemist. I don't even have a toothbrush.'

'Ah, there I can help you.' He reaches into his sports bag and produces a toothbrush still in its packet. 'I'm always leaving them behind at friends' places, so I keep some spares.' He holds out some toothpaste to go with it and I smile.

'Thanks, you're a star.'

'All part of the service.'

I try to take them, but he holds on firmly.

'What?' I ask.

He looks at me blankly, his face a picture of innocence. I pull harder but he only tightens his grip, drawing me closer.

'Come on, are you giving them to me or not?'

He tilts his head and smiles. 'You *can* talk to me, you know.'

'About my dental hygiene?'

He laughs. 'If you like. Or maybe, I don't know . . . how it went with your mum?'

I nod to show I'm giving it some thought, and then stare at the window behind him as if I've seen something. The moment he turns around, I snatch the toothpaste and brush out of his hand. He shakes his head as if he can't believe he allowed himself to be tricked, and I grin in triumph. 'Right now, I'm off to the bathroom.'

'Good luck – you'll need it.' He pulls a face and I decide not to ask.

I've barely turned my back to him when he calls out. 'Ivy?'

I spin around, bracing myself for another invitation to talk. 'Yes?'

A small white box hurtles towards me and I catch it mid-air. 'Don't forget to floss.'

I huff, wondering how he does it. Somehow he always manages to make me smile, even when I'm doing my best to be annoyed at him.

Taking a lamp from the dresser, I open the door and head across the creaky landing and down the stairs. The wood groans and I curse under my breath. It's like the house *wants* to announce my presence to the darkness.

Easing open the bathroom door, I see why Tom pulled a face. A large wooden box sits against the wall, a white toilet lid on top of it. Next to it is a ceramic sink and a shower cubicle covered with thick mould. I lift the lid and it doesn't smell too bad, most of the odour masked by sawdust. Even so, it feels odd relieving myself on a compost toilet and I find myself missing the wonders of the modern sewage system in a way I've never done before.

I'm surprised when I turn on the tap and hot water gurgles into the sink, steaming the mirrored cabinet above. The glass is mottled with rust and, like everything else, looks past its best. Aside from collecting their own rainwater, I guess the islanders rely on the boatman to bring the things they need – food, medicine, oil and gas, furniture. No wonder everything in the house is dated.

A bar of yellow soap sits in a puddle on the edge of the sink. I sniff it and recoil from the vaguely medicinal smell, then wash as quickly as I can. Shivering, I take a towel from the rail and dry myself, then change into the nightdress and pull on my jumper. As I brush my teeth, I wonder what else Tom has got in his sports bag. Maybe some hand cream or lip balm. Judging by the state of his stubble, he clearly doesn't have a razor.

I turn off the tap as best I can, unable to stop the last dribble of water, and the lamp gutters and spits. I fiddle with the tiny dial, my breath quickening. It's only a short walk back to the bedroom, but I'd rather not do it in darkness. The flame momentarily flickers out and I glance up and gasp. A pale face stares out of the mirror: a girl my age with long straight black hair parted in the middle, sharp cheekbones and full red lips.

You're not who you think you are.

I spin around, half-expecting to see someone, but the room is empty. When I turn back, the girl is gone and all I see is me.

12

By the time I get back to the room, my heart rate has almost returned to normal. I try to convince myself it was just the low light – the mirror was badly tarnished and the flickering lamplight distorted my reflection. It's been a long day and I'm tired. But whichever way I look at it, I know it wasn't my imagination.

Tom's been busy while I've been gone: both the beds are made and his sleeping bag lies across mine as an extra cover. The small act of kindness fills me with gratitude. He was only trying to help earlier; maybe I should tell him what's been happening.

He has his head in a book and barely notices as I place my lamp on the bedside table between us and then climb under the covers. He seems even taller lying down, his long legs stretching right to the end of the bed and his feet poking up under the blankets. He wriggles his toes and I'm reminded of the way he moves his shoulders when he eats.

'I take it you found something to read then?'

'It's about witchcraft. Apparently, you cast a circle as protection. If you need to pass through it, you have to cut a doorway as an opening and then reseal it. I think that's what your mum was doing in the hallway when we arrived.'

I rub my arms, feeling suddenly cold, and he eyes me with concern. 'You OK?'

'Yeah, it's just weird hearing you talk about witchcraft.'

'You should read this stuff – honestly, it's completely bonkers.'

'Somebody must take it seriously for them to publish all these books.'

'True.' He shrugs. 'But then think of all the Flat Earthers out there, not to mention the people who think the moon landing was a hoax. There's no shortage of gullible people willing to believe anything.'

He leans out and shoves the book back onto the shelf. As he does, several red notebooks jump out from the opposite end, as if pushed by an unseen hand.

'Maybe the witches did it.' He catches my gaze and grins, and I do my best to smile. My mum must seem gullible to believe in this stuff. I get it. Any thoughts I had about telling him the things I've seen are quickly forgotten.

He picks up the notebooks from the floor and his eyes widen.

'What is it?' I ask.

'I'm not sure, some kind of journal maybe.'

He hands it to me and I recognise the handwriting. The note my mother left was written in the same scrawl. I flick through the notebook, frowning at the Welsh. I only know one word of the language and unless my mother has written about a train station with a ridiculously long name, it's not going to help. I turn the pages and find symbols like the ones on the boarded-up door and other, more disturbing drawings. One shows a bent-over woman with long black hair, her face gaunt and her skin covered with spidery veins. Her eyes have been shaded, making them look cloudy, and her scrawny arms are impossibly long and thin.

Seeing it makes my mum's story feel real somehow. The ink lines are scratchy and give the drawing a kind of energy, as if the witch could turn her head to look at me.

Tom leafs through a notebook and taps a page. 'There, I knew I'd seen it before.' He holds up the book. 'You see this symbol?'

I study the circle with lines crossing it and dots inside. It's vaguely familiar, but then a lot of the signs on the door had similar markings. He raises another paperback and I notice several paragraphs have been underlined and my mum has made notes in the margin.

'It's in this book too. It's a protective seal to ward against demonic magic.'

Coldness runs through me like an electrical current.

'The shadows your mum talked about – according to this book they're a sign of demonic magic.' He turns a few pages then reads aloud. 'Witches who follow a dark path may call upon demonic forces to take control of a person. The shadows don't have a will of their own – the witch calls up a demon and then makes it do their bidding.'

'The shadows are demons?'

He nods and continues. 'Demonic possession can have a mild or catastrophic effect on the host. This can include repetitive movements, such as twitching of the facial muscles or violent jerking of the limbs.' He turns the page. 'When a demonic entity is in between hosts, it can be seen as a dark shadow.'

Realisation closes my throat.

'Maybe that's what your mum thinks she's protecting us from.' He huffs and adds, 'It's what she thought was inside *me*.'

A creak sounds on the landing and we turn and look at the closed door. It comes again, slow and drawn-out, as if someone is trying to move quietly.

C-*r-e-a-k*.

Tom frowns at me and mouths, 'What's she doing?' and I shake my head.

He eases the blankets off and I wave at him to get back into bed, but he goes to the door and drops to his knees. He's going to look through the keyhole. I imagine my mum outside, sprinkling salt or wafting around smoke, and feel a surge of protectiveness towards her. Whatever she's doing, I don't want Tom to see.

I throw off the covers and swing my feet to the floor. 'Just leave it,' I hiss.

Ignoring me, he puts his eye to the keyhole and it comes again.

C-*r-e-a-k*.

And then there's a different noise: a slow screeching sound as if someone is running their fingernails down the door.

He jumps back and stares at me.

'What is it?' I whisper. 'What's she doing?'

'She's . . . she's not there.' He blinks at me in disbelief. 'There's *no one* there.'

'What?'

He rakes his hand through his hair and stares at me, dumbfounded. 'But I heard her. She was outside.'

I push him aside and peer through the keyhole. All I see is the shadowy landing. 'It's dark; maybe you just didn't see her.'

'But she was right there. I heard a noise and the door moved. I felt a rush of air, I should have seen *something*.'

He looks at me as if expecting me to have the answer, but all I can do is shrug. If it wasn't my mum, then I don't want to think about what was scratching at the door. Gathering my courage, I pick up a lamp. 'I'll go and speak to her.'

The floorboards creak ominously as I step onto the landing, but there's no sign of her. 'She must still be up here,' I whisper. 'We'd have heard if she'd gone downstairs.' I walk to her door, then pause and listen.

'Is everything OK?'

My mother's voice comes from nowhere. I turn and she's standing at the bottom of the stairs, holding up a lamp. Her long blonde hair is more dishevelled than ever, her eyes two shiny black buttons in the dark.

'Tom – well, *we*, thought we heard something.'

Her fingers flutter to her throat. 'What did you hear?' I glance at Tom and she adds breathily, 'You must tell me if you see or hear anything.' The fear in her voice sets my nerves on edge. I'm about to tell her, when Tom cuts me off.

'Sorry. It was nothing. My mistake. Goodnight.'

He grabs me and bundles me back into the room.

'What the hell –'

He silences me with a look, then puts his arm around my shoulder and closes the door. We stand and listen to the groan of the staircase as my mother walks up the stairs, followed by the creak of the landing and the click of her door closing. He holds me tightly, so close I can feel the warmth of his body through my nightdress, and I pull away. Tom is going back to the mainland tomorrow. Whatever happens, I need to get used to being here by myself.

'You heard someone scratching at the door, didn't you?' he asks.

'Yes, but my mum was downstairs.'

'I've been thinking. She must have been standing to one side so that I couldn't see her. She had time to creep back down the stairs while we were talking.'

'But why?'

'I don't know. To make us believe whatever crazy stuff she does. To make us think there's something in the house.'

'Like what?' I glance into the murky corners of the room and wonder if he feels it too: that we're being watched. He shakes his head and whispers, 'The shadows she keeps talking about, the thing she's been writing about in her diary – these demons.'

He points at the bookcase. 'I've no idea what's going on in your mum's head, but these books can't be helping.' He walks over to his bed and gets in. 'It doesn't make sense. I mean, if you thought you were under attack from demons, would you take up witchcraft?'

'What's that supposed to mean?'

'If your mum's not a witch, she's doing a good impression of one.'

I jump into bed and pull up the covers. I don't know why a group of witches would want to hurt me, but my mother is only trying to protect me. Besides, what does Tom know? Just because he's spent an hour reading about the occult doesn't make him an expert.

He adds more forcefully, 'Come on, most people would use a Bible or a crucifix to protect themselves. Or they'd call in a priest.'

'Are you religious?'

'No, but I'm seriously thinking about taking it up.'

I make a noise somewhere between a laugh and a snort of derision, and he turns over and props himself up on one elbow. He looks at me earnestly, his voice serious. 'Your mum needs help, Ivy. Maybe the boatman can tell us something. He must know her history. Perhaps he can put us in touch with her doctor or someone else in the family.'

I purse my lips, feeling it would be a betrayal of my mum, but maybe I should go and see the boatman. I could confront him with my mother's story about witches and ask him outright. He was happy enough to talk about the folklore of the island before; even if he hasn't seen anything himself he can tell me what the other islanders believe.

Tom eyes me sympathetically. 'Once we get to the mainland, I'll help you find a doctor who'll come out and visit her.' When I don't say anything, he adds quickly, 'Or we can try and find someone else in your family, whatever you think is best.'

'Thanks.'

The word comes out tight and ungrateful, and I soften it with a smile. I'm thankful that he cares enough to want to help me. At the same time, I have no intention of returning to the mainland. I've only just found my mum – I'm not about to leave her.

'You're still coming back with me, right?'

I nod and smile more convincingly this time.

'I know that look.'

'What look?'

'The *half-nod* – the one where you nod and give a funny little half-smile, usually followed by you biting your lip. The one that tells me you're lying.'

I stare at him then look away, careful not to show my feelings.

'And if I'm not mistaken, you just gave me the *ice glare*. If we were at work, you'd walk away from me now – off to harass some poor visitor with facts about mandibles when all they want to do is look at pretty butterflies and forget their problems for half an hour.'

'Do you even know what mandibles are?'

'Teeth or those long spindly things on their heads. My point is that you'd rather do anything than have a real conversation with me.'

I cross my arms, unsure which appals me more: the fact he's given my facial expressions names or that he knows so little about butterfly anatomy, despite doing the same job as me for nearly a year. 'You mean antennae? Mandibles are jaws – caterpillars have them but butterflies do not.'

'Whatever. I know you take yourself off to the storeroom whenever the guys at work are arranging a night out. I even know about your hiding place. I looked in the window once and saw you squeeze yourself between two cardboard boxes at the back.'

I turn over with a huff, wondering how the conversation has managed to change so quickly. One minute we were talking about demons and the next he's admitting to spying on me at work. Undeterred by my cold shoulder, he continues. 'I never understood why you clammed up when I asked about your home life. It makes sense now, but I still don't see why you never came out with us. If anyone dared to invite you, you'd get this look on your face: the *brick wall*.'

'Well, thanks for the fascinating insight into my character. It's been educational, but I'm going to sleep now.'

He laughs. 'I know you want to argue with me, but you don't in case you reveal too much about yourself. That's why you always walk off when you're angry, isn't it?'

I thump my pillow. 'No, I just don't engage in mental combat with the unarmed.'

He scoffs and starts to say something else, but I cut him off. 'Look, I'm tired. Why don't you save the witty comeback for the morning? It will give you time to come up with something really clever.'

The room goes blissfully quiet for several long minutes and then he whispers, 'Did you hear that?'

I sit up in bed, my heart pounding. 'No. What?'

'A scraping noise . . . oh, wait, it was just you putting up another row of bricks.'

I throw myself back down with a sigh. 'Go to sleep, Tom.'

'Goodnight, Breeze Block.'

Pulling up the covers, I turn over and curl into a ball. The sound of waves fills the room and a few minutes later there's a different noise: gentle snoring. I listen to Tom for a while and then my own breathing slows and becomes heavy. Sleep comes swiftly after that, closing around me like a cocoon, and I'm held in blackness for a long time. And then I'm somewhere else – taken to a place shrouded in mist.

The vapour pulls apart to reveal a gleaming tower: the lighthouse. I push open the door and climb the stone steps. At the top is a familiar room, its floor littered with black feathers. Nine long grey chrysalides lie on the ground in a circle, the bottom of each touching at the centre. I kneel before the one closed chrysalis and touch its thick papery casing, its surface obscuring a network of glowing arteries. Hidden inside is the face of a woman.

Chanting fills the room, at first just a whisper.

Eko eko azarak. Eko eko zomelak. Eko eko azarak.

I stare around but I can't see where the noise is coming from. It builds louder and louder, until I have to cover my ears with my hands. I look at the woman's sleeping face and somehow I know I have to set her free.

I claw at the chrysalis, pull and rip at the casing. I have to wake her. She has to wake before it's too late. I tear through layer after layer of the tough, papery material and then connect with something else – living tissue. Shoving my hands deeper, I push and pull at stretchy membrane, my fingers slippery with blood, but it's not enough.

I'm suffocating, overcome with panic that I can't breathe. My lungs are burning. I have to wake her . . . I need to . . . Gasping for air, I tear through a layer of skin and scream. The woman inside is me.

13

My eyes snap open and I take a sharp breath. A cloying sense of *wrongness* clings to my thoughts like the wrinkled skin on hot milk. The memory of the dream is right there, just beneath the surface, yet I can't break through to reach it. There was something I had to do, something important . . .

Go back to sleep, Ivy. It was just a dream.

The lamps have guttered out and the only illumination is the red glow of the lighthouse, seeping through the curtains like blood through a bandage. I pick up my phone from the bedside table, relieved to see it still has charge. Three forty-five. *Great.*

I stare at the ceiling, my eyes fixed on a patch of peeling paintwork, while I think about the events of yesterday evening. Even if witches exist, why would they be interested in me? The wind whines and moans outside and I think about the whispered voice I heard behind the door. It sounded urgent, desperate even.

C-r-e-a-k.

My body tenses. It's just my mum going to the bathroom; any moment now I will hear the groan of the stairs. But I don't. A minute passes and then there's another soft creak. What's she doing? I push myself up in bed, but all I hear is the crash of waves and the swish of blood in my ears.

And then I hear the noise I've been dreading: a scraping sound, as if someone is dragging their fingernails down the door. Maybe my mum's doing some kind of protection spell. But why do it in the middle of the night? I swing my legs out of bed. Whoever's there, I won't be made to feel scared. I glance over at the snoring lump, deciding not to wake him. He was freaked out enough last time, and I don't need a boy to hide behind. I'm capable of checking out the hallway myself.

I switch on the torch of my phone then tiptoe across the room and pause at the door. Should I ease it gently, or . . . *Oh, to hell with this*. I yank it open and something blurs at the edge of my vision: a figure with long hair.

I step back, my heart racing, and my phone slips from my hand. I try to grab it and it turns over in my fingers, the light momentarily blinding me. Cursing, I fumble and catch it just before it hits the floor. The torch has gone out and I switch it back on. Holding the phone out before me, I make my way along the landing. My breath quickens as I imagine what might be lurking in the darkness, but there's no witch with cloudy white eyes and tangled black hair standing in the shadows. There's no one at all.

Yet *someone* was here just now. I need to warn my mum. I walk to her door and then stop. What if it was her? She could have darted back into her room when I dropped my phone. I don't think she'd frighten me just to make me believe her stories about witches, but what if Tom's right? There's only one way to be sure: I need to go downstairs and check the house.

No, Ivy. You need to stop coming up with stupid ideas and get into bed.

I hurry back into the bedroom and jump under the covers, relieved to hear Tom still snoring. Whatever's out there can stay out there. Pulling the sleeping bag over my head, I curl up and shut my eyes. Usually when I can't sleep, my brain likes to entertain me with reruns of my most embarrassing moments. Right now I'd gladly watch a highlights reel of my worst fails, but my mind has other ideas. It wants to convince me that someone is standing over my bed. Only it's not one person; something tells me there's a group of them.

My breath comes fast under the covers, the air moist and stinking of mould. I *know* there are people standing around me. I can sense their presence, feel the weight of their stare in the pinprick crawl of my skin. I imagine eight scrawny women with impossibly long arms grinning down at me. Only I'm not imagining it. I can *hear* the raspy catch of their breath.

No, witches aren't real. They don't exist. It must be Tom's snoring, or the muffled crash of waves. Keeping the covers clamped over my head, I tell myself that I've been silly to believe my mum's stories. Witches aren't real. I repeat the thought over and over until my brain stumbles over the words and I fall into a shallow sleep potholed with nightmares.

When I open my eyes, daylight is streaming through the window and Tom is sitting on the bed opposite, looking at me intently. I wince and shield my eyes. His face is preferable to that of a witch, but it's still unsettling to wake up and see someone staring at you.

'What time is it?' My voice sounds raspy and I clear my throat.

'Nearly noon. You OK? It sounded like you were having a bad dream.'

I sit up and rub my head, trying not to think about last night. And then I remember the figure I saw on the landing. That part wasn't my imagination, it was real.

I glance behind him and notice my bag is on the bed, next to his stuff. He sees me looking and scratches his cheek. 'I packed your things. I didn't think you'd mind.' He sounds worried, but I'm not angry. If anything, it makes me feel sad. It's not like I had much to pack, and as coercion goes it's a pitiful attempt. Something a kid might do.

A sigh escapes me. 'Tom, I know you think I –'

He stands abruptly. 'Just come and see David with me. You can make up your mind after you've talked to him. If you decide to leave, then you'll have your stuff with you.'

'But –'

'Please, Ivy. Just talk to him.'

'OK, fine.'

He smiles and I look away, feeling uncomfortable. I'd already decided to see the boatman, though not for the reason Tom thinks.

He grabs his washbag and heads for the door. Once he's gone, I get out of bed and notice something on my pillow – a book. I'm not sure how it got there, or how I managed to sleep without rolling into it. The cover is faded, the title embossed with silver letters that have lost their gleam. *The Life of Merlin*. Tucked inside is a long cormorant feather.

I open its pages and it smells old and fusty, the yellow paper crammed with tiny print. I don't know much about Arthurian legend, but I thought it was fiction – the characters and events made up rather than based on history. Yet the footnotes are full of dates and locations, as if the feasts and battles actually took place.

The feather marks a chapter near the end: 'Merlin's Dark Desires'. I scan a few paragraphs and then come to a line that makes my stomach drop.

Merlin was able to resist his demonic nature (1) throughout most of his adulthood, but that was to change at the end of his life if various accounts are to be believed.

My eyes flick to the footnote at the bottom of the page.

(1) Merlin was born to a virtuous woman, a nun who was impregnated by an invisible demon. Prompt baptism saved the infant from the consequences of his diabolic parentage, thus redeeming the 'strangely hairy and talkative child' when he began to display unnatural gifts. Though Merlin inherited his prophetic and magical abilities from the demon (some reports suggest the wizard was sent to Earth by the devil himself), he used his supernatural gifts for good and devoted his life to furthering Arthur's rise to power.

A bad taste rises to my throat and I start to shut the book, when my eyes are drawn to a paragraph further down the page.

In his later years, Merlin became infatuated with a beautiful young woman of Avalon. It's widely accepted that this relationship led to his removal from the world, though there is some disagreement as to the course of events. Several twelfth-century texts suggest the woman tricked him, promising to return his affections if he taught her magic. But she used his spells against him, trapping him in a glass tower, or in some versions a tomb or cave.

Other texts claim the girl was pure and innocent in her intentions, but add that she was so alluring that the ageing wizard couldn't be expected to resist her. These same writers point out that the identity of Merlin's father was common knowledge and for any woman to have dealings with such a creature was to run a grave risk, it being known that the female desire for forbidden knowledge invariably exacts a sexual price.

A hot, sick feeling washes over me. One minute it's the girl's fault for being so attractive Merlin couldn't be expected to keep his hands off her, and the next she's to blame because she should've known to stay well clear of him. A footnote lists more than a dozen scholars' names and I notice that they're all male. Not a single woman's opinion has been included and it makes me feel sad and angry, thinking of all the other female voices that have been omitted throughout history.

I don't want to read any more of this tripe, yet somehow I can't stop myself.

Various accounts suggest Merlin used demonic magic in an effort to make the girl return his affections, so determined was he to have her. It was this decision to call upon the dark power within him which led to his subsequent loss of reason and spiritual 'entrapment'.

A sudden pain throbs at my temples. I rub my head and the book falls from my hand, landing on the floor with a thud. I reach to grab it, but I can't see. Light flickers at the edge of my vision, turning the world white. The pain is searing, the light so bright it's almost blinding. I slump onto the bed and press my face to the pillow with a groan. What's happening to me? The light stops flickering as a rush of images and feelings flood my mind.

A teenage girl with waist-length black hair and full red lips stands looking out of a glass tower. Below her, a vast forest stretches in every direction, the dense canopy of trees dotted with castles. The girl watches the sun dip behind the purple mountains in the distance then nervously glances over her shoulder.

The room is large and empty, its walls and floors made entirely of glass. In the centre of the space is a column of swirling white energy that comes up through the floor and reaches to the ceiling. Seeing the portal fills her with excitement and trepidation. She knows that the room is rarely used and she's not allowed to be in here, but he said that's why it's the perfect place to meet. She doesn't like keeping secrets from her sisters, but he says they would be jealous of the attention he's giving her if they knew. Besides, she's fifteen now, not a child. She's old enough to make her own decisions.

Merlin materialises before her without warning and she marvels as the air shimmers around him. He wears a lavish velvet robe and holds a long black sceptre. At the top is a large clear crystal, held within the open jaws of two silver dragons, their serpentine bodies wrapping around each other as if they're fighting. His gnarled fingers are covered with jewels and his long grey beard is styled into two points at the end. She's no stranger to magic, but she can't help being in awe of him. It's hard to believe the most powerful wizard in the land once tutored her eldest sister, the Queen of Avalon. And even harder to believe he would want to teach her, the youngest of them.

He strides towards her with open arms, kissing her twice on both cheeks, and a familiar waft of musky incense fills her nose. The embrace is uncomfortably close and each kiss lingers a moment too long, but she says nothing, not wishing to appear rude or uncultured. King Arthur and his men lie sleeping under her sisters' protection now, but she's heard tales of their extravagant feasts and dances. She knows she's not allowed to enter the portal and cross to the other side, but Merlin has lived in the earthly realm amongst nobles. She wants to greet him in the proper custom, as a lady of the court would. So she allows his embrace and smiles when he kisses her.

'Are you going to show me what you've learned?' he asks.

She lowers her gaze and he takes her chin in his ringed hand. 'You have been practising, haven't you?' He laughs and the lines around his eyes deepen into crinkles. She pulls away and nods, hating the way her cheeks are flushing. Merlin has taught her all kinds of magic over the past few weeks, but she still feels embarrassed performing in front of him.

He gestures for her to stand before him. 'Come, there's no need to be shy with me.'

She nods dutifully and steps forward. It's not just the fear of getting it wrong. There's something in the intensity of his gaze that unnerves her. He seems to love watching her, scrutinising her every syllable and hand gesture, and his delight never wavers, even when she makes a mistake. If anything, he seems to enjoy correcting her: lifting her arm to improve a gesture or standing behind her and putting his hands on her stomach and pulling tightly, making her draw up the energy from her feet. She's grateful that he's so patient with her – not like her sisters, who get cross when she's slow to learn a new conjuring.

They've spent all week on a new spell and she's been practising hard to get it right. She adopts the stance, raising her arms and chanting quietly as the energy flows up through her feet and legs and into her arms. She speaks the words he's taught her, '*Papilionem ostenderem*,' and a butterfly appears above her head. It beats its delicate blue wings and dances on the air. She continues to chant and another pops into existence, and then another.

She wants to smile, but her head hurts from having to focus. She's been able to shift into animal shape since she was small, but bringing a new living creature into existence is far more difficult, and the butterfly is so fragile. Her concentration wanders and one of the creatures stops fluttering its wings and drops to the ground. She steals a glance at Merlin, who is watching her intently.

'*Papilionem ostenderem*,' she says again, only this time she stumbles over the words. A pitiful creature appears in the air, one of its wings twice the size of the other and its antennae missing. It flaps uselessly and drops to her feet with a sad little thud. She tries again and dozens more appear, but their colours are dull, their wings misshapen and tattered.

Angry at herself, she lowers her arms and the insects drop around her feet. All week she's been creating perfect butterflies, but she gets so nervous in front of him. It's obvious she made a mess of the spell, so why isn't he correcting her?

Her sisters would be chiding her by now, but he appears delighted.

'Magnificent!' he cries, clapping his hands.

She tries to return his smile but all she can think about are the poor creatures on the ground, their bodies littering the glass floor in a squirming carpet. He strides over to her and the sound of insect wings being crushed makes her wince. She wishes she could put them out of their misery, but she doesn't know how to magic them out of existence. 'Can you help them?' she asks.

Merlin looks down his nose at the dying creatures. 'Did you know that in the earthly realm boys would fasten threads of flax to the bodies of butterflies and fly them like tiny living kites?' He tells her this as if it should amuse her. She gulps and shakes her head.

'You have an exceptional talent. You simply have to let the magic flow through you. You have to feel it – in here.' He runs a hand over her belly and she flinches from his touch. He's laid hands on her before, but that was to correct her posture. Not a caress.

Before she can say anything, he raises his sceptre and intones, '*Papilionem ostenderem.*' The spell sounds like a song on his tongue, sublime in its simplicity. As the words leave his mouth, the butterflies at her feet rise up, fluttering all around them. Each is a vivid colour – blue, pink, green, white and orange, their fragile wings perfectly formed.

She laughs to see the creatures returned to life and he leans forward and whispers in her ear. 'You have to let the energy rise inside you. You have to open yourself to its power; you have to give yourself to it completely.'

133

She nods, confused, her heart beating as fast as the butterflies' wings.

'I can help you . . . if you give yourself to me.'

He leans forward to kiss her but she turns her head away. The dancing butterflies vanish as quickly as the ageing wizard's smile. His knuckles tighten around the sceptre, his gemstone rings flashing as hard as his eyes.

'You look forward to my visits, do you not?' he asks.

'Of course, but –'

'You're eager to accept my teachings, and yet when it comes to giving me something in return . . .'

The girl bites her lip. When he met her by the lake weeks ago and offered to tutor her in magic, he didn't mention wanting anything in return. Before she can decide on the proper response, he runs a finger down her cheek. 'You truly are a beauty. Those eyes, as green and wild as a mermaid's, and those lips . . . red lips made to be kissed.'

She wants to turn and run away, but shock keeps her rooted to the spot. This is all her fault. She had no idea he felt that way about her and now she's going to offend him. Her words come out in a shameful rush.

'I'm sorry. I didn't realise you . . . I'd never have taken up your time if I'd known.' She prepares to beg for his forgiveness, to apologise for embarrassing them both, but Merlin raises his sceptre, forcing her lips shut. Panic rises inside her. She feels helpless, a tiny insect under his command.

His breath is hot on her neck, the cloying, musky smell of his incense overpowering. 'I know you feel the same way. You just have to open your heart to me, give yourself to me.'

Her gaze darts around the room. She wishes she could call for her sisters, but no one knows she's here and her mouth is sealed up.

'I can help you. You want that, don't you?' he murmurs.

She nods, desperate to be free from his control, and he releases his hold on her. Gasping for breath, she raises her arm and utters the first spell that enters her mind, casting a net of protection before her. The silver cage glitters in the air for a moment, and then Merlin raises his sceptre and it falls to the ground.

He surveys her childish work with a scowl. 'I didn't want to do this, but you leave me no choice.' He utters something in a language she doesn't recognise, the words full of harsh consonants. '*Kallo vaer ditazh, zelab katch nichtum.*' His face turns pale and his eyes roll back in his head as he repeats the spell. She's never seen him like this. It's as if the chant is using him and not the other way around.

The girl watches in horror as a swirl of black energy appears at her feet. It buzzes like a swarm of flies, filling the room with the stench of decay, then circles around her in a whirlwind, rising up her body. This is nothing like the magic he's taught her before. Nothing like the magic she or her sisters have ever done. This feels dangerous, depraved.

The shadow swarms into her mouth and she pleads at him with her eyes. *Please stop this.* But he doesn't. She can feel his magic swirling in her gut, turning her body to ice. She gasps and splutters for breath. Is this how it feels to drown? Icy hooks pierce the soft flesh of her insides, tug at her heart. They pull at her emotions, trying to make her feel things she doesn't want

135

to feel. Love, warmth, longing. No. This isn't right. She doesn't feel that way for Merlin; he can't make her feel things for him that she doesn't.

The girl calls upon every ounce of magic in her, all the protection spells her sisters have taught her over the years. But Merlin is too strong. 'One way or another, I *will* have you,' he whispers.

The shadow slides deeper, questing and clawing, demanding that she give him her love. Desperate, she visualises her heart as a wooden chest. She crams her emotions inside and locks it with a key. She feels him trying to prise open the lid, but she won't let him. Her body shakes with the effort; blood trickles from her nose. Before the wizard realises what he's done, the girl drops to the ground, her lifeless eyes open and staring.

14

I push myself up in bed and take a deep breath. I've never experienced anything like that before. It was like watching a movie or reading a book, only it felt real. I knew exactly how the girl was feeling: the animal-like panic, the desperate need to hide her emotions. I don't know why, but I feel as if I know her. And then it occurs to me. The face I saw in the bathroom mirror last night, the girl with long black hair and full lips – it's her.

I pick up the book hoping to find answers, and my attention is drawn to the next page.

Some believe that Merlin now resides in Avalon (a place of paradise beyond this world where men do not age), ruled over by the sorceress Morgan le Fay and her sisters.(3)

I glance down at the footnote.

After he fell at the Battle of Camlann, King Arthur was taken by boat to an island by his half-sister Morgan le Fay. It's possible that Morgan extended the invitation to Merlin also.

I turn the page, my eyes widening as I read.

Several locations have been put forward, including Bardsey Island off the west coast of Wales, which is the nearest island to

Camlann on the mainland. Exactly how they entered the mystical realm is a matter of speculation. One theory suggests that a portal exists between the worlds, acting as a gateway between Earth and Avalon. Morgan and her sisters were said to live in a shining fortress, a palace made entirely of glass. A glass tower features in many stories associated with Merlin, leading some scholars to propose that the tower itself may act as a gateway. However, as a portal has yet to be found in this world, one must presume it is either invisible or does not exist.

In my vision, Merlin and the girl were in a glass tower and there was a shimmering portal. That's where he called upon the shadows that rushed inside her. That's where he killed her.

I turn back to the section about Merlin using demonic magic to make the girl fall in love with him, then Tom enters the room.

'Are you getting up some time today?'

I hold up the book. 'Why did you put it on my pillow?'

'What?'

I wave it at him. 'This.'

'I didn't. Are you all right?' He takes the book from me and opens it to the page with the feather. After reading for a moment, he smiles wryly. 'All those times I've wished a girl would fall in love with me. Shame I didn't know about demonic magic. I might've given it a shot.'

'How could you say that?'

'Come on, you're telling me you've never wanted an ex back? Never had feelings for someone who didn't feel the same way?' I don't answer and he pulls a face. 'Looks like it's just me in the loser camp then.'

I snatch the book from him and he gives me a strange look.

'Lighten up, would you, Ivy! It was a joke.'

I gaze at an unfamiliar mark on the back of my right wrist. The wine-coloured stain looks like a burn, or a birthmark. Something like that can't appear overnight, so how did it get there?

'Ivy?'

I can't keep it in any longer. I feel like I'm losing my mind. I have to tell someone what's been happening.

'Last night I woke up and there was someone in the house. I saw them run across the landing. It was dark and I couldn't see properly, but . . .' I pause, unsure how to tell him.

'You saw your mum?'

'No, at least I don't think it was her.'

His eyes widen. 'Who, then?'

'There's something I need to tell you.'

He sits on the bed opposite and I tell him my mum's story and he listens without interrupting. When I'm finished, he rubs the back of his neck. 'Let me get this straight. Your mum saw a group of witches around your cot the night you were born. She managed to grab you, but then they used dark magic against her. These shadow demons, or whatever they are, possessed her father and made him try to hurt you. So she took you to the mainland, but then she realised the shadows were inside her too. That's her reason for abandoning you.'

'Yes, she was trying to keep me safe. She had no choice.'

'And you think what? That you saw one of these witches last night?'

'Yes. Maybe. I don't know.'

He stares at me round-eyed, a sceptical look on his face, but I can't stop now. The words I've been holding back tumble out of me. 'I know it's hard to believe but I've seen things, Tom. Just before the woman with the trolley attacked me, I saw a swirl of dark shadow on the ground. It passed over her face and she changed; it was like she was possessed. And the guy in the anorak, he kept staring at me and . . .'

Tom stands up and raises his hands. 'I'm sorry but whatever you think you saw, you didn't. You can't have. Your mum has been putting ideas in your head, trying to make you believe in demons and witches – scratching at the door and sneaking around in the night. She's messing with your mind, can't you see that?'

I think about the vision I had and the girl I saw in the mirror last night. I don't know how it's connected to all of this, but it has to be. 'It's not just that. Something is happening to me. I don't feel like myself, I . . .' My voice cracks and I stop speaking, afraid of what I might say next.

'Then get the boat back with me.'

We stare at one another and I want to tell him there's no use leaving the island – the shadows found me on the mainland before and they will again. But I don't because I know what he'd say. My mum isn't the only one who needs help.

Tom puts his hands on his hips. 'David is leaving in less than two hours. Are you still coming to speak to him, or –'

'I said I'd come.'

I grab my bag and avoid his gaze as he gathers up his stuff. I wish I hadn't told him anything now. Of course he wasn't going to believe me.

When we get downstairs, my mum is standing at the kitchen stove. She wears a cheerful floral apron and her hair is pulled back in a neat ponytail. She smiles and waves a wooden spoon in our direction.

'I'm doing scrambled eggs on toast. Hope that's OK.'

'Thanks.'

I pull out a chair and a rush of sadness fills me. This is what I should have had: a mum, a childhood, a home.

We sit down and Tom eyes her suspiciously, as if he's expecting her to scramble his eggs in a cauldron. After a few minutes, she places two plates of food on the table. Her fingers brush mine as I take my plate and she looks at me and smiles. I wish now that I hadn't gone to bed so early last night. There are so many things I want to know about her and my family, but with all the talk of witches, I didn't get to ask.

We eat in silence, Tom leaving his eggs untouched and munching on the toast. We're almost finished when she turns from doing the washing-up.

'You slept OK?'

Before I can answer, Tom replies. 'Actually, we heard a noise in the night.'

Her smile fades, replaced with a frown. 'Oh.'

I glare warningly at Tom but he keeps speaking. 'Ivy saw someone on the landing.'

'What?' She steps towards me and searches my face. 'Why didn't you tell me?'

The panic in her voice makes my throat constrict. I lower my fork, the eggs congealing in my stomach. 'I only caught a glimpse. I thought it was you.'

She turns and leans over the sink, her bony shoulders slumped. 'This can't be happening,' she wails.

I stand and go over to her. 'Mum?'

She takes a few steps in one direction and then turns back, her hands fluttering at the knot of her apron. 'I've kept them out all these years!' She pulls at the cord, making it tighter instead of loosening it. 'Are you *sure* you saw someone?'

'Yes. There was a woman. I saw her long hair.'

My mum lets out a strangled sob. 'If they're in the house, then my protection spells have stopped working. I have to close the portal.'

Tom almost chokes. 'The *what* now?'

She turns on him, her voice strained with impatience. 'The lighthouse is how the witches come through to our world.' She looks at me and adds, 'I can try to close it, but it will be risky. I can't be sure what will happen, and if it goes wrong . . . I was hoping it wouldn't come to this, but if they're in the house I have no choice.'

'Where do these witches come from exactly?' asks Tom.

She paces back and forth, tugging at the apron before finally ripping it off. I know what she's going to say before she opens her mouth because I've *seen* it.

'Avalon – it's where Morgan le Fay took King Arthur after he died. There's a reason why twenty thousand saints chose to be buried on the island – they could sense the energy of the other world leaking through to ours. The lighthouse is a gateway between dimensions. That's why the birds keep crashing into it. I have to prepare, there's so much to prepare.'

She rushes to the wooden dresser and opens the large cupboard drawers at the bottom. I watch her pull out a box of black candles and then her head and shoulders disappear inside as she searches for something at the back. Tom leans across the table and whispers, 'A portal to Avalon?'

Ignoring his pointed looks, I call to my mum.

'Is there anything I can do to help?'

She reappears from the cupboard, banging her head. 'No, and I want you to stay away from the lighthouse. You mustn't go near there once I start the ritual, no matter what you see or hear.'

Tom pinches the bridge of his nose as if he can't believe what he's hearing. 'Sorry, but I'm going.' He pushes back his chair and picks up his things. 'I don't know how long it will take to walk to the harbour and I don't want to be late. Are you coming?'

My mum is on her knees, frantically sorting through jars of incense.

'Mum?'

She doesn't answer and I raise my voice. 'Tom's leaving now. I was going to walk with him to the harbour and then come back.'

She scrambles to her feet and rushes past me, muttering something about needing to find a book. I've no idea what 'closing the portal' involves, but I'm not letting her do it alone if it's going to be dangerous. I follow her into the hallway and call out as she runs up the stairs. 'Do you want me to stay?'

She clutches the banister and hangs her head. 'No, it's better if you go. I need to start the ritual as soon as it gets dark. There's a lot to prepare, I need to concentrate.' She hurries off to her bedroom and I stare at the floor, my shoulders slumped. I was hoping we could spend some time together and get to know each other properly, but it doesn't look like that's going to happen. Maybe I should just let her get on with things. I'll easily be back before nightfall.

Tom appears and hands me my bag. 'You OK, Shorty?'

The pity in his eyes makes me want to crumple. 'Yeah, just give me a minute.'

I dive into the bathroom, taking a moment to splash my face with cold water before joining him in the hallway. He shifts his weight impatiently as I open the front door. The world outside has been obliterated, the surrounding buildings hidden by a thick white mist. We step into the chilly vapour and I crane my neck upwards. The tower is obscured by fog, the lantern the only thing visible: a floating glass eye with a Cyclops stare.

Tom readjusts the bags on his shoulder and sets a brisk pace, seemingly keen to put the place behind him. The sun is feeble and bloated above us, a poached egg hanging in a milk-white sky. Apart from the distant crash of waves, it's eerily quiet. No gulls crying and wheeling overhead and no wind tugging at our clothes and battering our ears. The mist has thrown a heavy blanket over everything, dampening the colours and sounds. It sits on my lungs and gets in my hair, the saltwater so thick I can taste it.

I look towards the sea, hoping to get my bearings, but there's no line to mark the horizon, just a vague blur where one band of pale blue merges into another. Not being able to see the cliff edge is unnerving and I'm glad we have the track to follow. After ten minutes or so, Tom points up ahead. 'Is that the village?'

I squint, but I can't see anything apart from the outline of the mountain in the distance.

'Are you sure you don't want to come back with me?' he asks.

'I can't leave her, Tom, not when she's like this.'

He nods and I'm relieved when he doesn't push the issue. He takes a moment then asks, 'Do you want me to let anyone know you're here? If you give me their number, I can call your foster parents or whoever once I get back to the mainland.'

He's right. I should let them know where I am; I don't want them to worry about me. At the same time, I can't risk them coming out here. Jim and Richard want the best for me, but they're not going to believe the things I've seen. No one would.

'Can you tell them I'm staying with a friend and I've lost my phone?'

'I guess. I mean, I can if you want, but someone ought to know you're here. There must be someone you can tell, a friend of the family, a mate, or –'

'No,' I snap. 'There's no one.'

He looks at me in surprise and a huff escapes me. I know he's fallen out with his parents because they won't give him money for his venture, but they're still paying for him to go to university, they still care. It's not his fault he's privileged, but at the same time not everyone grows up with people who are there for them. I don't have sisters who can help me out in a crisis, or an uncle who can give me a job, or mates who'll let me sleep on their sofa.

'You're telling me you don't have a single friend?' he asks.

'Not any more.'

He goes quiet as if considering this, and then says, 'I'm sorry, I didn't realise.' He says it like he actually means it and I feel bad for snapping at him. He doesn't know about Katie and what happened in the care home – how could he?

145

The silence grows between us, filled only by the distant crash of waves. Eventually the shape of a building emerges from the fog – the schoolhouse or church maybe, it's hard to tell. We walk towards it when we see something that makes us stop. A group of dark shapes stands further along the track: half a dozen or so people gathered together. They are oddly still, some of them leaning towards one another as if in conversation.

'I thought the island was deserted,' says Tom.

His voice is frayed with uncertainty, but it's nothing compared to the rope of anxiety twisting in my gut. The mist is too thick for me to see how many there are, but what if there are eight of them? Could they be the witches? I slow my pace and Tom strides ahead.

'Christ. For a minute I thought . . .'

I catch up with him and realise what he means. The figures are tall gravestones. What I thought were human heads are the bulbous tops of Celtic crosses and what seemed like figures are their upright bases. A loud cackle cuts through the quiet, making the hairs on my arms stand on end. The noise comes again, followed by a guttural grunting. Tom pauses and searches the sky.

'Cormorants,' I say.

'What?'

'Big black seabirds – we saw them on the crossing yesterday.'

He looks doubtful, but then I guess he was too busy trying to keep his lunch down to pay much attention to the wildlife. Another cackle cuts through the air, this time even closer. Several fly overhead in a group, their long thin legs hanging behind them, their immense wings outspread. Black hags, the boatman called them. I know they're meant to be an ill omen,

146

but to me they're magnificent: wild, otherworldly creatures. Seeing them sends a thrill of excitement through me, but when I look again they've gone, vanished into the mist.

We continue along the path and the empty holiday cottages loom up next to us, their dark windows like sunken eye sockets. We pass by them and then the disused schoolhouse, stopping when we come to David's farmhouse. The quad bike and trailer are parked outside but there's no sign of life, not even the lonely bleat of a sheep. Tom jumps over the low slate wall and knocks at the door. When no one answers, he glances at me nervously.

'He's probably down at the harbour,' I say.

'Yeah, of course.'

He smiles briefly, as if embarrassed about being worried, and then heads down the path. Even if the boatman was expecting us to stay here for longer, surely he wouldn't have gone earlier than he said? Tom walks off in the direction of the bay, and I hurry to keep up with him. By the time we reach the top of the hill, he's a dozen paces ahead.

The track drops sharply away beneath me and I look down, expecting to see the crescent-shaped beach, but there's only swirling white vapour. Stepping into nothingness is unsettling, and it doesn't help that the ground is uneven and I nearly lose my footing. Not that it seems to worry Tom, who jogs down the hill, his feet sliding on the loose gravel. I think about asking him to wait, but he's already halfway to the bottom.

Eventually a boat comes into view, cream and black and considerably bigger than the catamaran we arrived in. Tom looks back at me and grins, his relief evident, and I smile too. Even though I'm not going with him, the idea of being abandoned here isn't exactly pleasant.

Tom trudges along the foam-covered pebbles towards the boat, and I follow him. Maybe it's the damp air, but the smell of sulphur is stronger than ever. It must be coming from the seaweed, strewn across the shingle in thick dark ropes. I think about the dead seal pup and wonder if that's where the rotting smell is coming from. Or maybe it's the harbour wall itself, which is covered with tiny rough barnacles and furry lime-green lichen that seems to almost glow in the pale mist.

'Hello, anyone there?' shouts Tom.

David's head appears on deck. 'Hi, come on up!'

Tom waves me over and then climbs the metal ladder. The boat isn't as big as I thought, so presumably David must do several trips when he takes the sheep across. I can't see them from here, but I can hear their plaintive bleats and the faint clatter of hooves.

I climb the ladder and Tom hauls me aboard.

'Missing the open sea, eh?' laughs David.

Tom's face pales and I realise why he only ate toast this morning. He forces a smile. 'Yes, that's right. I was hoping to go back with you today, if that's OK.'

The boatman eyes me warily. 'Decided to leave early, then?'

I shrug. 'David, I wanted to ask if –'

An alarmed bleat sounds behind him. The noise is followed by another and another, and then there's a panicked snort and the clatter of hooves.

'What on earth?' He strides towards the sheep, but then stops and peers down at his feet. I can't see what he's looking at, but something is wrong. A waft of decay reaches my nose and I grab Tom's arm.

'We should go.'

'What? Why?'

A swirl of shadow moves across the deck and grows bigger, rising up to stand in the vague form of a human, its black outline hazy and indistinct. A second later, it slides across David's face. He stares at me, his eyes bulging, then tilts his head to the side, making the bones in his neck pop and crack. Again and again he repeats the motion, like some kind of automaton.

Tom stares, open-mouthed.

'Please, Tom, we need to run.'

David stops moving his head and charges at me. I rest my weight on my back leg and find my stance, ready to throw him, but I don't get the opportunity. Tom hurls himself at the boatman, grabbing him around the waist and shoving him into the metal rail behind. The older man straightens and rubs his back. I think he's returned to normal, but then he sees me and his face twists with malice.

David lunges at me again and this time Tom tackles him by the legs. The boatman goes down with a thud, his head cracking on the deck. Tom scrambles to his feet, then checks him over, feeling for a pulse in his neck. When he pulls his hand away, it's covered in blood.

'It's not your fault. You didn't mean to hurt him,' I whisper.

He looks at me blankly, as if he can't take in what just happened. The boatman groans and begins to stir, and Tom turns and gestures for us to go.

I race for the ladder and scramble down, half-dropping onto the shingle, and Tom jumps down behind me, landing awkwardly. He gathers up the bags with a wince and looks down at his ankle. I take his arm and wrap it around my shoulder and we stumble across the pebbles, both of us glancing back at the boat.

We're twenty paces away when David appears on deck. His face seems normal, the grimace gone. Holding on to the rail with one hand, he touches the back of his head then looks at his fingers in surprise. I wait for him to shout down to us, but it's like he hasn't seen us.

Tom hops on one foot and I take the bags so he can get his balance. We watch as the boatman unwinds the rope from the harbour and a moment later we hear the engine rumble into life. The boat pulls away and turns in a wide arc. Tom mutters in disbelief, 'He's leaving.'

The boat picks up speed, leaving a trail of churning white foam in its wake, and then it's gone, swallowed by the fog.

15

We stop to rest at the top of the hill, and Tom bends to rub his ankle. A thin film of sweat covers his forehead and his hand is trembling. He holds my gaze for a beat then looks away, his eyes filled with anxiety. I wish I could reassure him that everything will be OK, but how can I? He straightens up and stares toward the misty sea, his face unreadable. He hasn't said a word since we watched the boat leave, but I have to know.

'Did you see it?'

He nods, not taking his gaze from the horizon.

'You saw the shadow?'

'Yes.'

I expect him to ask me about it and demand that I tell him everything I know, but he doesn't. He releases a heavy breath and limps off down the path, his shoulders slumped.

When we reach the farmhouse, I check the quad bike and find the key in the ignition. The petrol is low but it should be enough to get us to the cottage. The thought of my mum doing this ritual alone sends a jolt of worry through me. I need to get back – and quickly.

Tom gives me a sceptical look. 'Have you driven one before?'

'No, but it can't be that hard.'

I arrange our bags in the trailer and he climbs inside. Once I'm sure he's comfortable, I straddle the bike and start the engine.

'You OK?' I call, glancing back.

He doesn't answer, his attention taken by his phone, and I almost don't dare to hope.

'Do you have network coverage?'

His stricken face tells me the answer.

David warned us there was no mobile signal and no way to contact the outside world if we got into trouble. He's the only person who knows we're here, and our only way of returning to the mainland. My heart sinks, but then I remember the confused look on his face when he realised his head was bleeding. If he's anything like anorak man, he won't remember what happened and will return to the island as planned.

I try to sound positive. 'He said he was coming again in a week.'

Tom's jaw tightens. 'And if the same thing happens?'

I twist back around in my seat, unable to answer.

The truth is that I don't know anything. I don't know why a group of witches from another world would want to hurt me, or why the shadows didn't possess the boatman on the crossing over. My mum said that with some people it can take longer for them to get inside, but they always find a way. Maybe it will be her attacking me next time, or Tom.

I squeeze the throttle and the bike gives a throaty roar and then dies. I start it again and it lurches into life. Concentrating hard, I ease the throttle and do my best to keep it steady as

I take us onto the track. The trailer rattles along behind me and Tom curses when we hit a bump. I can't blame him for being angry. If I hadn't talked him into coming, he'd be on the mainland now. Instead he's here with me – stuck in a nightmare.

We pass through the village and then I turn and take us down through the fields, gripping the handlebars so tight my palms hurt. A splatter of rain hits me and I glance at the darkening sky and realise the fog is lifting. Seeing the lighthouse fills me with foreboding. I should have begged my mum to leave with me, but what good would it have done? The shadow would still have possessed the boatman; we'd still be stuck here.

The rain is coming down faster now, wetting my nose and cheeks, and by the time we get to the cottage my hair is dripping. I switch off the engine and go to help Tom, but he's already out of the trailer and heading for the front door. Picking up the bags, I follow him as he limps down the hall.

The kitchen is empty, the house silent. I walk to the bottom of the stairs and call up.

'Mum?'

No answer.

I turn to Tom. 'Do you think she's started the ritual already?'

He flicks his hair and frowns, but says nothing. I hurry back along the hallway and he shouts after me. 'She told you to stay away, Ivy!'

Ignoring him, I open the front door. The rain is beating down at an angle, bouncing up from the gravel track and making it hard to see in the murky red twilight. My mum is heading towards the lighthouse. She must have seen us arrive and hidden from us, but why?

'Wait!'

She pauses a moment and then quickens her pace.

I chase after her, my feet splashing in puddles. I know she can hear me, so why doesn't she turn around? She opens the door and slips inside, just as I reach it.

'Mum?'

I hear the sound of a bolt being drawn and then she sighs. 'Please, Ivy, it's not safe. Go back to the house.'

Tom is standing under the porch, sheltering from the rain. He gestures for me to come inside but I can't let my mum do this by herself. I throw my shoulder against the wood but it barely moves. And then I remember the boarded-up door with its strange symbols.

I dash through the rain and run past Tom. He follows me into the kitchen and watches as I frantically snatch open cupboards and drawers. Eventually I find what I'm looking for under the sink: a hammer with a claw. I run to the bottom of the stairs and go to work on the door. There are so many nails, it will take ages.

'Please, Tom, can you help?'

He hobbles over and stands in my path. 'Your mum told you to stay away from the lighthouse! You saw what happened to the boatman. What if more of those shadow things appear?'

I shove him aside. 'Fine, I'll do it myself.'

I tug at one of the wooden boards fixed diagonally across the door. It won't budge. I haven't pulled out enough nails. I lever out more but it still doesn't move.

'Damn it!'

I try again and Tom grips my shoulder. 'Will you just stop, please?'

'No. Either help me or get out of my way.'

He huffs, evidently realising I'm not going to change my mind, then reaches over my head and rips the board away in one brutal motion. I pick up the hammer and pull out more nails and he tugs at another board, and another. Eventually we remove the last one.

The door creaks as I push it open. Inside is so dark I can't see a thing.

'Can you get me an oil lamp, please? There should be one in the kitchen.'

I wait for him to go then peer into the gloom. The passageway feels damp and airless and when I hold out my arms, my fingers touch rough stone walls. I walk forward and something brushes my face. I gasp and pull away a handful of cobwebs, my scalp crawling with the thought of what might be in my hair.

'Ivy?'

I turn back and Tom is holding up a lamp. His face is contorted in the flickering light, his features a confusion of shades and hollows: his cheeks gaunt and his eye sockets so deep that his head resembles a skull. He looks like the witch from my mum's drawing. I rub my eyes, relieved when he catches up to me and appears normal. To our left is a green door – this must be the one my mum entered and locked behind her – and a little way ahead is a flight of narrow stone steps.

'What was that?' asks Tom.

I glance back the way we came, but I don't see anything.

'Can't you hear it?' he asks.

155

I close my eyes and make out a soft rumble of thunder. Only it doesn't sound like a noise from outside; it seems to be coming from the tower above us. We walk over to the stone steps and look up them.

A high-pitched wail cuts through the air – the cry of the wind or a bird, perhaps. It comes again and this time there's no mistake – the scream is human and full of fear.

16

I hurriedly climb a dozen or so steps and find myself in an open landing area, a large green metal tube running up the body of the tower. I glance around, certain I've been here before. I've never seen inside the lighthouse, yet somehow I know that I've touched its rough stone walls. I've walked up the staircase, my hand on the metal railing, my feet echoing on the concrete steps. Remembering my dream makes me feel faint and I stop to catch my breath when Tom appears behind me. He peers up the dimly lit stairwell and from the look on his face, he doesn't want to know what's at the top either.

'You don't have to come with me. It's OK, really.'

My voice echoes and bounces against the walls, and I glance up at the windows high above us, and then back to him. His face is taut with anxiety and I think he might leave, but he shakes his head.

'No, come on.'

He says it without a smile and I start climbing again before either of us can change our minds. The wind howls and pummels the stone walls, and the suck and slap of the waves is so loud it sounds as if the sea is crashing into the lighthouse itself.

I run up another flight of steps, then make the mistake of leaning over the railing and looking down. The ground speeds away and I stumble back, my head spinning with vertigo.

'Are you OK?'

Tom appears on the stairwell beneath me. He's moving as quickly as he can, but I can tell his ankle is hurting him. I start to answer when another low rumble sounds overhead. We hold one another's gaze and Tom's eyes fill with warning. The noise fades, until there's only the sound of the wind whistling through cracks in the stone.

My mum's voice calls out from above and I grip my locket. I don't understand the words – they sound like another language, Latin maybe, but I can tell she's afraid. I start to run again, and am almost at the top when Tom shouts.

'Ivy, wait!'

I turn around and he winces in pain.

'I can't keep up. My ankle.'

My mother yells something, her voice panicked.

'Please, Tom, go back to the house.'

He says something, but I don't stop to listen. I race up the last few steps and pass through a wooden door, surprised to enter an empty room with an iron ladder fixed against one wall. From the vivid light flooding down, I'm guessing I'm in a service area that leads to the lantern.

Grabbing the rails of the ladder, I climb up and see a white domed ceiling with curved walls made from dozens of panes of glass. The circular space is surprisingly small, most of it taken up by a two-foot-high metal platform that holds the lens in the centre. Tall and thin, it looks like half a dozen balls of glass placed on top of one another.

Squinting at the brightness, I step off the ladder and onto the metal walkway that surrounds the lens. My mother stands to my right, her back pressed to the wall. She wears a long black robe, her face a ghoulish red. She glares at me and then jerks her head to the side.

I follow her gaze, and the air is punched from my lungs. A creature prowls opposite us, half hidden by the optic. It's tall, maybe twice the height of me, and walks on two legs, the top of its body leaning forward at an odd angle. Only it's not a thing of flesh and blood. It's made of shadow: a swirling mass of black smoky air, its outline blurred and wispy.

I hold still, praying it doesn't see me, when a movement catches my attention. Looking closely at the optic, I see that the glass is smashed, leaving a gaping hole down one side. A shadowy creature emerges from it and enters the room. This one is short and squat and jumps like a toad; its legs fat and its back mottled with diseased-looking skin.

A rumble sounds and a different creature emerges, its clawed hand appearing first and then a long snout. A forked tongue flicks from its mouth as it climbs out.

My mum shouts, 'Quickly – to me!'

With the tip of a knife she draws an outline of a rectangle in the air. I run over and she pulls me next to her and then closes the invisible door. The creatures grunt and sniff as if they can tell we're here but can't see us.

My breath comes hard and fast. 'What are those things?'

Another rumble builds and the red light glows brighter, the air pulsating around it. Arms and shoulders writhe and creatures pull themselves through the hole in the glass, twisting and snarling. More and more of the things emerge. Some swish long scaly tails, some crawl on eight legs, and others flap torn and tattered wings – hideous, impossible things made of darkness and hunger.

She shakes her head. 'This wasn't meant to happen. They weren't meant to come through!'

'Can you make them go?'

'I don't know. I need to get closer to the portal.'

Shielding her eyes, she peers at the optic. No creatures are emerging from it now. Instead, there's a hazy image of a man with a long beard inside it. He glares into the room, his black eyes blazing, and every muscle in my body tenses. Corruption seeps out from him, washing over me in waves, and my stomach shrinks inside me.

Before I can ask if my mum sees him too, she turns away from me and raises the knife. I grab her arm and pull it down. 'What are you doing? I thought you'd cast a circle to protect us.'

Her eyes fill with tenderness. 'I'm sorry. I wish there was more time.' She pulls me close and holds me tightly, as if she's trying to make up for a thousand missed embraces, and I hug her back. It feels so good to be held by her, I don't want to let go. She pulls away from me and clutches my shoulder.

'I love you so much. I never wanted to give you up. Please remember that.'

Tears sting my eyes and I wipe them away. I don't know what she's planning to do, but I don't want her to leave the circle. She kisses me on the forehead then straightens her shoulders and fixes me with a look that tells me to be strong.

I nod, and she raises the blade and traces a doorway in the air. She steps out then turns and closes it behind her, sealing me inside.

I bite my lip and watch as she climbs onto the metal platform. As soon as she does, the creatures turn in her direction, grunting and sniffing the air. Holding the knife with both hands, she raises it above her head and points it at the optic.

'*Creaturae noctis, et abierunt!*' she commands.

The red light flickers and the shadowy forms lose definition, their outlines becoming mere wisps of smoke. Whatever she's doing is working.

The tall creature skitters towards her, its body swirling into a vague blur and then reforming. It towers over her, but she has her back to it and doesn't see.

'Mum, be careful!'

As soon as I call out, I realise my mistake. She turns to look at me and the knife drops from her hand. The creature grabs her and jumps into the broken optic, dragging her inside.

I stare, open-mouthed. They've vanished. She can't have gone, not just like that.

Something tugs at my arm.

'Ivy?'

Tom shakes me by the shoulders and I gaze at him.

'I heard shouting.'

My voice cracks. 'She's gone . . . my mum . . . it took her.'

'What took her?'

I look back but there are no creatures prowling around the room, just a thick swirl of smoke writhing around our feet.

161

Reaching down, I grab my mum's knife. I don't know why, but I feel safer for holding it. I open my mouth and a string of words flies out.

'*Eko eko azarak, eko eko zomelak.*'

Raising the blade above my head, I repeat the line again and the base of my skull prickles with pins and needles. Somehow I know what the words mean . . . only I don't. It's right there on the tip of my tongue, and yet I can't reach it. I just know I have to say them. My life depends on it.

The shadows swirl around Tom's legs and he gives a panicked shout and tries to swipe them away. I want to help him but the chant has taken hold of me and I can't move.

'*Eko eko azarak, eko eko zomelak.*' I chant again and again, my voice growing louder. Power flows up my feet and surges through my body like electricity.

The shadows spin around Tom in a whirlwind, the vague shape of arms appearing within the mass of darkness, clutching at his body and pulling him down.

Still the words fly from my mouth. '*Eko eko azarak, eko eko zomelak!*'

I chant and chant, and then my arms drop and somehow I know it's done.

Tom writhes on the ground and the shadows pull apart and twist around on themselves, forming a long thin funnel that whips about his body. He yells and a narrow stream of darkness pours into his mouth.

'Tom!'

He groans deep in the back of his throat and I turn away, afraid he will stare at me with bulging eyes, his face fixed in a grimace.

A window smashes overhead, glass shattering everywhere as a huge black seabird crashes into the room. The pane opposite breaks as another bird flies inside, and then another. More and more of them follow until the air is full of cormorants. They beat their powerful wings and I hold up my arms and shield my face. The birds screech and dive, their sharp bills snapping at the shadows and driving them away.

One of the cormorants does a somersault mid-air and lands before me. I look down, but it's not the webbed feet of a seabird I see. On the ground are human feet: bony and dirty, the thick toenails curled under. I look up and a woman in a tattered black dress stands before me, a pair of huge, feathered wings protruding from her back. Long dark hair hangs about her shoulders, tangled with feathers and bits of fishbone. Her cheeks and forehead are covered with a spiderweb of black veins and her eyes are completely white. No pupils, no irises, yet somehow they are looking right into me.

She opens her lips and the cry of a seabird comes out. I stare, unable to comprehend what I'm seeing, and she shimmies her shoulders and repositions her feet on the floor. Her long white throat undulates and she makes a wet, convulsing rasp, like she's gulping down a fish. This time when she opens her mouth, a cracked voice fills the room.

'We heard your ca-a-all.'

The words are sharp and stuttering, as if she hasn't spoken for centuries. Too shocked to wonder what she means, I stare at her face. Her mouth changes shape, her lips stretching thin and making the tendons of her neck stand out. She repeats the motion, her lips twitching up at the edges like she's trying to smile.

163

'We found you – sister.'

She lisps the last word, her tongue poking out between her teeth as if she's forgotten how to shape the letters. I glance at Tom, who lies on the ground covered with black feathers. Instead of seabirds flocking around him, there are dark-haired women. Somehow I know that they won't hurt him, even before I see one of them stroke his forehead.

The bird-woman tilts her head and surveys me with rheumy white eyes. A glistening transparent film slides over her eyeballs like a tiny shutter opening. The strangeness of it fills me with revulsion, yet somehow I'm not afraid.

The woman raises a scrawny arm and I watch entranced as her fingers dance on the air, her talon-like nails clicking together. The tiny flicking motion does something to me and I feel my mind slow, like it's full of feathers. I fight the urge to close my eyes and she steps behind me and clamps a damp hand to my forehead, pulling me back into her. She smells brackish, of rock pools and vast windswept beaches, and I feel as if I'm being held by the sea. A rhythmic guttural sound emanates from her throat, then she cackles and a rush of seawater closes over my head. My mind rocks shut like a clam and everything goes black.

17

I open my eyes to find myself back in the attic bedroom, red light seeping through the curtains and Tom breathing heavily in the next bed. Hideous shadowy creatures prowl the corners of my mind and I press my face into the pillow. It was just a nightmare. Tom's safe and so is my mother. I turn over, and a weight shifts at the bottom of the bed. The bird-woman peers at me and I cry out.

'Sh-sh-shush now.'

She reaches a hand towards me and I scramble up the mattress, my heart pounding, as massive feathered wings open from between her shoulder blades. I blink at her in disbelief, taking in her razor-sharp cheekbones, long hooked nose and milky-white eyes. The veins under her skin glow in the red half-light, giving her an oddly mottled appearance. Something about her seems incredibly old, ancient even. My nerves stretch out with the seconds; her existence is so impossible I can't trust my own mind. If I screamed, would Tom wake me and say I've been dreaming or would he see her too?

A soft grunting noise comes from the back of her throat, the words stuttered and barely comprehensible. 'Am I m-much ch-changed?' Her mouth briefly widens, her pale lips stretching thin before wrenching upwards. It's a strange parody of a smile and yet something about it – about her – is disturbingly familiar.

She clamps her hands onto my knees and crawls up the bed, her sharp fingernails digging into my legs. My muscles tense and I hold my breath as she leans close, her long, dirty hair hanging over my body. Freakishly white eyes search mine as if she's looking for something buried inside me. I start to cover my face and she notices the red mark on my wrist and smiles with something like recognition. She reaches to touch it, but I snatch my hand away.

Heaving a sigh, she retreats to the bottom of the bed and my body trembles with relief. I wait for her to say something but she just sits there, her shoulders rounded. *I hate seeing her like this, bone weary and ground down. Where is the beautiful woman with ice-blue eyes? She's always been the fiercest amongst us, the most passionate and brave.*

How can I know these things? The voice inside my head is my own, but the thoughts belong to someone else. Something's not right. *I'm* not right. I must be dreaming. The creatures in the lighthouse, my mum being taken, it can't have happened.

'None of this is real, it can't be,' I mutter.

Her hand squeezes mine and I'm filled with a sinking realisation. Whether this is real or some projection of my mind, I'm not going to wake up.

Tom groans as if he's in pain and my heart constricts. I don't know what the women in the tower did to him, but what if he doesn't wake up? What if he does and tries to attack me? Instinctively, I turn to the bird-woman for help. She smiles and something tells me that she can heal him. It makes no sense – my mum warned me the witches wanted to kill me, yet instinct tells me I can trust her. I feel certain she'd never hurt me, even though I've only just met her.

'My mum, what happened to her?' I ask.

The bird-woman shakes her head and the air leaves my body. She can't have gone. Not like that. Not taken by those *things*.

'I have to get her back. Please.'

She moves up the bed and holds my hands in hers then gently bumps her forehead against mine. The intimacy of the gesture takes me by surprise, and fills me with inexplicable longing at the same time. I have a feeling we've sat like this before, sharing our hurts and hopes, comforting one another. It makes me homesick for something I've never had.

'First you m-must remember.'

She draws in a sharp breath and I get the impression that talking is exhausting for her. The more she speaks, the clearer her diction becomes, but every word is extracted at a cost.

'It will be easier if your memories return by themselves. That's why we've been whispering to you, making our ma-mark on your door, leaving the book.'

Thinking about the book reminds me of the man I saw in the portal. The image was hazy and indistinct, but I would know his face anywhere. It was the man from my vision.

'I need to remember Merlin?'

She smiles encouragingly and I wish I understood.

'Do you know who I am?' she asks.

I search her face, certain that I know her but unable to recall her name.

The woman lays her hand on her chest. 'My name is Morgan le Fay.'

I nod, but none of this makes sense. I know who Morgan le Fay is, but only as a character of legend. That doesn't explain the existence of this bizarre bird-woman on my bed.

She makes a soft gulping sound. 'You were once a sorceress of Avalon, one of my sisters. Your name was Moronoe.'

I try to pull away and she tightens her grip on my hands. 'I know this is hard for you to believe, but what I say is the truth. A portal between the earthly realm and Avalon has existed since time began. In our world, we chose to build a glass tower around it.'

She looks at me expectantly but my mind is spinning away from me. Stroking my hand, she adds, 'Here on Earth, the portal is located on the island. For the longest time it was a mere shimmer in the air, and then they built a lighthouse on it.'

'Who did?'

She shrugs as if it doesn't matter. 'Humans are sometimes able to sense the energy of the portal, but they cannot see it. The men who built the lighthouse were no doubt drawn to put a structure there, but they wouldn't have known why.' She smiles sadly. 'In Arthur's time, the portal opened into the air and we stepped onto grass.'

I begin to feel light-headed, as if I'm no longer inside my body but floating on the edges of reality. I cast around my mind, looking for something that will help me make sense of things. 'So King Arthur was a real person?'

She laughs. 'Very much so. My half-brother was a good man. We had what you might call a *complicated* relationship, but few men in history have proved to be as courageous as he.' She gazes into space, her eyes wistful. 'After he fell in battle, we brought him to the island and carried him through the portal to Avalon. Of course, the lighthouse didn't exist then. So many things have changed in the world of men.'

'How long have you been in this world?' I ask.

'We've been trapped here since the sixth century.'

'Over one thousand, five hundred years?'

'That is correct. We've taken the form of cormorants to conserve our energy, and only fly as our true selves in winter when our powers are strongest.' She sighs sadly, her expression darkening. 'But we are becoming weak.'

Her grip tightens on my hand. 'There's no easy way to tell you this. You died in the glass tower in Avalon a very long time ago, and your spirit was pulled into the portal and came to this world.'

I look at her, wide-eyed, and she continues. 'Your sisters and I never stopped searching for you. We were there on the night you reincarnated. We wanted you to grow up knowing the truth of your identity, but then Merlin sent his demons.'

I gaze at the unfamiliar red mark on my wrist and an unwelcome thought washes up on the shore of my mind, one that has been sailing towards me through the mist for days.

You're not who you think you are.

Realisation drops anchor deep inside me. The girl I read about in the book and saw in my vision, the face I glimpsed in the bathroom mirror, is me. That's why the mark on my skin suddenly appeared. I'm seeing it because it once belonged to her. She's inside me, her thoughts and memories affecting my mind.

'You're telling me I died over a thousand years ago?'

'When we found your body, we tried to revive you but your spirit had already slipped into the portal. If you had died anywhere else, we could have brought you back. We knew that your soul would seek out an unborn child, but time exists differently in the portal and we didn't know *when* you might emerge into the earthly realm. At first, we had no idea it was Merlin who had killed you. As soon as we left Avalon, he enchanted the portal so that we couldn't return.'

I think back to my vision. I know Merlin tried to kiss the girl – tried to kiss me – and that he killed her, but something doesn't make sense.

'Why does he want to stop you going back?'

'To prevent us from avenging your death, and because he wants Avalon for himself.'

She stands up and pulls her shoulders back, her wings opening and then resettling. 'Merlin became obsessed with you and used demonic magic to try and make you love him. He had no interest in taking Avalon before, but I fear that working with demons has set him on a dark path – one of greed and reckless pursuit of power.'

Morgan paces to the window on bare feet then turns to face me. Her voice is quiet and fraught with guilt. 'I am the eldest. I am responsible for you all. I should have known what was happening. I failed you and I am sorry.'

Mum was wrong – the witches weren't trying to hurt me. They came to me the night I was born, but it was Merlin who sent the shadow demons, not them. The tightness in my chest eases a little. I'm relieved to know the truth, yet I don't feel any better. The impossibility of it all makes my head hurt. I realise there are people who believe King Arthur once lived, but magical beings who come from another world? I'm not sure which I find harder to accept: that Avalon is real or that I once lived there.

'Why my mum, why me, though?'

Morgan smiles sadly. 'The portal brought Moronoe's spirit to this point in history at random. She sought out the first infant vessel she could find. There was no choice involved, no act of destiny – simply a coincidence of place and time.'

My head pounds as another thought occurs to me. None of this would have happened if it weren't for Merlin. I would have grown up with a family and the girl in the story, Moronoe, wouldn't have died and the witches would be where they belong – in their own world.

Morgan strides towards me, her feathered wings ruffling. 'He knows that if we reunite and become nine, we'll be strong enough to open the portal and take back Avalon. He'll do anything to stop that happening, even if it means sending his demons and killing you again.'

'And my mum? Where is she?'

'If she was taken into the portal then she's in Avalon, in the keep of Merlin.'

'We can't leave her there! Please, you have to help me.'

'Your mother was only able to open the portal because Merlin allowed it. He no doubt intended for his demons to snatch you. Even if he allowed you to open it, he would kill you as soon as you stepped through.'

'There must be something we can do.'

She clasps her hands together in a gesture of entreaty and takes a deep breath. Whatever she's about to say, I have the feeling she's been building up to this moment for a very long time.

'I cannot make any promises, but we will do our best to rescue your mother. You have a choice: deny who you are or reclaim your power and join us.'

She extends her arms to me but I stay on the bed.

'Join you?'

'It's time for you to become a witch once more.'

I blink at her, unable to form a reply. I came here to find my mum, not to be reunited with witch sisters from another lifetime. I don't want any of this. I want to be with my mum, preferably starting a new life together far away from this place, somewhere ordinary where nothing ever happens. Like Coleford.

She steps closer and peers into my eyes. 'The witch inside you is already waking.'

Her words curl into me like fish hooks. She says it with such certainty, as if she can see her sister within me. It makes me feel that there's nothing I can do and I may as well as accept it, but how can I? It's bad enough knowing there's someone else inside me, without trying to *wake* her. I don't want to see her face in the mirror, I don't want to hear her thoughts or relive her memories. If that's what reclaiming my power means, I don't want it.

Something flutters in my chest, a thump of an extra heartbeat just missing the rhythm of my own. I can *feel* her inside me, knocking to be let in – or trying to get out.

I lean back on the bed and cross my arms. 'I don't know who I was before, but I'm not that person any more. I'm sorry.'

A cackle bursts from Morgan's lips, the noise so violent and unexpected I'm not sure if she's angry or amused. 'Just because you can't feel the magic inside you, doesn't mean it's not there. You can drain the oceans of water and fill them anew, and the tide will still flow. Magic is the tide. You have only to wade into the water to feel its pull.'

She straightens her shoulders and adds firmly, 'If you want to save your mother, you must remember who you are and become a witch once more. Your sisters and I can train you in magic. It's the only way.'

I get to my feet and look at Tom sleeping in the next bed. His face is clammy, his hair slick with sweat. 'Will he be OK?' I ask.

Morgan frowns. 'If the demons are driven out of him, there's a chance he will survive. I will do my best, but I'm not as strong as I once was. I may need to call upon your energy.'

I chew my thumbnail, wary of what she'll ask of me, and yet knowing I can't let him stay like this. It's my fault he's on the island. I would never forgive myself if I didn't do everything I could to help him. Morgan raises her eyebrows and something deep in my gut tells me I can trust her.

I nod and she pats my arm, then steps towards the bed.

Her wings open and she jumps up in one clean motion, her feet landing on either side of him. Crouching over his middle, she extends her arms and presses her palms against his chest. Her long hair hangs over his body, bits of shell and fishbone gleaming in the tangled black tresses. She arches her back and there's something so wild and primal about her that I feel self-conscious for watching. She brings her hands over his face and makes a flicking motion, her long fingernails clicking together, and he opens his eyes.

I rush to his side. 'Tom, it's me. Can you hear me?'

He stares ahead with a fervid gaze, apparently unaware of the otherworldly creature perched over him. I look at Morgan, but her face is fixed in concentration. She gulps greedily at the air, making a glugging noise deep in the back of her throat, and the sound takes on a rhythm of its own, as if she's chanting. There are no words but something about it is familiar, like hearing a badly hummed version of your favourite song. On and on she chants, the sound rising and falling, swelling and retreating like the tide.

Her wings unfurl and beat the air, sending a gust of wind into the room. And then something happens that's so strange I wonder again if I'm dreaming. Her hair lifts from her shoulders and floats upwards, defying gravity to swirl above her head. It makes me think of a mermaid swimming underwater. Her face glows as if lit from within, her eyes no longer cloudy white but ice blue, with huge black pupils at their centre. Everything about her seems brighter, her whole being infused with eerie transcendence.

A thin film slides across her eyeballs with lizard-like speed, so quick I almost miss it. She grasps my hand, and heat flutters in my abdomen and vibrates against my ribcage like the beat of a moth's wing. Instinctively, I reach out and grip Tom's shoulder, willing him to be well, and the energy leaves me all at once like an arrow firing, as if my worry had pulled my feelings taut and touching him has released them.

Morgan squeezes my hand tighter and warmth floods along my arm like liquid sunshine. Tiny dots of light spark and flicker at the edges of my vision as a sense of wellbeing infuses every cell of my being. If this is magic, it is utterly exhilarating. I feel as if I'm standing on the edge of a cliff with sea spray hitting my face, about to soar into the sky. Tom's eyes remain closed but he's no longer twisting his head back and forth. He's breathing hard, his cheeks flushed. The energy continues to surge through me and into him, and the warm glow in my chest grows stronger. The sensation is intoxicating, but more than that, it feels good to know that I'm helping him.

Morgan nods her approval and I hold her gaze and smile. And then I see a face reflected in her black pupils – a girl with long dark hair and red lips, her eyes blazing with witch-light. A girl who isn't me.

I release her hand and the energy stops abruptly like an elastic band snapping back. Morgan leans forward on her haunches then takes a shuddery breath and jumps awkwardly to the floor. Her face is fish-pale and sickly, her eyes clouded over once more. She looks sunken in on herself, and I have an urge to take her in my arms and give her my energy; anything so that she'll be well. Whoever I was in a previous life, I know that I needed her to be strong. Without her, everything is lost.

'Are you OK? Morgan?'

She shakes her head. 'I cannot drive the demons out of him, at least not tonight. He is too weak and would not survive. I have done my best to soothe him. He needs time to rest and regain his strength, as do I.'

Tom is sleeping soundly, his chest gently rising and falling. Whatever she did just now – whatever *we* did – seems to have worked. And yet it's cost her so much.

She glances back at him. 'You must not wake him, even if he cries out. You must let him sleep. I will return tomorrow and do what I can.'

'Thank you.'

My fingers tingle and I hold up my hands, marvelling at the gentle thrum of magic within them. The energy is no longer coursing through me, but I can still feel its presence, the afterglow like the taste of warm honey on my tongue.

'Morgan, can I try it again? Can I heal him?'

She raises her eyebrows. 'Your energy is strong but not focused. It will take time for you to direct it unaided.'

I nod, disappointed that I can't do more to help him. I'm still fearful of waking the witch inside me, but the feeling of magic is so thrilling that I want to experience it again. The realisation is unsettling.

She tilts her head. 'You will begin training with your sisters in the morning?'

I glance at Tom and push down my fear. I don't know what will be expected of me, but I have to help him. Whatever it takes, I need to rescue my mum. 'Yes,' I answer quietly.

Morgan crosses the room and pulls back the curtain, the red glare of the lighthouse accentuating the deep hollows of her face. She sways on her feet and my heart reaches out to her. She might look like a nightmarish creature, but I owe her so much.

I pull up the sash window and icy drizzle hits my face. She stands tall, the smell of the sea seeming to revive her a little,

176

then shuffles her feet. I move to one side and she grabs hold of the window and hauls herself up. Her wings beat the air and then she jumps out. I rush forward, relieved when she rises up a few seconds later. She flaps her wings once, twice, and in the blink of an eye she is a cormorant. Wiping the rain from my face, I watch as she swoops around the tower then turns and heads out to sea.

18

I wake to the cries of cormorants, their raucous honks and cackles so loud it sounds as if they're in the room with me. Tom is lying on his back, snoring quietly. I swing my legs out of bed, relieved to see that some colour has returned to his face. Morgan said she would drive the demons out of him once he's regained his strength, so I just have to hope they're dormant for now. He murmurs something and I touch his shoulder. No healing energy flows into him this time, and I can't help missing the spark of magic in my fingers.

Several dark shapes swoop past the window and I hurriedly throw on my clothes. I don't know where I'm meant to meet my sisters, but if I don't go out soon their cries are sure to wake Tom, and Morgan said to let him sleep. Fastening my coat, I pause and glance back, wishing I could stay by his side. I have a sudden urge to go over and hug him, but I don't. Getting emotional isn't going to help. Now more than ever, I need to be strong.

Downstairs, I use the bathroom then quickly eat some breakfast and head out. Pulling the door closed behind me, I stare up at the lighthouse. It looms as pale as a ghost in the early morning mist, its menacing presence a constant shadow over my thoughts. My breath catches when I think of my mum. What if Merlin hurts her, or he . . . I clutch my locket, refusing to think that way. I have to do whatever Morgan asks of me. Magic is real, I've felt it myself. If becoming a witch is what it takes to get her back, I'll do it. I just hope I learn fast.

There's no sign of the cormorants, but I can still hear them. Following the sound of their cries, I turn my back on the tower and walk along the gently sloping path that leads to the beach. The sea is a rolling expanse of grey, the swell rising and falling like some great panting beast that's yet to fully wake. I trudge across the shingle, picking my way through mounds of seaweed and quivering white foam that bubbles and froths in the breeze. A faint purple haze hangs over the water and despite the cries of the birds there's a soft stillness to the air, the swash of the tide hypnotic.

A little way out to sea, I spot a family of seals lying on an outcrop of rock. One of the weighty adults lumbers over to an infant and pats its flipper on the creature's upturned belly. Arcs of sea spray shower them as they wriggle on their fronts and launch themselves into the water, their smooth grey heads dipping and reappearing above the waves, round eyes gleaming like black glass. It reminds me of when we first arrived, and I find myself wishing I'd pointed them out to Tom. What if he doesn't wake up? What if I don't get to spend any more time with him? No, Morgan will help him – she has to.

Looking along the beach, I can't see Morgan, or any other winged women. I know that last night really happened, but standing here now with my shoes sinking into the shingle and the salty air in my lungs, it's hard to believe it wasn't a dream. And even harder to believe that I'm meant to start witch training with my 'sisters'.

Several cormorants fly above me, their massive wings outstretched. They call to one another as they soar, their throaty grunts loud over the swell of the tide. I spot another four of the birds bobbing on the sea. They swim low in the water, gliding effortlessly. One of them takes to the air then dives head first into the waves, plummeting as hard as lightning, before emerging with a fish in its bill.

I duck as a cormorant swoops low over my head and then lands on an outcrop of granite a few paces away. It holds out its glossy black wings, the scallop-shaped feathers iridescent in the pale light, and then turns and repositions itself, its webbed feet slapping against the wet rock. Its face is covered with bare scaly skin and surrounded by pale feathers, its green eye watching me. With its flat forehead and cruelly curved bill, it's a strange reptilian-looking thing. It makes a gulping noise and I step closer, wondering if it's trying to communicate.

A hand grips my shoulder and I gasp and spin around. A woman in a tattered black dress stands before me, her long dark hair plastered to her forehead. Her skin is so pale it's almost translucent and her eyes are pure white. Unlike Morgan, she's tall and broad-shouldered with generous womanly curves. She smiles, revealing a flash of sharp teeth, and then glances over my head and frowns.

A cormorant is heading straight for me. As it gets closer, I see its face. A woman's face: small and pinched, with a furrowed brow and sharp, angry eyes. It flickers and changes, the image becoming one thing and then another. A cormorant's face. A woman's. Cormorant.

Its vicious beak opens like I'm a fish it's about to swallow and I lift my arm, sure it's going to crash into me, when the bird somersaults and turns into a woman. She lands with a thud, her bare feet skidding into the pebbles. She wears the same clothing as the first woman and has the same long dark hair and white eyes, but is much shorter – and angrier. She shoves the bigger lady, who shrugs as if they've had this argument before.

Another of the birds lands as a woman to my right, her feet thumping into the shingle. A moment later, a different one appears to my left and then another behind me. I turn and look in every direction. Seven women stand around me, their huge, feathered wings fluttering in the breeze. Some of them laugh with joy, a few regard me in seeming disbelief, and the smallest one glares at me like I owed her money in my previous life.

They pace around me. There's something unnerving about the way their bare feet step effortlessly across the pebbles, their movements synchronised. Every now and then they talk amongst themselves, their honks and grunts so strange that I begin to feel light-headed. The short one breaks the circle as if she's going to talk to me, but the women on either side pull her back.

Ignoring her smaller sister's protests, the tall woman strides forward and holds her throat. She makes a strangled noise and the short one honks in derision, earning her a shove from her neighbour. The first woman tries again and makes the same sound. She snaps her mouth shut, her fleshy cheeks turning crimson. A different woman in the circle grunts, and before long they're all making the same awful noises. I cover my ears, wondering if I've done something wrong, and then I realise. It's not anger on their faces, but frustration. They want to talk to me, but don't know how.

I approach the tall one and hold out my hand. 'Hello.'

To my surprise, she shakes it firmly. 'Ha-ha crack-ko.'

The others cackle loudly and shake their heads and I realise they're laughing. The woman glares at them and tries again. 'Ha-low.' She sighs with seeming relief then turns to the others and waves her arm dismissively. This time when she tries speaking, her throat convulses and a spasm of syllables comes out, the noise so unnatural it sounds as if she's about to throw up. Amongst the rough croaky grunts are snatches of words. She keeps on talking and after a while, I catch a distinct phrase.

'Not speak-ka in a long time.'

I'm so pleased for her that I clutch her arm. 'Yes! You've not spoken for a long time.'

Her face lights up and tears fill her eyes. 'Moronoe. Sister, my sister.'

I smile awkwardly and she points to her bosom as if I should know her. 'My na-name is Glitonea. You remember?' Her face fills with hope, and an image flashes into my mind of her hugging me when I was sad. She's the motherly one of the group: always there with a kind word and a shoulder to cry on, and cake . . . she made the most amazing cakes.

I find myself nodding, even though the memory belongs to someone else, and she throws her arms around me. Suddenly they all rush forward, hugging and kissing me. Their long wet hair covers my arms and back, their damp sandy hands stroking my cheeks. Cackles of happiness ring in my ears.

Glitonea pulls away and addresses the others. 'I speak-ka. I teach.'

I want to ask what she'll teach me, and if she can help me to heal Tom, but I don't get the chance. She grabs my hand and studies the crowd as if daring anyone to challenge her. When no one does, she nods decisively and turns to me. 'We don't have much time. Come.'

Like Morgan, it seems the more she talks, the easier it becomes. I start to follow her, but the rest of the women have other ideas. They gather around me, stroking my hair and caressing my arms.

One of the women steps forward and thumps her chest as if there's something lodged inside her. She tries to speak, her eyes glistening, but I can't understand the noises she makes. She laughs and points to each of her sisters before her finger lands on me. As she does, I feel it – a sharp tug behind my ribs. Somehow I know that I once had a special relationship with her, as I did with each of the women. We hold one another's gaze and there is a moment between us, a deep and powerful knowing. Even though we've only just met, I know that I once belonged to her and the rest of her sisters, as they did to me.

The women turn to each other, placing their arms about

one another's shoulders and honking sadly. One by one they turn and move away, each walking in a different direction. Their wings open and beat the air, taking them into the sky, and a moment later they're cormorants. My chest aches with emptiness. It's like there's a knot of kite strings stuffed behind my breastbone and each line leads to one of the bird-women. The further they fly from me, the tighter it pulls. Even though I'm a different person now, the feeling of connection fills me with raw, ravenous wanting. It's not just that I miss them. I desperately want to go with them.

A hand grasps mine and I turn and see Glitonea. She smiles sadly, as if she's aware of how I'm feeling, and points along the beach. 'Ka-low.'

I shake my head and she points again. 'Ka-low.'

'I'm sorry, I don't –'

She sweeps me off my feet, her arms strong beneath me. I search her face, my heart beating fast. Surely she's not going to . . .

She runs a few steps then opens her wings and launches into the sky. I cling to her neck, not daring to look down. When I do, the ground is moving so fast my stomach flips.

'We're flying,' I gasp. 'We're actually flying.'

She raises her eyebrows and grins, seemingly surprised by my reaction. We follow the line of the coast and I'm torn between peering at the beach below and staring at her in awe. With her long hair streaming in the wind, she looks like a warrior flying into battle. I think about Tom, imagining what he'd say if he knew, and my smile broadens. I wish he was here to see me. Glitonea adjusts her arms beneath my legs and I cling to her neck as we fly higher, my heart lifting with each powerful beat of her wings. Something sparks and comes to life inside me, and I know that I've done this before. I was once like her. I too could fly.

19

After a few minutes she drops back onto the shingle, bending her knees and lowering me down. She points to an opening in the rocks and I smile with realisation.

'Cave, is that what you meant?'

She nods as if she said it right all along. 'Ka-low.'

An echoey pit-pat and splash of water sounds from deep within and I get the impression it goes a long way back. It's so dark and enclosed – why bring me here? I glance along the misty shoreline, wishing we could go somewhere else, when she walks inside.

I follow her and the ground shifts beneath me, my shoes sinking in deep silt.

Before me, a dozen or so boulders lead down like stepping stones. The air reeks of sulphur and rotting things. The further I go the harder it is to see, so that I can only just make out her broad back, as she picks her way over the rocks with ease, despite her bare feet.

Water drips on my head and trickles into my eyes. As I wipe my face, my foot slips on something squelchy and I grab the wall of the cave. I start to go after her, when I see something down below that makes me falter.

Glitonea is standing in a shadowy chamber, knee-deep in a pool of water, her eyes two points of eerie white light in the gloom. The darkness must be playing tricks on me as she looks completely different: her skin is flaky and peeling, like she's covered in mud, and her hair is sparse and stringy. Water splashes and plops, tapping out a disjointed rhythm all around us. Why isn't she saying anything?

The cave feels airless suddenly and I struggle to breathe. I don't know what she plans to teach me, but I feel as if I shouldn't be here. I glance over my shoulder at the entrance, wishing I'd stayed with Tom. I should have at least waited until he woke up. But then Morgan wouldn't have told me to leave him and meet my sisters if he was in danger.

Glitonea holds out her right arm and a dot of golden light appears above her palm. It rises slowly, zigzagging one way and another like a firefly, before hovering high in the air. She mutters something and the light brightens, revealing a scene from another planet.

The cavernous roof is covered with stalactites. There are hundreds of them: fat white columns creeping down like melted wax, tiny needle-sharp shards packed together in rows, and huge icicle formations that hang over our heads like giant teeth. Dozens of stalagmites rise up from the ground, the pale mounds and columns filling the cave.

Glitonea gestures to one of the boulders that line the edge of the pool, but I don't move, unable to pull my gaze from the strange hovering light and the alien world around us. She wades out from the water and points again at the rock. 'Sit,' she says.

I do as I'm told and she sits next to me, angling her body so we're holding one another's gaze. The light flickers and dims and her image changes: one moment she looks like the woman I saw on the beach and the next old and decaying. I glance away, feeling uneasy, and she turns my chin to face her.

She takes a deep breath and gestures for me to do the same. I inhale slowly, my chest rising and falling in time with hers, and then she starts to chant – noises that aren't quite words, yet are somehow familiar. She nods for me to join her and we sing for the longest time, until my eyes lose focus so that I no longer see the details of her face. There is only a patchwork of light and shade, tiny dots swirling thickly in the air.

Tapping her forehead, she stands up and says, 'Make a picture.'

She clambers onto the boulder, her ragged dress dripping with water, and in the course of a single step her fleshy calves transform into the thin legs of a bird. When I raise my gaze, there is a cormorant standing on the rock. It beats its mighty wings and I shield my face as the bird becomes a woman once more.

Glitonea grabs my hands and pulls me to my feet. 'Make a picture,' she says again, this time pointing at the centre of my forehead.

I close my eyes and imagine myself as a cormorant: muscular wings on my back, my body covered with feathers. I think about looking down and seeing thin legs and webbed feet. I visualise it so clearly, I almost believe it could happen. I open an eye and squint, but unless I'm a bird wearing thick black tights

188

and shoes, nothing has changed. Frowning in concentration, I try again, but all I give myself is a headache.

She sighs as if it should be easy for me, and my shoulders sag. Part of me wants to know how it feels to do the impossible, but what if I get stuck and can't turn back? What if it hurts? The more I keep trying, the more ridiculous I feel. I can't simply *think* my way into being a cormorant. I decide to tell her this, when she leans forward and searches my eyes.

'Wake the witch inside.'

I don't want to ask whoever I was before for help. I'm already becoming aware of her memories. What if she takes control of me completely? Maybe Glitonea and the others *want* that to happen so they can have their sister back.

I swallow hard, about to ask what will happen to me if I do, when she presses her finger to my forehead. Electricity surges down my spine and sparks along my arms and legs. Magic ripples through me like a stone dropped in some vast, unknowable ocean. I am a wave breaking on the shore, a bird diving into the sea, an autumn leaf falling. There and gone again, me and not me.

'Picture the bird,' she commands.

I dig my fingernails into my palms and focus with all my might, imagining myself as a cormorant. Sweat covers my forehead as lightness rushes through my body, hollowing out my bones. I am abruptly too hot and shivering all over. My hands tingle and I'm filled with an overwhelming sense that I can do anything. The heat intensifies and my bones creak. Something is happening. I'm changing.

The realisation fills me with panic. I thought I could do this, but I can't. The idea of becoming another creature – of physically transforming – is terrifying. I tell myself that I *have* to become a witch to save my mother, but it's like a shutter has come down in my brain. Magic drips through my fingers, leaving my hands with the sensation of holding a pile of wet seaweed. I am no longer hot, but cold as the stone beneath me.

An image of a girl with long dark hair and red lips flashes into my mind.

Let me help you.

Something thumps wildly in my chest, like a bird is battering its wings against my ribcage. Moronoe's face grows bigger and brighter, her words loud.

You must let me help you.

The stronger she becomes, the weaker I feel. I shake my head and her image fades as quickly as it came.

I open my eyes and inspect my hands. My fingers are my own, but when I touch my jaw I feel feathers. I try to sit and hear a snap. Stars prickle at the edge of my vision as the pain hits me, white-hot and searing. I look down and see a shard of bone protruding from my right thigh. The skin surrounding it isn't pink and covered with blood. It's black and bumpy like the leg of a bird. I pull at the hole in my tights and tear open the material. The scaly surface covers several centimetres of my leg. I try to cry out but my tongue is swollen and flaps like an eel in my mouth, and all I make is a strangled juddering sound. I turn my head and tiny bones crack and pop in the tunnel of my neck.

Glitonea is saying something but I can't understand her words. She looks afraid. I grab her, desperate now, and she presses a firm hand against my thigh. I sigh with relief as a cool sensation flows through my veins, easing my pain. Panting hard, I peer at my legs. The bone retracts before my eyes and disappears back into my flesh, the skin knitting itself together. I check the rest of my body and feel my own skin instead of feathers. Overcome with gratitude, I turn to hug her, but draw back when I see her face.

Her eyes have sunk into their sockets, the bones protruding to reveal the shape of her skull. Most of her hair has fallen out and her scalp is covered with scaly white patches. She croaks something, pointing towards the cave entrance, and I fight back a tear.

'I'm sorry I couldn't do it. I shouldn't have tried.'

She grips my arm, her voice raspy. 'You can't give up.'

Before I can answer, she takes an unsteady step back and shrinks to a cormorant. I watch her flap weakly out of the cave, feeling helpless. I don't have what it takes to be a witch. I've failed them. Because of me, the witches won't be able to go through the portal and return home, and I'll never see my mum again.

20

I clamber up the rocks and stumble onto the shore, blinking in the harsh light. There's not a single cormorant in the sky and I can only hope that Glitonea has gone to find her sisters. I hate to think of her suffering because of me. I should have done as she asked; I should have let the witch inside me help.

As I head across the beach my thoughts turn to Tom. I don't know how long I've been gone, but it feels like hours. What if he wakes and there's no one there? I walk as fast as I can, willing my aching legs to go quicker.

The house is quiet as I enter the hallway and make my way through the kitchen to the stairs. The wood creaks as I step onto the landing and I startle as a figure emerges from the shadows. Morgan is no longer wizened, but looks how she did the first time we met. Her face is grave and I'm almost too afraid to ask.

'Is it Glitonea? I couldn't do it and she had to heal me . . .'

Morgan raises her hand, silencing me. 'I've every hope your sister will recover with a few days' rest.'

Relief washes over me and Morgan forces a smile. 'She told me what happened and it sounds like you made progress. You can't expect your powers to return instantly. It may take a day or two.'

I raise my eyebrows, thinking that sounds ambitious for someone who only managed to sprout a few facial feathers in her first lesson; that and break a thigh bone. Maybe there's something easier I can start with. 'Can you turn into anything, or is it just cormorants?'

Morgan frowns as if I should know the answer. 'We've taken the form of cormorants as it's easy to find food and we have few predators. Becoming a winged creature takes less energy, but we're able to transform into anything – as will you be once your powers return.'

I nod, even though I don't really believe it. I accept it's possible – my failed attempt earlier has convinced me of that, but I still can't imagine actually turning into a bird, or a frog, or a cat, or anything else for that matter. The idea feels utterly surreal. But then so does standing here, chatting to a witch with wings.

A groan sounds from the bedroom. Morgan steps to one side, letting me go past, and I realise why she looked so worried before. Tom is thrashing in the bed, his skin covered with angry red blotches and his forehead drenched with sweat. My heart lurches and I rush to his side.

'What's happening to him?'

'The demons inside him are stronger than I thought.'

'Please, you have to do something. You have to help him.'

She wrings her hands as if there's something she doesn't want to tell me. 'First you must know what you are asking. I can drive the demons out of him, but I cannot destroy them. They will remain in the house as shadows.'

I glance about, unsure what she means. 'Can they get inside him again?'

'No. They will not be able to re-enter his body. Nor can they enter a sorceress – you and I are immune, as are your sisters. But that does not mean you are safe.' She opens her wings wide and her glossy black feathers flutter in an unseen breeze. 'The demons take the form of shadows in this world, but if they grow strong enough they can become corporeal.'

'You mean they become flesh and blood?'

She nods. 'They have been tasked with one thing, and that is to kill you. Only this time they will not require a human host.'

The idea of those grotesque things becoming real makes my skin crawl. There were so many of them, I wouldn't stand a chance. A strangled sob comes from the bed and I turn to Tom. His grey sweatshirt is covered with damp patches and he's panting hard. He lashes out an arm, fighting an enemy that only he can see, and I clench my fists.

He shouldn't be here; this shouldn't be happening to him. If he'd walked back to the farmhouse the first night we arrived, he could have returned to the mainland with the boatman. He only stayed because he was worried about me. I should never have dragged him into this.

I pinch the bridge of my nose, wishing the past two days had never happened and we were back at work. I know I can take him for granted sometimes, but it's only because I don't like to admit how much he means to me. Part of the reason I loved my job was because I looked forward to seeing him. It's not just that he makes me laugh; he brightens my day in a way I can't explain. He gets me in a way other people don't. Work wouldn't have been the same without him. Nothing would be the same without him.

He twists his head, a look of torment on his face, and I make up my mind.

'Please Morgan, get them out of him.'

Her face fills with tenderness, as if she can tell how much I care for him. 'I have not used demonic magic in my own workings – and nor would I – so there are limits to my understanding, but I will do my best. You must remember that Merlin is a powerful wizard and the offspring of a demon; his magic will be stronger than most.'

I nod and she presses the back of her hand to Tom's forehead. The room darkens as if a cloud has passed over the sun and the temperature drops, turning my breath white. The air is so cold, I can feel it biting at my cheeks and slicing into my throat.

Opening her wings, she jumps onto the bed and straddles Tom's waist. She draws herself up and mutters. '*Exorcizamus te, omnis immundus spiritus, omnis satanica potestas, omnis incursion infernalis adversarii, omnis legio, omnis congregatio et secta diabolica.*'

Tom's eyes rove beneath his closed eyelids. His head wrenches to the side, his lips parting to reveal a film of spittle at the corner of his mouth. Something about him looks different: his nose is a fraction wider and his jaw squarer. His features are hazy and indistinct and at first I think there's a shadow hanging over him, but it's not that. Something is moving *inside* him. It's like his face is re-forming, his bones rearranging the contours of his face. Only the movement isn't smooth. His flesh ripples like it's full of maggots.

I watch with sickening fascination as a different set of features appears beneath his own, and then another and another, some of them human and others grotesque misshapen creatures, his face constantly morphing while his body writhes in the bed. Morgan pushes down on his chest, her eyes no longer white but two inky pools of black.

'*Exorcizamus te, omnis immundus spiritus! Omnis satanica potestas, omnis incursion infernalis adversarii, omnis legio, omnis congregatio et secta diabolica!*'

Tom rears up and spits at her. The saliva glistens and drips from her cheek, but she doesn't wipe it away. She keeps her palms pressed to his chest, her expression grimly determined. Tom writhes harder, his body twisting and turning, and then his head snaps in my direction. He glares at me, his face full of hatred, and cold foreboding washes over me. I can *feel* the malevolence seeping out from him. Some human instinct tells me that whatever's inside him is beyond all reason or understanding. It is evil itself.

I step back and Morgan beats her wings furiously. She looks like a creature of the night about to rip out his throat. Tom bucks and fights but she holds him down. He gnashes his teeth, his legs thrashing under the covers, and I silently plead for him to stop. But he doesn't. He struggles and kicks and eventually manages to throw her.

She tumbles to the floor and in the next second he sits up and makes for me. Morgan leaps on top of him, landing with her bare feet on his hips and her hands on his shoulders. She screeches and the sound is like nothing I've heard before: a wail of rage so terrifying it could rip the flesh from a rodent's back and slice the scales from a fish.

She shoves him onto the bed. '*Exorcizamus te, omnis immundus spiritus!*'

His body arches and his lips open, letting out a stream of darkness that swirls and curls around on itself like a snake. A foul smell rolls through the room – rotting flesh mixed with the acrid stench of sulphur, and I cover my mouth and fight the urge to gag. Morgan pushes up his shirt and something is wriggling beneath his bare chest and stomach. Faces appear under his skin, pushing at his flesh like they're trying to get out.

She reaches into the swirl of darkness coming from his mouth and pulls out a shadowy, severed head. Holding it with one hand, she claws at it with the other, slashing it to pieces. She grabs another and another, clawing and biting. Her head jerks from side to side as she pounces on each monstrous form. She snarls and snaps, claws and rips, tearing the darkness to shreds and sending it scattering into the corners of the room like cockroaches.

Eventually the stream of darkness slows and Tom slumps back onto the mattress, his chest heaving. Morgan licks her lips and beats her powerful wings, her long hair flying wildly as she twists her head from side to side, ready to swoop at the smallest movement.

I call out, my voice weak. 'Is it over?'

She rocks back on her haunches, her tattered black dress rising up to expose sinewy white thighs. If she hears me, she doesn't turn around. She snarls like a creature possessed, her hands held before her, fingers curled into claws, talon-like nails ready to strike.

'Morgan?'

Her head snaps towards me and I shrink beneath her piercing black gaze.

And then her wings drop limply, her eyes fading to white once more. She half-collapses onto Tom, then awkwardly rolls off his body and climbs down from the bed, a shrivelled husk of a woman.

'I must conserve my strength,' she gasps. She stumbles towards the window and I rush to her side. She holds my arm for support and speaks through ragged breaths. 'In the morning, you must train with your sisters. You are safe with them in the daytime, but they cannot protect you at night.' She glances behind her. 'If he wakes, get him to eat something.'

'And if the demons take physical form?'

She sucks in a shaky breath. 'I'm sorry. I've done all I can. Try not to watch for the shadows; look to each other for the light.'

I push up the sash window and she grabs hold of the frame. Her thin hands are gnarled and it takes a couple of attempts to haul herself up. She doesn't so much launch into the sky as fall head first. I look down and my heart plummets as the seconds pass. One, two . . . I fear she might not return when a cormorant rises up, its body buffeted by the wind.

I shut the window and a stab of raw emotion pierces my heart. It's her, the witch within, telling me how much she loves her sister, how much she loves all of them. Moronoe's grief is so strong I can taste her bitterness. Swallowing hard, I stare at my hands and force them to stop shaking. Controlling my own feelings is hard enough without another person's threatening to overwhelm me, and it takes all my strength to push down her pain.

I need to make sure Tom is OK, but my feet don't want to budge. The demons that were inside him are now in the room – turning around means facing what's in the shadows. My breath comes shallow and fast, turning the air white. Twisting my head, I risk a quick glance. Everything looks how it did before, and yet it *feels* different. The hairs on my arm lift as I realise why. The room isn't just unnaturally cold, it's buzzing with awareness.

Tom coughs feebly. I walk over and the back of my neck prickles as if dozens of eyes are watching me. He's sleeping fitfully, his face shadowed with dark circles. I drop onto the bed next to him, suddenly exhausted, and the windowpane shakes as if someone is slapping their palm against it. An icy breeze sweeps over me, brushing my hair, and I spin around. Something darts in the corner of my eye: a shadow crossing between the wardrobe and the chest of drawers. I hold still, my muscles stiffening. I only caught a glimpse, but I'm sure I saw it rear up from the skirting board and flash across the wall.

Tom moans in his sleep.

Dragging my gaze from the wardrobe, I take the sleeping bag from my bed and put it over him. I rub his arm under the covers and whisper, 'I don't know if you can hear me, but you're not alone. I'm here with you.'

A sudden howl of wind sets the windowpane trembling and then a floorboard creaks on the landing and a faint tapping sounds deep inside the house. Old places are like that: the wood resettles and the pipes contract. It doesn't mean anything is there.

Stop it.

I think about the gloomy stairway and kitchen, my mind roaming through the rooms of the house, imagining them slowly getting darker. And then I picture the island's empty holiday cottages and the closed-up schoolroom and the crumbling abbey and its lopsided gravestones. The families that live here have all gone now, and so have their farm animals. Nothing human is left.

Something crumples inside me. 'Please, Tom. You have to wake up.'

He doesn't stir or make a sound. I miss him so much. I miss his ludicrous laugh and the way he flicks his hair, and how he rests his arm on my head and calls me Shorty. I miss him so much it's an actual physical pain in my chest.

The lighthouse comes on, bathing the room crimson. I need to light the oil lamps before it gets any darker. And I need to eat to keep my strength up, even if I don't feel hungry. Tom too – I should fetch him something in case he wakes. I start to light the lamps when I hear a whisper behind me.

21

I turn around and Tom's eyes are closed. Perhaps he spoke in his sleep. I walk over and perch on the bed opposite him.

'Tom?'

His eyelids flicker open and he stares at me blankly, his eyes pink-rimmed and wet. What if he doesn't know who I am? What if he's *changed* in some way? I get to my feet, unsure what to do. 'Can I get you anything? Are you hungry, thirsty?'

'Am I awake?' he croaks.

'Yes. We're on the island, in my mum's house.'

He reaches a hand to his chest and groans when he feels his ripped sweatshirt. 'I'm awake,' he mutters. 'I'm awake.' He says it over and over, his head turning from side to side as if he's having a bad dream. Anxiety sweeps over me and I clutch his arm.

'Tom?'

He frowns at me, a faint glimmer of recognition in his eyes. 'You're . . .'

I lean close, willing him to say my name. 'Yes?'

'Shorty,' he says.

A tiny laugh of relief escapes me. 'Yes, that's right.'

'No, you're hurting my arm.'

'Oh, sorry.'

I pull away and he whispers. 'You know I . . .' He coughs convulsively, unable to finish the sentence.

'Bruise like a peach?'

He smiles and then winces. 'Water. I need water.'

'I'll get you some. I'll be back in a minute, OK?'

He lifts his head, his eyes swimming with anxiety as he peers around the room. The red glow from the lighthouse is broken by shards of darkness, the flickering oil lamps making the shadows leap and lick at the walls. The wind moans a low warning outside and he stares at the window as if fearful that something unearthly will climb through it.

'I'll be as quick as I can.'

He gives a feeble nod and I stand and gaze at him a moment longer. It's so good to have him back, I don't want to let him out of my sight.

Taking one of the lamps, I head downstairs. I've been dreading going into the house knowing my mum's not here, but the darkness doesn't seem quite so bad now that Tom is awake. In the kitchen, I pour two glasses of water then search through the cupboards. Amongst the canned potatoes and peas are some tins of soup.

I smile, remembering Tom eating tomato soup in the staffroom once. He kept dipping his bread in the bowl and making slurping noises. When I glared at him, he grinned and only did it more. I open two tins and pour their contents into a pan, wishing we were there now. He could annoy me every minute of the day and I wouldn't care, just as long as he was OK.

It takes a while to get the stove to work and I have to strike several matches, but eventually the gas catches with a whoosh. While the soup is heating, I find myself glancing over my shoulder. Perhaps it's the pool of darkness under the table and by the dresser, but the kitchen seems different: bigger and colder, and yet not as empty as it should. Being here without my mum feels wrong, and my heart clenches to think I may never see her again.

The walk back upstairs tests my waitressing skills – carrying the tray and the oil lamp together is no easy task – and by the time I get to the room, half our dinner has washed over the side. I step through the doorway and force a smile. I can't imagine how Tom is feeling, but I have to act normal. I have to stay positive for his sake.

'Good news. I found some soup.'

He lies with his back to me, not moving.

I set the steaming tray on the bedside table then wipe my hands on my skirt. Still no sign of life. Perhaps he's fallen back to sleep.

'Excuse me, sir, but I believe you ordered some water?'

I shake his shoulder and he twists his head and stares at me. It's like before when . . . No, whatever was inside him has gone. I startled him, that's all. Ignoring the chill spreading in my stomach, I pick up a glass and make my voice light.

'Come on, you can't drink lying down.'

He struggles to sit up and I hover over him, relieved when he finally manages it. While he gulps down the water, I reposition the pillows behind him and then take his empty glass. He leans back and a fit of coughing wracks his body. Just when

I think it will never end, his shoulders stop shaking and he wipes his mouth.

Dialling up my smile, I reach for the food. 'Right, if you're quite done . . .'

But he isn't. I sit on the edge of the bed and rub his arm while he coughs and coughs. His lips are dry and flaky and there are dark circles under his eyes, his face at peak paleness. I don't think I've ever seen anyone look so ill.

He catches me looking and huffs. 'Do I look as bad as I feel?'

'Depends. Do you feel like crap?'

'Worse.'

In truth, he looks like he's been possessed by demons and gone three rounds of exorcism with a witch. But now probably isn't the time to share.

I glance at the tray, noticing the steam has gone from the soup. The room is icy cold, yet I haven't seen Tom shiver once. Perhaps he's so cold that he can't feel it any more, I think that can happen with hypothermia. Or maybe it's a side effect of demonic possession and it will wear off with time. If I had a phone signal I could look it up, though I doubt it will be on WebMD.

I place one of my blankets around him and he fingers his throat.

'What happened to me? Those things, are they still . . .' He stops speaking and stares at something over my shoulder. My pulse races as I turn my head, but apart from the flickering lamplight and the rain splattering against the window, nothing moves or makes a sound. Maybe he overheard Morgan saying that she could drive the demons out of him, but they would remain in the house. I could ask him, but of all the conversations I *don't* want to have, it's right at the top of my list.

Picking up a bowl with one hand, I reach for a spoon but it slips from my grasp, splashing me with lukewarm soup.

'Are you going to eat that or wear it?' he asks.

I smile. '*You'll* be wearing it if you're not careful.'

Something darts across the corner of my eye: a shadow that has no business moving by itself. Tom stares at the door, then back to me, and I know he saw it too.

'What kind is it?' he asks, his voice shaky.

I unglue my gaze from the door, realising he means the soup. 'Tomato. Is that OK? I thought you liked it.'

'Are you sure it's not leak?'

A beat passes and then I get the joke. 'Funny.' I glance behind me, but nothing moves. At the same time, the darkness looks different. The pool of grey by the wardrobe appears denser, as if the shadows have gathered together. I blink, and it looks normal again.

'Good job it's not alphabet soup. Spill that and it could spell disaster.'

I smile, aware of what he's trying to do. He's trying to keep our attention on each other, hoping that if we don't see what's happening in the room then it can't hurt us.

I pick up his spoon but he reaches out and stops me.

'I can take it from here, thanks.'

His soft brown eyes look as anxious and trapped as I feel. A moment of pained understanding passes between us, and I look away and tut in mock anger.

'Just eat it, would you.'

He peers into his bowl. 'What's left of it – the tide's gone out in mine.'

As he eats, I notice his hand is trembling. He sees me looking and drops the spoon on the tray, then picks up the bowl and drinks from it. I think about reprimanding him for his table manners, but right now he could lick the soup off his fingers for all I care.

We finish eating and the silence is unbearable. If we're talking, we can at least pretend everything's normal. I ache to turn and look behind me, but that would mean admitting I know something's there.

'How long have I been asleep?'

'Are you OK after –'

We talk over one another and then stop.

'You've been in bed for a day,' I tell him.

He raises his eyebrows as if he was expecting a different answer. Keeping an eye on a dark corner of the room, he says, 'I'm OK; at least I think I am. Everything feels a bit unreal, like I'm not actually here.' I look at him blankly and he rubs his head. 'I was in the lighthouse and the shadows pulled me down and then I was somewhere else. I knew I wasn't dreaming, but at the same time I knew it couldn't be real. Sorry, you have no idea what I'm talking about, of course you don't.'

My mouth twists at the irony. 'Go on, tell me.'

'There was a man in a glass tower,' he says.

A beat of anxiety pulses in me. 'What did he look like?'

'He had a long grey beard and wore a robe. He had your mum with him.' He lowers his voice, his eyes brimming with pity. 'In a cage.'

'What?'

'I didn't know whether to tell you, but it felt so real and . . . I'm so sorry, Ivy.'

This can't be happening.

'Are you OK?' asks Tom.

I poke around inside my head for a normal-person response. Heartbroken? Angry? Powerless? A heavy numbness sits in my chest where my heart should be. I push the heels of my hands into my eyes and try to breathe slowly. 'Was she OK? Did he hurt her?'

Tom's expression darkens, telling me everything I don't want to know. 'She was crying and looked in a bad way, but I didn't see him actually touch her. He kept muttering something; it wasn't any language I've heard before. It was like he was doing a spell.'

My blood pounds in my ears, drowning out the roar of the waves outside.

'Did she say anything to you? Did you talk to her?'

'No. It was strange. It felt so real, but I knew I wasn't actually there. I was here in bed with these *things* inside me.' He coughs and holds his throat. 'They were so vile, Ivy, so full of hate. I could feel them drawing on my worst thoughts and feelings, twisting my emotions. They wanted to make me like them.' He coughs again, his eyes watering. 'I can still feel them.'

'No. They've gone. They're not inside you any more.'

'The bird-woman, I thought she was going to kill me.' He snatches a quick breath and speaks between coughs. 'It *was* real, wasn't it? It wasn't just a nightmare?'

'Try not to think about it. It's over now.'

He stares at something behind me, his eyes widening as if his nightmare is not over but very much alive and crawling towards him along the skirting board.

I spin around. The shadows by the door are growing darker and lighter, expanding and deflating like they're coming to life. There's a skittering movement as something jumps across the wall, and then a patch of grey in the opposite corner begins to slowly pulsate.

'What's happening, Ivy?'

He pleads at me with his eyes and I look away. How can I tell him that the demons that were inside him are now in the room with us?

'Rest now. We can talk more in the morning.'

I adjust the sleeping bag on his bed and he grabs my arm. 'You know what's happening. I can tell you're afraid. The demons we read about in that book, is that what's inside me? Your mum said the lighthouse is a portal to another world – is that where the bird-woman came from? Are more things going to come and –'

'Please, this isn't helping.'

I know how frightened he must be, but I'm worried that if we talk about them it will make them real somehow; we have to look to each other for the light. We have to keep it together – *I* have to keep it together.

Movement flickers in the corner of my eye, near the door. A patch of shadow draws close, like someone stepping into the room. I tear my gaze from it, hoping Tom doesn't see.

'The best thing you can do is sleep.'

He laughs bitterly. 'Sleep! How am I meant to sleep with . . .'

He looks around and swallows the rest of the sentence as if he can't bring himself to say it.

'I know, but you have to try.'

Another fit of coughing takes him. 'Just tell me . . .' *Cough.* 'I deserve to know . . .' *Cough.*

Unable to speak, he leans forward and holds his chest. His shoulders shake as he brings up a string of thick, black phlegm. He wipes his mouth and stares at his hand.

'What the hell *is* that?' he asks.

It drips from his fingers onto the bed, filling the room with a foul stench. Amidst the slime are lumps of something fibrous, something that looks suspiciously like human tissue. I grab a towel and wipe it away before either of us can look too closely.

Throwing the towel to the floor, I reach behind him and yank out the pillows. He falls back with a defeated sigh and I straighten the blankets over him then jump into my own bed. I brace myself for another barrage of questions, but he turns his back to me. I don't know whether it's exhaustion, shock at what just happened, or if he just plain hates me right now, but I'm relieved. The more he demands to know the truth, the worse I feel for not telling him.

Shivering, I curl into a ball and rub my arms while the sea pounds against the rocks outside and the wind answers with a mournful lament. The lamplight flickers at the edge of my vision, but I don't look at the shadows. I can sense them, though, shifting around me, the darkness growing stronger.

After a few minutes, Tom's breathing slows and becomes heavy, tiredness seeming to get the better of him. I stare at the shape of his back under the covers, hoping that his sleep is dreamless and wishing I could have told him how I feel. A ball of emotion swells in my throat and I try to push it down, but it only gets bigger.

The room darkens. I raise my head and check the oil lamps, thinking they must have gone out, but they're burning the same as before. And then I realise – it's not the light that has dimmed. The darkness itself has grown stronger. It crowds around my bed like a mob of people, the black shapes blotting out the lamps and glow of the lighthouse. I can *feel* the darkness pressing down on me like it has an actual physical weight.

Squeezing my eyes shut, I whisper, 'I'm sorry, Tom. I should never have asked you to come to the island with me, and now we might never leave.' I release a shuddering breath. 'I should have told you everything, but I didn't want to scare you. I didn't want to see the panic in your face, knowing it might be the last time I ever saw you.'

The darkness is like a hand around my throat.

I have to get the words out; I have to tell him the truth before it's too late. My voice shakes, but I don't stop. I tell him everything that's happened since we were in the lighthouse – about the cormorants smashing through the windows, and meeting Morgan, about the witch inside me and how Merlin killed her, and how I have to train with the others so they can enter the portal. I tell him about my failed attempt at turning into a bird, and how the demons are in the house and could take physical form.

I open my eyes and the darkness has receded as if whatever was there has taken several steps back. My throat is dry, but

I carry on talking. 'You're right, I *am* afraid. Not just of what's in the shadows. I'm afraid that whatever it takes to become a witch, I won't be able to do it. I'm afraid that my mum will die in a cage and Morgan and the others won't be able to go home. And I'm afraid of losing another friend, knowing it was my fault.'

The room lightens, the darkness that was crowding around my bed no longer there. A gasp of relief escapes me and I look over at Tom, remembering how he was always trying to get me to confide in him. Maybe he was right. Talking can help.

'I told you. You should do it more often, Breeze Block.'

I sit up, shocked that he's awake.

'Tom?'

He murmurs something and turns over in bed.

'Are you awake?' I hiss. 'Tom?'

I heard his voice clear as anything; was he listening to everything I said? It's only then that it hits me: I didn't speak out loud when I said that talking can help, so how did he know to answer me?

22

The next morning I come downstairs to find Tom in the kitchen, holding a saucepan in one hand and scratching his side with the other. He's wearing the same ripped sweatshirt as before and his hair is messy and sticking up. I stand unseen in the doorway, watching as he peers in various cupboards and gyrates his hips while singing Beyoncé's 'Flawless'.

He repeats the chorus, proclaiming that he *woke up like this*, then lifts the pan and drinks, noticing me at the same time as dribbling milk down his front.

'Morning, Shorty.'

He wipes his mouth with the back of his hand and I cautiously step into the room. I don't know what I was expecting him to be like this morning – my life has detoured so far from normal that I don't know what normal is any more – but it wasn't this.

'Do you want the good news or the bad?' he asks.

I pull a face and he continues.

'The good news is that we have everything we need to make pancakes.'

I risk a noncommittal, 'OK.'

'The bad news is that I have no idea how to make pancakes.'

'Toast is fine.'

'Cool.'

I pull out a chair and he hands me a plate stacked with toast, which he appears to have been scoffing in between raiding the cupboards. 'Wait, I'm not done with that bit.' He snatches back the top slice and shoves it in his mouth. After a few quick chews, he swallows then takes another swig from the pan.

'You know there are mugs?' I ask.

'Saves on washing-up.' He shrugs. 'Want some? I can put yours in a mug if you like.'

'Thanks.'

He takes a mug from the counter and dips it into the saucepan, then bangs it on the table, sloshing milk over the side. I smile, resisting the urge to comment on the mess he's made, and he throws himself into the seat opposite and eyes my breakfast.

'Help yourself,' I offer.

'No, it's OK. You have it.'

I can tell from how he rubs his thighs that he's still hungry. When he doesn't take any, I nudge the plate towards him. He grabs a slice and waves it in my direction. 'So, any exciting plans for today?'

I sip my drink and blink at him.

'No? I thought you were going witch training with your fish-loving sisters.'

'What?'

'You know, your sisters from a different mister.'

My face flushes and I lower my mug, feeling stupid. So he

did hear everything I said last night. 'You don't believe me?'

He flicks his fringe. 'The crazy thing is that I do.' He huffs and then mutters, 'God knows, I wish I didn't.'

I frown, unsure how to take that, how to take him. He's acting so weird. Is he angry I didn't tell him everything when he asked last night? Does he blame me for making him come to the island? Watching his reaction, I ask, 'So how are you feeling this morning?'

'Actually not that bad, considering. I've had worse hangovers – tequila is evil, I tell you – and I woke up to find I was still alive, which is always a bonus. And no, I don't blame you.'

'What?'

'I said tequila is evil.'

'No, the other bit. What made you say you don't blame me?'

He shrugs. 'I don't know. You seemed worried about it last night, something about it being your fault I was here.'

'Oh, right.'

For a moment it seemed like he'd heard what I'd just been thinking, but I must be mistaken. Still, something doesn't feel right. I take a bite of toast and try to sound casual.

'Do you remember what you said to me before you fell asleep last night?'

'Sleep tight, hope the demons don't bite?'

'Are you OK, Tom? Only you're acting a bit . . .'

He drops the saucepan and it clangs on the table. 'I don't know, Ivy.' He sighs and rubs his head. 'All of this is so surreal. Actually, I feel like I've gone beyond that. I've left surreal and have entered the hysteria stage.'

'Stage of what?'

'Insanity, I suppose. I tell myself to get on with things like I always do at a new place – forage in the fridge for breakfast while everyone's still sleeping and pretend to be house-trained so they'll let me stay another night – and then it hits me and I remember I've entered the Twilight Zone. The only thing weirder than what's happening is how calm you're being.'

'Calm? I don't know about that.'

I think about how terrified I was the first time I met Morgan and how the last couple of days have been like a dream. At the same time, there's something so achingly familiar about her and the others that spending time with them has felt like coming home.

'Hmm, you seem to be coping pretty well to me.'

He makes it sound like an accusation. I finish my food and he crosses his arms and presses his lips together.

You should have told me, Ivy. You should have told me when I asked you what was happening last night.

I lean across the table, my pulse racing. He didn't open his mouth, and yet I heard him clearly.

He takes the last slice of toast. 'Anyway, I'm glad you told me. I'd rather know what's happening than be left in the dark. I have a million and one questions. The first one being, how the hell are we going to . . .'

He drops his toast, his mouth falling open. I turn in my seat to see Morgan in the doorway. She enters the room and beats her immense wings, bringing the briny smell of the sea with her. She takes her time, walking slowly, and my heart fills with pride. Her dress might be tattered and torn, her hair dirty and full of bits of the sea, but to me she is flawless.

She cackles and Tom jumps up from his seat. I stand and go to him, remembering what he's been through and how frightened he must be at seeing her again.

'I told you about Morgan last night, about how she helped you.' I rub his arm and he nods slowly, never taking his eyes from her.

Morgan looks him up and down, though mainly up. 'I am pleased to see you on your feet.' Tom drops back into the chair and mumbles an incoherent reply, and she turns her attention to me. 'Your sisters are waiting for you under the cliffs.'

Tom gives me a pleading look.

'You'll be fine with Morgan,' I assure him.

His expression says otherwise.

Standing behind his chair, I squeeze his shoulder and whisper, 'She won't hurt you, I promise.' I feel it deep in my bones. Not because Morgan is an angel of virtue – part of me knows she's capable of acting out of self-interest and she can make bad decisions as well as good. I know it because she loves me and would never hurt anyone I care about.

Tom gives a tiny shake of his head and Morgan steps closer. 'You have no cause to fear me,' she tells him.

She throws me a knowing grin and time folds in on itself, revealing a thousand other smiles in her cloudy-white gaze, a thousand moments of laughter and love, a world of sisterhood. Excitement fizzes in my belly; the witch inside me has so much to tell her, she's missed her so much. I know how she feels. There's a lot I have to talk about too – like

216

how come I was able to hear Tom speaking when he didn't move his lips.

Not wanting to mention it in front of him (or even think about it too loudly), I turn the conversation to the most important thing on my mind. 'Tom saw something while he was asleep, didn't you?'

He cuts me a look, unhappy at being put in the spotlight, and then seems to catch himself and nods. 'Yeah, I saw Ivy's mum.'

Morgan narrows her eyes, her expression darkening. 'What did you see exactly?'

'There was a man wearing a long robe, standing in a glass tower. He was speaking in a weird language and Ivy's mum was with him, locked in a cage. It felt real and yet I knew I wasn't actually there. How was I able to see it?'

She arches her eyebrows. 'My guess is that your mind became linked to the demons under Merlin's control.' Tom looks horrified and she adds, 'If you haven't seen anything since, hopefully it won't happen again – though I would like to offer you some healing.'

He coughs. 'Um, that's very nice of you, but I don't know if . . .'

She beats her wings and he gulps. 'OK, thank you.'

I touch Morgan's arm, almost too afraid to ask. 'What does Merlin want with my mum? Will he hurt her?'

She speaks quietly, choosing her words carefully. 'Merlin knows that once you step into your power, we will be strong enough to enter the portal. He will be devising a counter-attack.' I frown and she explains. 'If Merlin has kept your mother alive, then it is for a reason. He perhaps wishes to make a bargain with you. If she has a use, then her life has value to him. We can only hope that we reach her quickly.'

She glances at the door and I nod to show I understand. The sooner I become a witch, the sooner we can rescue my mum.

23

I find them below the shallow cliffs, lounging around a rock pool. Several dangle their feet in the water, splashing noisily. One sits behind her sister, picking bits of the sea out of her hair and eating them, while another stands and tosses pebbles into the pool. With their long wild tresses flowing in the wind, they have a look of mermaids about them.

I'm halfway across the beach when they see me and rush over. Damp sandy hands stroke my cheeks as salty wet lips cover my forehead in kisses. My ears echo with their cackles and I find myself smiling, wrapped up in their joy. As they circle around me I search the group for Glitonea, and my heart sinks when I realise she's not there.

A head breaks the surface of the pool and my spirits lift at the sight of her. Grinning, she takes a gulp of water then lies on her back and spurts it over herself in a great fountain. The others laugh as she hauls herself out and shakes her wings, splattering water everywhere. Her hair is adorned with curls of seaweed, her broad shoulders cloaked in frothy sea scum, and her arms plastered with grit. Tiny white spider crabs skitter across her goose-pimpled flesh as if making a home in her cleavage. She steps towards me, carrying a waft of fish with her.

She throws her arms around me, pressing her cold wet flesh against my body, and memories flood my mind. *My sister, how I've missed you!* Moronoe's thoughts sound clear in my head and I know that whenever she was upset, she would seek her older sister out. There was no cut knee or unkind word that one of her hugs couldn't soothe.

Glitonea pulls away and wipes her eyes, and the others crowd around and put their arms about her shoulders, their expressions mirroring the tender sadness of her own. She shoos them away as if to say it's merely the wind stinging her eyes, and they hug her tighter.

Taking my hand, she turns and addresses the group. 'Today we teach how . . .' Before she can finish the sentence, the women push forward, honking and grunting as if annoyed that she's taking charge again. The short angry one lets out a cackle so fierce they all stop and look at her. But whatever she says doesn't seem to persuade them to her way of thinking as they go back to squabbling. Glitonea rolls her eyes at me and I have a feeling this often happens when Morgan isn't around to lead.

Once they've finished arguing, the women step forward and introduce themselves: Mazoe, Gliten, Tyronoe, Thiten, Gliton and Thiton. Some squeeze my hands, some hug me, and the short one named Thiten thumps me hard on the arm. Mazoe can't stop laughing and I suspect she always honked with glee, even before spending hundreds of years in bird form. A couple make only guttural sounds, but most say a few words I recognise. The more they talk the easier it becomes for them, and before long they're speaking in full sentences – telling me how much they've missed me and how much they love me.

Taking hold of one another's hands, they circle around me, their bare feet sinking and twisting in the sand. Their steps are perfectly synchronised, limbs and heads moving at the same time, their voices singing as one. 'Moronoe. Moronoe. Moronoe.' They say it over and over and I feel a tug behind my breastbone. I turn on the spot, staring at their faces as they dance faster. 'Moronoe. Moronoe.' They throw the word to one another across the circle until it becomes a chant. The world whirls around me and I step sideways and hold my head.

I know they miss their sister, but each time they say her name I feel myself shrinking inside. 'I'm Ivy,' I say. They don't hear me and I have the oddest feeling that I'm fading away. I don't want to be erased. I don't want to be forgotten. I need them to know who I am now. 'Ivy, my name is Ivy!' I shout.

I turn around, trying to latch on to something fixed, something solid that I can hold on to, but there's only a blur of pale faces, feathered wings and streaming hair. Closing my eyes, I repeat my name inside my head, a drumbeat fading to a whisper. I feel her rear up inside me – Moronoe. She wants me to say her name, to scream it to the sea and sky. I fall to the sand, my head spinning, and the dance stops abruptly. Concerned faces peer down at me, blocking out the dark clouds above, and then the women look at one another, their alarm turning to disappointment.

Glitonea steps forward and I lower my gaze, feeling that I've let her down. She warned me in the cave that I have to wake the witch inside me for this to work. If I'm going to save my mum, I have to do whatever they ask of me.

Grabbing me under the arm, she hauls me to my feet. 'Come.'

The women make their way to the shoreline, their expressions as sombre as the sky, and I hang my head and follow them. Glitonea points at me and calls out, 'Thiten, Mazoe, Gliten.' The short angry one and two others stand next to me, while the remaining women walk towards Glitonea. Running along the beach, they spread out and form a circle. They look alert and excited, their bodies tense, as if they're about to charge at one another.

As if prompted by an unheard cue, each woman extends her right arm towards the centre of the circle and turns her palm upwards. Hovering above each is a tiny golden flame. The women hold their free hands over the flickering lights, circling their palms until the flames expand into glowing spheres the size of bowling balls.

An angry honk sounds and I turn to see Thiten glaring at me. She nods towards my right arm and I turn over my hand, startled to see a tiny flame. Copying the other women, I hold my palm over the flickering light and a golden ball of energy pulsates between my hands. It pushes outwards, expanding and contracting, warming my fingers.

Magic rushes through me and my palms itch with possibility. I turn my face upwards and the savage wind matches the ravenous hunger I feel. I want this. I want this feeling that I can do anything. I want this power. As if hearing me, the ball of energy burns brighter. A laugh of wonder escapes me and I'm sure I see Thiten smile before she remembers to scowl.

A woman opposite me, Gliten, I think, lets out a fearsome cackle and extends her arms, sending a stream of energy shooting across the circle. It makes a drawn-out screeching sound, like one of those fireworks that spins around and around but doesn't do much else, and then hits Mazoe, who's standing next to me. She stumbles to the side and hurls one back. As soon as the ball leaves her hands, another one appears to replace it. This one is tinged dark blue, strands of colour swirling amongst the gold. More balls are thrown across the circle and then one hits me, landing in my stomach like a fist.

I double over, the air knocked from my body, and the women laugh good-naturedly and encourage me to return fire. I extend my arms but my ball doesn't move. It hovers stubbornly in the air. I narrow my eyes and focus, willing it to fly across the circle. More cries of amusement sound around me. Even Thiten laughs, until a missile takes her off guard when it smacks into the side of her head. She throws out her arms and a ball of black energy thunders across the circle. Her adversary manages to duck just in time. The ball lands in the sea with a steaming sizzle, and Thiten throws another. This one doesn't miss.

It seems the signal for open combat has been given. Thiten and the two other women next to me sprint away along the beach. I look up and realise why. Glitonea and her team are rising into the air, their wings beating furiously. A ball of energy screams past my ear and thumps down, showering me with sand.

I turn and run as energy arcs across the sky like fireworks, lighting up the stormy clouds and disturbing a colony of gulls, who squawk in protest. The balls are different colours – red, blue, green, black – but they all land with the same force. I dive and roll, cursing as another missile nearly hits me. Instinctively, I hold up my palm and a dome of black light appears, shielding me from further attack. Two women hover in the sky above, their wings beating fast. They point down and say something to one another, and I get the sense they're impressed by my ability to dodge if nothing else.

I catch up with my team and realise they're planning to use the boulders beneath the cliffs as shelter. Thiten rises into the sky and gestures that she will provide cover while I scramble over the rocks. Before me is a narrow crevice, just wide enough for me to squeeze into. I push my way inside. Cackles fill the air as the women shout instructions to one another, the ground beneath me shaking.

Thiten lands on top of the boulder and peers down, her white eyes blazing.

'To win, the other side must knock us out,' she shouts. I look at her, confused, and she explains. 'The winning side are the ones left standing.'

My martial arts class could be tough, but this sounds like a whole new level of brutal. Maybe I haven't understood right. 'So . . . ?'

'So we need you!' She kneels down and grabs my hand, lifting me up. I find my footing on the boulder and she spins me around. 'Fight!' she yells. The second heart inside me beats wild and strong and I let it. Opening my palm, I watch the flame expand into a ball and then extend my arms. I will it to move forward, but it doesn't budge.

Thiten barges into me, nearly knocking me off the rock.

'Watch it!' I yell.

She frowns at me as if I'm deliberately being difficult. 'Throw it!'

I grit my teeth, knowing exactly *where* I'd like to throw it.

I stare at the energy throbbing between my hands and command it to move. It drops down, hovering just above the rock, and I fall to my knees. Why won't it work?

Thiten kicks me hard and I fall to my side, gasping in pain.

'You let Merlin kill you – are you going to let him kill your mother too?'

Rage claws at my throat and I clamber to my feet and let out a scream, throwing my arms and sending a black ball of energy shooting forward. It knocks Thiten clean off the rock. I bite my lip and stare at the sky, commanding myself not to cry, but it's too late. Tears are streaming down my face. Gulping back a sob, I wipe my eyes. I'm not someone who loses control. I *never* lose control.

The other women land on the boulder and crowd around me, the game at an end. Glitonea places a heavy hand on my shoulder and I shake my head, unable to face her.

'Thiten is fine,' she whispers. 'She is a hard one.'

Thiten flies up then lands on the boulder and wipes a trickle of blood from the corner of her mouth. She looks angry as hell, but she steps back and lowers her gaze. I've been in my fair share of fights – it doesn't take much for things to kick off in a care home – and I can tell she knows she had it coming.

I hold my aching side and my face flushes with shame. Not because I hurt Thiten. I'm ashamed because I cried and made a fool of myself. I'm ashamed of being weak.

Glitonea wraps a comforting arm around me.

'Do it again,' she whispers. 'Send the energy.'

I open my palm and a sphere of black light appears. I throw my arms out, making sure not to aim at anyone, but it doesn't move. Closing my eyes, I take a deep breath and try again. Nothing. Heat creeps into my cheeks. I can sense them staring at me, wondering why I can't do it. I did it before, so why not now? I think about Thiten, remembering how upset I was, and try to feel that way again, but it doesn't work. It's not that I don't feel angry. There's a seething pool of rage inside me – but I can't let it out.

Keeping my eyes shut, I whisper silently in my head.

Moronoe, please help me.

I wait, hoping to feel something stir inside me.

Nothing.

I open my eyes and the women look as stricken as I feel.

'I'm sorry we lost,' I say quietly.

They turn away from me, each one facing a different direction, some sniffing back tears and others clutching their chests. One bites her lip and then they all do it; another clenches her fists and her neighbour does the same. It's almost like they're acting, pretending to restrain their feelings, but I know they're not. I can tell their suffering is genuine from their expressions. It's as if they're passing a single emotion between them.

It starts to rain and I wipe my eyes, startled to see the women are changing. Suddenly they are haggard creatures:

226

spines curved and wings drooping, their skin wrinkled and their hair sparse and grey. I blink and they look normal again, their appearance flickering from one form to another.

One by one they fly away until only Thiten is left. She opens her tatty black wings, the feathers ragged, then turns to me and hisses, 'It's not a game to us. It is life or death.'

24

The rain is coming down in sheets as I dash along the path back to the lighthouse. A cackle cuts through the frigid air and a group of cormorants soar overhead, their bodies blown and buffeted by the wind. My heart lifts, longing to fly with them, and then I remember that their sister is Moronoe. She's the one they love and miss; she's the one who belongs with them – not me.

I watch as they circle the tower then head inland towards the mountain. With their huge wings outspread they make a forbidding sight, and I imagine how scared the islanders must have been to see them fly as witches. My mum only stayed here because she thought her enchantments were stopping them from coming through the lighthouse. She couldn't have known it wasn't them she had to fear, or that they're trapped here, unable to go home.

Home.

It's such a small word and yet it holds so much: memories of joy for some and pain for others. For me, the word has always had a hollow ring to it. People talk about how they long to go home, how there's no place like it, but I wouldn't know. I've never had anywhere that felt like home. Not that I'm special. I'm sure most kids in the system feel the same way and I've seen what can happen to the unlucky ones, the damage that can be done by adults who are meant to 'care'.

I stop and take shelter under the lighthouse, letting my body slump to the ground. Whenever I feel myself sliding into self-pity, I remind myself that things could have been so much worse for me. There was someone once, a person I belonged to and who belonged to me, someone who felt like home. Sitting on the step, I bang my head against the door behind me. Getting upset about Katie won't change anything, but there's still a chance I can help the witches get home and save my mum. I need to focus on what I *can* do.

I hold out my right arm and turn over my hand, thrilled to see a tiny golden flame flicker above my palm. I run my other hand over it, enjoying the warmth as the energy expands and contracts. A second heartbeat thuds in my chest and somehow I know that magic has always been there, lodged deep inside me, waiting to be found.

Taking a deep breath, I imagine the ball moving away from me. Nothing happens.

I try again, squinting through half-closed eyes as I extend my arms, but it doesn't move. I picture Thiten's face and remember how angry I felt, but it still doesn't budge.

Please, Moronoe, I don't understand why it's not working.

I wait, but nothing stirs inside me. No image or feeling comes to mind.

Please, I need your help. If I can't become a witch and reunite with your sisters, then they won't be able to go home.

229

A girl with long black hair appears in my mind. Moronoe. I wait for her to say something but she shakes her head, a tear rolling down her face. At first I presume she's mourning her sisters, but then she points at my chest and a thought surfaces loud and clear.

Only you can open it.

I will her to say more, but her image fades as quickly as it came. What does she mean, only I can open it? Does she mean the portal?

A shadow slides over the ground and I look up and see a cormorant. It flies straight at me then somersaults in mid-air, landing as a woman. Morgan looks surprised to see me here and I force a smile, worried she's going to ask me about what happened on the beach. She gestures for me to make room and I shake my head.

'I need to get back to Tom.'

'I checked on him earlier, he's fine.'

She waves at me to shoo and I shift along the step, letting her sit down. As I do, a memory that isn't mine flashes into my head: Morgan wearing a blue gown cut to accentuate her slender waist, her glossy black hair curled and fastened with a silver comb. Her bright blue eyes glitter with excitement as she makes her way around a lavish banquet table, stopping to talk with people and throwing back her head and laughing. She catches my gaze and beckons me over. She loves being the centre of attention, but she loves showing off her sisters even more. She's proud of our accomplishments rather than our looks, and though she has a taste for the finer things, the most exquisite cloth and luxurious food, she values craftsmanship and artistry above all else. She aspires not to beauty, but to the perfection of her craft – to magic. She makes me want to do better, to excel at spell work. I want to achieve great things: not to compete with her, but to be like her.

She shifts on the step next to me and my gaze travels along her bruised and dirty legs, taking in her mud-splattered dress and filthy hair. Not for the first time, the sight of her fills me with despair. I hate seeing her reduced to this.

'How was combat training?' she asks.

She narrows her eyes and I find myself sympathising with Moronoe. It can't have been easy being the youngest of nine sisters, feeling that every skill had already been mastered by someone else. I've had a taste of what it's like to fail at magic, and I can't say I like it.

'I couldn't throw the energy. I did it once, but then I couldn't get it to work again.'

'Why was that, do you think?'

I hang my head and try not to show my frustration. She says it kindly enough, but I don't have time for soul searching. I need her to tell me what to do.

'I don't know. The first time it happened, I was angry. I tried feeling that way again, but it didn't work. Why would it work and then stop?'

She looks at me blankly. 'Only you can answer that.'

There must be *something* she can tell me. 'OK: what will it take for me to become a witch? How will I know when it happens?'

She chuckles. 'You will know.' I frown and she leans over,

231

nudging my shoulder. 'There isn't a series of tests for you to complete like a knight on some epic quest, if that's what you imagine.'

I know she's trying to make me feel better, but I can't bring myself to smile. Not when my mum is locked in a cage. I don't have time for riddles, I *need* to do this.

'I couldn't turn into a bird. I haven't been able to throw energy. What if I can't –'

Her voice turns steely. 'We continue. We continue until we can no longer . . .' She stops and takes a sharp breath. 'We cannot do this for you, but we will keep trying our best to help you. *You* can only try your best.'

I nod, letting her words sink in. Have I been trying my best, though? I didn't let Moronoe help me in the cave and I refused to say her name on the beach. I find myself fiddling with the silver stud in my nose – a tiny act of defiance when I was fifteen years old. My foster family at the time insisted I only wore the clothes they chose for me. I went into town one day and got the piercing on a whim. Not to annoy them, though I knew it would, but because I wanted to feel like an individual. At that age, my identity was tied up in my clothes and how I wore my hair. Choosing how I looked *meant* something to me. I fought to hold on to it, the same way I got into fights in the care home if anyone touched my stuff – not just because it was mine, but because it was all I had.

I don't want to tell Morgan that I haven't been trying my best because I'm afraid I'll lose my sense of self, but now isn't the time to keep quiet. There's too much at stake.

'Sometimes I can sense Moronoe inside me. I can hear her

thoughts and see her memories. On the beach earlier, she wanted me to say her name but I didn't.'

Morgan nods, a faint smile curving her lips. I can't tell whether she feels sympathy for me or is pleased her sister is growing stronger. I'm afraid to know, but I have to ask.

'Is that what happens? Do I become a witch by letting her take control of me?'

Morgan's eyes widen. 'Every human has led many lives. People may carry the scars of their previous incarnations – a person who drowned may fear the water in their next life – but most don't remember their previous existence. But then you are not most humans. You are a sorceress, a magical being of immense power. It's hard for you to reconcile this, I can see that. But there are not two souls inside you. There has only ever been one.'

She watches my face as if waiting for me to respond, but I can't bring myself to nod. I *know* that Moronoe exists within me. I can hear her thoughts; I can see her memories and feel her emotions.

I get to my feet and brush the concrete dust from my legs. 'Tom must be wondering where I am.'

She nods and I glance at the cottage, remembering. 'There was something I wanted to ask you. Last night, I was thinking something and Tom answered me even though I hadn't spoken, and then this morning I heard his voice even though his lips didn't move.'

'I see.'

'Why did it happen?'

She shrugs. 'Sometimes a person can lose a part of themselves after a demonic clearing. It could be that his mind has lost some of its defences, leaving him more receptive to the thoughts and feelings of those around him. People have been known to change in all kinds of ways. Mostly the changes are harmless: subtle differences in personality that only those closest to them would notice.'

I don't say anything and Morgan asks, 'Is there anything else you've noticed about him?'

'Like what?'

She stands up, her wings opening wide and her feathers ruffling in the blustery wind. 'Tom was able to see Merlin and your mother in Avalon because his mind merged with the demons. It's possible they gained access to his thoughts in turn. If Merlin is able to influence him, it could put us all in danger.'

A chill runs through me as I remember how Tom could still feel the demons after Morgan exorcised them. He said they were drawing on his worst thoughts and feelings, trying to make him like them. I thought he was just traumatised by the experience, but what if they *are* still in him?

The rain is coming down hard, pounding against the gravel track and making the tiny stones jump into the air. Morgan glances at the darkening sky. 'A storm is coming. I must return to the others and make sure they are safe.'

I expect her to turn into a bird and fly away, but she doesn't. She shifts her weight to her other foot and wrings her hands. 'When I was in the house earlier, I sensed the demons in the shadows. I wish I could have destroyed them, but I'm not strong enough and I cannot put your sisters at risk.'

She drops her gaze and I can see how much it pains her to

tell me this. The idea of spending another night in the house fills me with dread, but I know the witches are weakening. I see it all the time, their appearance flickering as if they're finding it harder to conceal their true form: aged, decrepit, dying.

I touch her arm. 'I understand.'

She shakes her head, her expression grim. 'I'm not sure that you do. There are far more demons than I first thought and they're growing stronger – much stronger.'

25

I enter the kitchen and what I see makes me gasp. Every cupboard door and drawer stands open, packets of food and eggshells scattered across the countertop, a bag of flour on its side, its white contents spilt on the floor. My mum's jars of herbs are no longer on the dresser but lie strewn across the table, their lids removed. Everywhere I look are pots and pans and baking trays, as if they've been hurled to the ground by a dark force.

Tom leans against the oven and licks something from a wooden spoon, seemingly oblivious to the carnage around him. He pulls a disgusted face then seems to reconsider and goes back for another taste. From the way he smacks his lips and winces, it hasn't improved.

He sees me and nods towards a pile of cookbooks on the table, their cheerful covers easy to spot amongst the titles on witchcraft. 'I found some recipes and thought I'd give them a try,' he explains. '*Demon Dining for One* had a nice beef goulash, but the oven cremated it. So I made a frittata from *Fiendishly Good Cuisine.*'

'Are you OK, Tom?'

He rubs his head. 'Sorry, I may have spent too much time reading about demons.' He sniffs the spoon in his hand and holds it out to me. 'What do you reckon? I think it might need something, but I'm not sure what.'

'Putting in the bin?'

He smiles and says wryly, 'If it doesn't work out we can always get Deliveroo.'

'Well, then, we're saved.'

I consider asking him to step away from the wooden spoon, slowly and with his hands up, but then I remember what Morgan said. He might be acting oddly because this is his way of coping, or he could be changed in some way. Until I know for sure, I should probably tread carefully, which is just as well given the state of the floor.

I take off my wet coat and hang it on the back of a chair, and it immediately gets to work forming a puddle on the slate tiles.

'You're soaked,' he informs me.

I sneeze and he rushes over. 'Come and stand by the stove and warm up.'

'It's OK. I need to get some dry clothes. I'll be fine once I've had a shower.'

'No. You stay here, I'll get them.' He bundles me over to the oven then dashes upstairs and reappears a few minutes later with an armful of clothes and towels.

'Thanks.' I take them and glance at the smoke billowing behind him. 'You might want to check on . . .'

'Not my frittata as well!'

He jumps into action, grabbing a pair of oven gloves and clapping them together furiously, whether to dissipate the

237

smoke or intimidate the ancient appliance into obedience, I'm not sure. While he's remonstrating with the oven, I look through the pile of clothes and notice a black stain on one of the towels. He must have picked it up from the bedroom floor where I threw it last night. Not wanting to touch it, I drop it onto a chair and head out.

A cold draught swirls around my legs as I walk along the gloomy hallway. The door at the end is ajar, the boards we ripped off still where we left them, reminding me of our desperate dash to the lighthouse. I don't like seeing the mess of wood and nails everywhere – with the state of the kitchen, it feels as if the house is falling apart, and I decide to clear them up as soon as I get the chance.

Stepping into the bathroom, I wish I'd brought an oil lamp with me. There's only one window and it's already getting dark outside. Deciding to risk it, I use the toilet then shower as quickly as I can. Once I'm dressed, I go to the sink and wipe the condensation from the mirror. Apart from appearing tired, I look how I always do. I tell myself there's only one soul inside me, but I know she's there – Moronoe. I may not be able to see her, but I can sense her stronger than ever, curled up tight, waiting.

Trying not to think about it, I make my way back to the kitchen and am startled when the lighthouse comes on. I should be used to the ghastly red glow, but there's something jarring about the way it floods through the windows like a warning. Tom has lit some lamps and is sitting at the table with his back to the room, his nose in a book. I was hoping he'd have cleared up, but the floor is a minefield of pots and pans and the cupboard doors remain defiantly open. I don't know how he can bear to sit there with them gaping at him.

The wind howls outside, the rain pounding on the windows like it's trying to get in, and I shiver as I close the cupboards and salvage bakeware from the floor. I try not to glance behind me – if I start looking over my shoulder I won't be able to stop.

Grabbing a cloth, I set to work wiping the counter. Somehow we have to pretend that everything's normal. Eat dinner, do the dishes, go to bed. Don't look at the shadows. If we can just get through the night, then I can train with the witches again in the morning. Whatever it takes, I'll do it, even if it means letting Moronoe take control of me. I have to, or . . . I fight back tears, my fingers gripping the cloth so tight that water pools everywhere.

I can't fall apart. I won't.

I throw the smashed eggshells in the bin then pick up the bag of flour lying on its side, cursing as more spills out. The floor will just have to stay a mess. I don't know where the mop is kept and I can't see well enough to do a good job in the dim light anyway.

Tom hasn't lifted his head from his book once.

'How's dinner looking?' I ask.

He glances up and rubs the back of his neck.

'Dinner – how's it doing?'

He rushes to the oven and kneels down, opening the door a crack and coughing on a face full of smoke. As he lifts out the pan, something that looks like egg and cheese slides to the far side. 'Do you know if that's meant to happen?' he asks.

'Maybe you need to flip it over.'

'Oh, it's kind of burnt on the bottom already. I guess there's always pudding.'

My stomach drops. 'There's pudding?'

'I've made a cake. The recipe called for glacé cherries, but I couldn't find any so I improvised.'

My gaze tracks over the used mixing bowl on the counter to the half-empty packets surrounding it: flour, baking powder, sugar, and a jar of olives stuffed with red pimentos.

'Can't wait.'

While Tom returns the dinner to the oven, I pull out a chair. Even though I haven't seen anything in the shadows, I prefer to keep my back to the dresser so that I can watch the room. I shove the books to one side to make space for some plates, and Tom appears with a cake. Instead of cutting it into slices, he's buried a carving knife in its middle, the handle sticking up to the ceiling.

He lowers it before me and it lands on the table with a hefty thud. I survey its crusted black top and he steps back and flicks his fringe from his eyes, his face full of hopeful apprehension. I wish I could say he reminds me of a *MasterChef* contestant, but it's more like he's brought down a wild beast and is presenting it to the village chief as a sacrificial offering. He coughs and I realise I'm meant to say something.

'Wow.'

He grins, seemingly pleased by my response, and I'm relieved I'm not expected to say anything else. While he turns back to the oven, I lean to one side and cautiously peer at the monstrosity, not wanting to think about how many ingredients he's used to make it. There might be enough food and gas to run the stove and heat the water for now, but my mum probably only has enough supplies for one person to last the winter. Being stuck here for months isn't something I want to contemplate, but I don't know how long it will be until the boatman returns, or what will happen when he does. We should start rationing.

Tom sits opposite me and asks, 'I wonder how they're getting on without us.'

I frown, distracted from mentally stock-taking the cupboards. 'Who?'

'It's getting dark,' he explains. 'I was thinking we'd probably be leaving work about now. I wonder how they're coping without us.'

I couldn't care less about Mr Neeson or how he's doing. Maybe we should make a list of the food we have left. We need to eat the fresh produce first and save the dried stuff and tins for last. If things get desperate, we may need to eat the cake.

Why doesn't she answer me? Can't she see I need to talk? It's my own fault; I shouldn't have spent so much time reading about demons. I need to think about something else. Something that doesn't involve my imminent death, or I'm going to lose my sh—

'Tom?'

'Yeah?'

It was just like before; I heard his voice as clear as anything, but his lips didn't move. He rubs his stubbly chin, seemingly unaware of what just happened, and I realise that he's been cooking all day to keep his mind off things. I cast around for something to say, something that will help to distract him.

'I can't see anyone missing us,' I offer. 'Mr Neeson's probably hired a new trainee already.' Someone young and pretty he can leer over, and pay less than the minimum wage.

Tom leans across the table and smiles. 'Nah, I reckon the place will fall apart without us. Uncle Mike's probably had to close down due to lack of custom.'

'I doubt it,' I scoff. 'You know what Dot and the others are like. They'll be making the most of their season tickets and visiting every day for the free heating. They smuggle in packed lunches and everything. Do you remember the guy who used to bring in a coffee flask?'

He frowns and I add, 'He was . . . hygienically challenged.'

Tom looks at me blankly.

'He smelt like he wanted to be left alone.'

'You mean Stinky Pete?'

'Yeah, him. He got into a fight with another old-timer once. I went over to break it up and found him lying on a bench, swigging from his flask. It wasn't coffee inside, but lager. Dot's the same. She sips a bottle of "water" she keeps in her handbag, supposedly to wash down her medication. She got so tipsy once, I had to help her to the bus stop.'

Tom laughs. 'She told me it was her bunions! Saga louts, the lot of them.'

'We used to get some right characters, didn't we?'

He nods. 'You were always so patient. I don't know how you put up with them.'

'I liked talking to the customers.'

And it's true. I always made a special effort to chat to the visitors who seemed a little lost or alone. I'd share an interesting fact about butterflies or offer to let them hold a pot of nectar. I loved seeing their faces light up when a butterfly landed on them; watching them smile felt magical, like I'd been able to give them a gift. Dot was different, though. I enjoyed our chats as much as she did and we sought each other out. I hope she's managing to get about; she doesn't have much family or many friends and I know she's lonely.

I sigh sadly. 'Like I say, I can't see anyone missing us.'

'Maybe not me, but they'll notice you're not there.'

You were the best thing about the place.

I stare at him, startled to hear his voice again. I was looking at his face and I know he didn't speak.

Tom huffs. 'I won't miss Uncle Mike being on my case, that's for sure. The man was like a software update: every time I saw him I thought *not now*.'

I laugh, remembering the way Tom used to dive into the undergrowth whenever our boss was on the warpath. Mr Neeson would hurry around the walkways, his short hairy legs working overtime, never seeming to notice the giant fern trembling with laughter.

Tom stands up and goes to the oven and I find myself gazing into space. The fact we were at work only a few days ago makes being here feel even more surreal.

He dishes up the half-incinerated frittata, then turns and hands me a plate. 'I know what you mean. It's weird to think we were there just days ago.'

I take the food, my eyes wide with surprise, and watch his shoulders do a tiny wriggle as he picks up his fork. If he's aware of anything, he's hiding it well. Is it the same for him? Can he hear what I'm thinking right now?

He glances over his shoulder then back at me, his voice strained with anxiety.

'Why are you staring?'

'I'm not.'

He twists in his seat and scans the room. 'The shadows – is there something there?'

'No. Sorry, I guess I'm just looking at you because I'm amazed at how good it tastes.' I cough on a lump of hard potato and add quickly, 'You're a really good cook.'

He raises his eyebrows. 'Hey, it's me you're talking to. You don't have to pretend.'

I smile with relief and we eat in silence, both of us picking around the burnt bits.

'So how did it go with your sisters?' he asks.

I pull a face.

'That good?'

'Worse. How was your day?'

He jabs his fork at a pile of books. 'I've been doing some reading. Did you know that Merlin once tutored Morgan? Apparently it was a huge honour to be his apprentice.'

I shift in my seat, my shoulders tensing. 'You know what he did, right?'

Tom glances at a book lying face down on the table, the faded black cover embossed with silver letters: *The Life of Merlin*. The same book the witches left on my pillow. Tom's lips don't move but his voice sounds loud and clear.

Yes, but we're only hearing one side of the story. How do we know Morgan is telling us everything?

Rage courses through me and I clench my fists as Moronoe rears up inside, ready to strike. Placing my hands on the table, I straighten my fingers and tell myself it's not Tom's fault, he has no reason to trust Morgan like I do, but that doesn't stop my stomach churning with bitterness. The strength of Moronoe's emotion frightens me, but if I'm honest, some of the hate I feel is my own. Merlin sent the shadow demons to kill me; he's the reason my mother abandoned me. He's the reason I grew up without a family, without a home.

'I despise him for what he's done.'

I'd still like to hear his side of things.

I slump back in my seat as an unpleasant thought worms to the front of my mind. What if Morgan's right and Merlin *is* influencing his thoughts?

Tom raises his eyebrows. 'You OK? What's wrong?'

I press my lips together and look away.

'Ivy?'

'Nothing. Just leave it.'

'Something's upset you. Tell me what's wrong.'

I shake my head and he leans across the table. 'Please, Ivy, just tell me.'

Suddenly I'm back in the care home, fourteen years old and sharing a room with Katie. She knew I was upset and wouldn't let it go. She kept asking and asking. I cover my face with my hands, not wanting to remember.

Tom pulls my hands from my eyes and a shadow flickers to my left. There's something strange about the chair where I left the towel. The darkness around it is expanding and deflating. It's as if someone is sitting there – not a person, but the shadow of a person.

'Ivy?'

I swing my gaze back to Tom. He hasn't seen. It's right

there, in the chair next to him, and he hasn't noticed.

And then I see something else: a footprint on the floor, its outline defined in the flour, shaped like the hoof of an animal. Another one appears before my eyes, and then another.

I cover my mouth and stare at Tom, but he has his back to the room and doesn't see. He shakes my arm, pulling my hand from my face. 'Who's Katie?'

A wound opens up inside me. He must have read my thoughts; I haven't spoken her name aloud, not to anyone, not for years. My heart beats fast in my chest as panic courses through me. What if it's not like last night, what if the demons . . .

'Ivy. Who is Katie?'

I struggle to get the words out. 'Katie was my best friend at the care home. We lived at the same place for years; we were like sisters and did everything together.' I stare at the floor behind him, dreading what I might see. The footprints are still there, but no more have appeared. It's as if whatever's there has stopped in its tracks, holding still, listening.

Tom's eyes search mine. 'Go on. You did everything together and . . . ?'

The shadow on the chair next to him has gone. I lean across the table and look to make sure, but all I see is a towel on the seat, the one with the black stain from last night.

Tom follows my gaze and looks confused. 'Ivy?'

I don't want to tell him, but then I remember how the darkness receded from my bed after I admitted how I was feeling. Maybe whatever was there has gone because I started to tell him what happened. I bite my lip and decide to keep talking.

'It was a long time ago. We were only fourteen. Katie started seeing this boy, and he was always getting her to sneak out of the home to meet him.' I take a deep breath. 'We used to spend all our time together and then suddenly I hardly ever saw her. I tried not to let it show, but she knew I was upset. One night she wouldn't leave it alone. She kept asking me what was wrong and in the end I told her.'

Tom frowns. 'You told her how you were feeling?'

'I tried to explain that I missed her, but she accused me of being jealous because she had someone and I didn't. I told her I wouldn't want someone like him, and that she'd get into trouble if anyone found out about them. We argued and I gave her a choice. Either stop seeing him or we couldn't be friends. I didn't mean it; she was all I had. I loved her more than anyone or anything . . .'

Tom touches my hand. 'What happened?'

'She climbed out the window and that was the last time I saw her. She didn't come home the next day, or the next. The care home staff went to the police, but they couldn't find her. I spoke to her boyfriend but he hadn't seen her. I looked everywhere I could think of; I went into town and talked to people living on the streets. It was like she'd vanished. I still don't know what became of her. I don't even know if she's alive or not.'

Tom's eyes fill with sympathy. 'We've all done things we regret. We've all said things and not meant them. You were young; you couldn't have known what would happen.'

I sniff back a tear, my chest feeling a little less tight. 'I know, but I should have kept quiet and not said anything. Katie would have seen what he was really like, or they would have got bored of each other. I might have been lonely for a while but she would have come back to me when it ended. I shouldn't have told her how I felt.'

No, your mistake was trying to emotionally blackmail her.

My breath catches, his words like a slap to my face.

'It wasn't your fault, Ivy. You mustn't think you did anything wrong.'

'Don't.'

'What?'

'Don't say one thing when you mean another.'

He runs his hand through his hair, bewildered. 'I didn't, I . . .'

I get to my feet before he can finish speaking. It doesn't matter what he says. I know what he really thinks. I heard it for myself. I will never be able to share the pain of how I feel. I will never be rid of it. There was a time I used to wish my hurt could be taken away from me, that I would go to sleep and wake up a different person, like a caterpillar discovering it has wings. But life isn't like that. The pain is a part of me. I have to accommodate it; my body grow around it. It's mine to carry and there's no use trying to share it.

'Talk to me. Please, Ivy, I don't understand what's happening.'

I shake my head, refusing to say another word. I was stupid to trust him. I should never have told him how I feel.

A shadowy form darts across the room, leaving a trail of white footprints on the floor. I point to warn Tom, when something stirs in the chair next to him. At first it's just a swirl of grey, its outline blurry and indistinct, and then it flickers and becomes denser, as if it's drawing the darkness into itself. A bad smell wafts from it, the rotting stench of sulphur giving way to a meaty, sucked-penny odour of flesh and blood.

Tom looks at the footprints then back to me, his face pinched with fear. He still hasn't noticed what's in the chair next to him. The black mass grows darker, pulsating and throbbing as it forms into a solid shape. Its rounded head hangs forward and I can make out the shape of its lopsided shoulders. It rises up, revealing a narrow torso made of muscle and sinew. Tom sees it and leaps to his feet, his chair clattering to the tiles. The creature lifts its head and I stifle a scream. Its mouth is an open wound, its eyes a mass of pale grubs wriggling in the sockets.

26

The creature lurches away from the table then drops its head as if it's looking down at itself. It only has one foot; the other leg ends in a misshapen bloody lump. Tom backs away but neither of us runs. We stare at it, wide-eyed, and I feel time slow down. The demon steps in our direction and I bite back a cry. Its face is a mangled mess of flesh, two tiny nostrils opening and closing in a flat nose, its red slash of a mouth making a wet rasping sound.

Tom rushes to my side and pulls me behind him and the thing jerks towards us, dragging its half-formed leg behind it, the twitching raw stump slithering across the tiles and leaving bloody tracks in the flour. It raises an arm, its finger probing its eye socket, and one of the grubs boring and twisting inside it drops to the floor.

Tom looks as if he's going to be sick. I can't imagine how it must feel to know that the thing standing before us was once one of the shadows inside him. I nudge his elbow then glance over my shoulder and he answers with a stricken nod. The creature is blocking our path to the front door, so the only option is the hallway.

We take several slow steps back, edging our way out of the room, and the demon leans to one side and then another, its nostrils puckering. It sniffs in our direction and we hold still, not daring to move as it shuffles closer. A long black tongue slithers from its mouth, its wet lips slapping together as if it's trying to taste the air. The pungent stink of it makes me gag and I clamp a hand to my mouth and retch.

The demon pounces at me and everything happens at once. I turn and run for the hallway and it snatches hold of my hair, yanking me to the ground and dragging me back. Tom lunges for the table and pulls the knife from the cake, slashing the creature's side, and I tug myself free and get to my feet. The demon wails but doesn't stop. It comes at me again.

Tom swipes with the knife but misses this time. 'Run, Ivy!'

I race down the hallway, the demon right behind me. It's moving fast, too fast for me to make it up the stairs. The passageway to the lighthouse . . . I rush towards it and wait for bony fingers to grab me but instead there's a yelp. It's trodden on one of the nails on the floor. While it's distracted, I snatch up a plank of wood and whack the creature's shoulder. It staggers back and lets out a cry, blood dripping down its arm.

I open the door, then slam it behind me and draw across the bolt. A howl of rage sounds from the other side, the wood bowing as if the demon is hurling itself against the door. I hurry along the passageway and look up the narrow steps of the lighthouse. If I go to the top of the tower and the creature breaks down the door, there'll be nowhere for me to hide – and what if more shadow demons come through the portal and take physical form? Turning back, I go to the door that leads outside.

The creature is still banging and howling, trying to get in through the passageway. My only chance is to go out.

I slide open the bolt and step into the night and the wind pounces on me, pushing me back into the building. Holding my arm up against the driving rain, I head for the disused engine room next door. It was full of broken furniture when I looked through the window before, so maybe there's something I can use as a weapon. I reach the circular white building as a group of cormorants flies overhead. One of the birds lands on the flat roof before me, and then another and another. I turn and bump straight into Morgan.

'You came!'

'Thiten sensed you were in danger. She insisted we come – they all did.'

The birds flap down to the ground and land as women. Their faces are taut with anxiety, their wings hanging low and their bedraggled feathers dripping with rain. They crowd around me and I try to thank them, but I'm too overcome with gratitude to get the words out. Despite being so weak, despite knowing the danger, they came for me – my sisters. Emotion tugs at my breastbone, a love so strong and deep it takes my breath away.

I point at the house. 'We have to go back. Tom's alone with the demons.'

Glitonea strokes my hair. 'Shush now, he's safe. It's not him they want.'

The witches move around me, three standing behind and two on either side, with Morgan holding my hand in front. Wrapping their arms around my waist, they usher me towards the building and lead me inside. The red glow of the lighthouse slants across the single bed in the centre of the floor and suddenly I realise. This is the circular room from my dream, the one with all the windows. This is where I saw eight empty chrysalides with their grey husks lying open, the ninth one still closed, the woman inside trapped in an abortive metamorphosis.

My feet root themselves to the spot and a sob builds in my throat. I want to beg them to let me go – I don't want to suffocate, I don't want to die. Morgan pulls me towards the bed and the witches support my weight and carry me forward. I tell myself that I can't collapse, that whatever's about to happen I have to be strong, but my body has other ideas and I take the last few steps bent double, my legs shaking. Strong hands reach under my arms and turn me onto my side as I crawl onto the mattress, the women hushing softly and stroking my hair.

Something bangs against a window and the demon's face appears. It must have broken down the passageway door. Its fingers scrabble against the glass and I call out to the witches for help. Stepping away from me, they form a circle around the bed and hold out their right arms, a tiny golden flame hovering above each palm. The dots of light float upwards and meet above my head, sending a wave of energy radiating into the room. The golden shimmer covers the walls, the windows, the door.

I glance back at the window and the demon has gone. Whatever the witches have done, it seems to have worked. I want to ask if we'll be safe, but the words stop in my throat when I see their faces change, one moment young and the next old and decaying.

Morgan sits next to me. 'How many demons have taken physical shape?'

253

'One. I ran but it followed me through the passageway.'

She lets out a breath, her shoulders relaxing slightly.

'But I think others were starting to form. I saw footprints on the floor.'

Her eyes dart to the windows and I shuffle up the mattress and draw my knees to my chest. Morgan directs the women to watch the door then turns back to me, her face stern.

'Tell me what happened before the demon became physical.'

I look away, not wanting to remember my argument with Tom, and something darts past the window to my left. Another figure moves outside to my right, followed by another.

Bang. Bang. Bang.

They're trying to break down the door. A window smashes and I cry out as an impossibly giant hand reaches inside, its long, broken fingers grazing the floor. A skull-like face appears at a different window, a mass of tentacles hanging from its mouth.

Morgan shakes my arms, her voice urgent. 'What triggered them to form?'

Something huge strides past the building, the bottom part of a spindly leg, then there's a clattering above us. Panic rises inside me. I have to get out of here. I try to get up, but the witches rush forward and hold me down. Fighting them off, I clamber across the bed and crawl to the floor on my hands and knees. I can't stand this. I need to get away. I need to breathe.

The women follow me, Mazoe and Glitonea rubbing my shoulders as I arch my back and drag in a lungful of air. Morgan crawls towards me and takes my cheeks between her hands.

Looking into my face, she inhales deeply and then blows out a long exhale. A transparent film races across her eyeballs and I glance at the faces around me, surprised to see the others breathing in time with her, their eyes flickering in the same strange way.

'What made the demon form?' she asks again.

I hold her gaze, the tightness in my chest easing a little as my breathing slows. There must be something I'm missing, some connection. And then I remember how the shadows retreated from my bed when I told Tom how I was feeling. They became physical when I refused to tell him why I was upset.

'I argued with Tom.'

'What about?'

'I was talking to him about my best friend, about how I fell out with her and how she left me . . .' My voice wavers and I stop speaking. It's not just that I feel betrayed by Tom and upset about Katie. There's a hard knot of pain inside me, a knot pulled so tight I don't think anyone will ever be able to get their fingers inside to prise it apart. All my life, I've been on my own. I've never had a proper home, a proper childhood. The one friend I had, I lost.

I glance about me and the creatures retreat, the hand withdrawing from the window. Holding my chest, I keep speaking. 'I trusted him. I shouldn't have told him how I feel.'

Morgan touches her chest in anguished sympathy and the others do the same. I rub my temples, my head pounding with the need to cry, and the women rub the sides of their heads. At first I think they're mimicking me, but it's not that. They're sharing my emotion, feeling what I feel. They smile at me sadly and I'm overcome with a sense of how much they love me; whatever they're doing, I know they're trying to help. A tear rolls down my cheek and I wipe it roughly away. The effort of not crying is suffocating. I feel as if my face is covered with thick papery casing and I can't breathe.

Morgan takes my face in her hands again, her fingers gently stroking my cheeks.

'Everything you've been through – all the hurt and suffering, it's not who you are. You don't have to fight it; you don't have to carry it. Feelings are real, but they are not you. Emotions are made to move through us, like the wind in the trees and tide through the sea.'

I rock back on my knees, my body moving with a will of its own. For so long, I've refused to let myself grieve for the things I don't have, things that so many other people have – parents, a family, friends, a home. I've pushed down my emotions, afraid they'll overwhelm me. But I can't go on like this. If I keep it inside, it will tear me apart.

A girl with long black hair appears in my mind. Moronoe. She wipes away a tear then smiles at me and whispers, *Only you can open it*. Suddenly I understand. When Merlin tried to make her fall in love with him, she locked her emotions inside a chest. She had no choice; it was her only hope of surviving. She's not here to open it any more, but I am.

I lay my hand on my heart and whisper, 'Moronoe said only I can open it.'

Morgan looks at me quizzically. 'Moronoe is not a separate person inside you. You *are* her. You have always been her – it is not Moronoe who must wake for you to become a witch. It is *you* who must wake to the realisation of who you are and always have been.'

I nod, feeling the truth of her words deep in the core of my being.

Morgan grips my shoulder and looks into my eyes. 'Pain, hate, self-pity, jealousy, love, fear . . . whatever it is you feel, know that you are free to feel it.'

Something shifts inside me like a lid being lifted. Rage builds in my throat and I let it. Glitonea's strong hands grip mine, steadying me as I lean up on my knees. A strangled sob escapes me and I snatch a lungful of air and scream out my pain and loneliness. My arms tremble as I lean forward, sob after sob wracking my body. I cry for myself – for the child who was abandoned, who grew up feeling she wasn't wanted by anyone, feeling that she wasn't good enough to be loved. I cry for my mum, knowing how painful it must have been for her to give me up.

My belly constricts and I drop my head, my body rocking backwards and forwards. I don't know whether I need to scream, thump something, or be sick. My spine is burning, my bones shifting and rearranging themselves, pushing and protruding against my flesh. I lick my lips and taste salt. I'm sweating despite the cold, my skin slick with it. The witches push my damp hair from my forehead and I groan as my body contracts again.

I glance at the expectant faces of the women around me, the chant of their voices enveloping me like a membrane. Another wave of emotion surges through me. Love – love for my sisters who came back for me, who willingly shared my hurt, who would give their lives for me. I clench my teeth until the muscles in my temples ache and then my skin tears and I gasp as something thick and wet bursts from my shoulder blades. I turn and see black feathered wings slither from my body and open wide.

Tears of relief run down my face. I'm weak and wrung out, but I can finally breathe. A calm, bright feeling tingles through me and I smile, more clear-headed than I've ever been. The witches help me to my feet and their eyes are no longer white but brilliant blue. They look so much younger, their skin pink and flushed, their hair clean and glossy. It feels like I'm seeing them how they really are. I peer down at my bare feet and tattered black dress and they laugh to see my confused expression.

'You did that,' whispers Mazoe.

The witches step back to form a circle then hold out their right arms. I do the same and a golden flame appears above my palm. I throw the ball of energy upwards easily and it travels towards the others. This time when they meet, there's a crack of thunder and blinding white light engulfs the room, blowing back our hair and what's left of the window panes.

Magic courses through me, igniting every atom of my being, and I know I have the power to do anything – the power to bring life into existence or to destroy it. A single heart thumps loud and strong in my chest. I search for Moronoe, wanting to share the moment with her, and she steps forward in my mind and throws her arms about me. She kisses my cheek and it feels like a goodbye. I hug her and silently promise to make this life a good one for both of us. No more hiding my feelings, no more being afraid to get close to people in case I get hurt.

Morgan strides out of the building with her head held high and I follow her, my heart full of pride. Ash and rain fall from the sky, littering the ground with steaming mounds of cinder. Smoke stings my eyes as I look in every direction, hoping to see Tom.

Something moves to my right, but it's not him. A figure with a stump for a leg drags itself along the ground towards me. A familiar burning sensation sparks down my arm and into my fingers. I hold out my hand and rage surges through me, sending a ball of black energy flying at the demon and turning it to dust. My wings beat the air and resettle on my back. Disintegrating the creature has done nothing to release the anger inside me, and my fingers itch with a desire to destroy more of the hateful things.

Maybe Tom's still inside. I start towards the cottage, but Morgan pulls me back.

'Are you still able to read one another's thoughts?' she asks.

'No, it only happened while we were in the same room.'

'I'm sorry, but you can't see him. Not if there's a chance his mind is linked to the demons. If he reads your thoughts and learns of our plans, then Merlin will know them too.'

'Tom wouldn't betray us.'

She fixes me with shrewd eyes. 'He may not be aware it's happening. You've spent time with him – have you noticed any changes in him? Anything to make you concerned?'

'No,' I answer a little too quickly. I pause and then add, 'There was something. Tom was reading a book about Merlin and I heard him thinking he'd like to speak to him. He thought you might not be telling us everything and he wanted to hear his side of things.'

'I see.'

'Does it mean anything?' I ask.

'Perhaps not, but it's safer for Tom if he remains in the house. I will send someone to check on him and explain why he has to stay away.'

She glances up at the lighthouse and a shadow of unease crosses her face. 'Merlin will not simply allow us to fly into Avalon and rescue your mother. We can expect a battle. I've seen what happens to those who use demonic magic; I can't imagine what working with them for over a thousand years has done to him.'

She pats my arm as if sensing my dismay. 'Don't worry, the demons he sends will be shadows; it takes time for them to become corporeal and they cannot enter us or Tom now I've healed him. And we have the element of surprise – Merlin has no way of knowing when we'll pass through the portal. He'll expect us to wait a few days to gather our strength and train you in combat.' She smiles wryly. 'Only a fool would dare attack him right away.'

27

We fly to the top of the lighthouse and it's the most incredible feeling in the world: the roller-coaster dip of my stomach as I launch into the sky, the cold night air streaming past my face as my sisters swoop around me, the grey-crested waves of the sea raging far below. Having wings feels wondrous yet natural, as if my body was always meant to fly.

We circle the summit of the tower twice, three times, and then the witches flap down onto the metal railing that runs around the outside of the lantern room. They land one by one, legs crouched and feathers ruffling, their long black hair whipping about their faces like snakes. I find that I land easily too, the movement second nature to me.

The glass walls are still broken from when the witches crashed through as cormorants, and rain lashes onto the optic and pings off the metal walkway inside. Exposed to the elements, the red light burns with raw intensity – not there to warn sailors of the rocks and guide them to safety, but an act of violence against the darkness itself.

I peer at the smoking mounds of ash below and a smile comes to my face, knowing I helped to incinerate the demons. Magic flows hot and strong in my veins and my body trembles with the need to release it. The sheer sense of power frightens me, but what scares me most is my hunger to use it.

Holding out my hand, I release the tiniest stream of magic. A bolt of black energy thunders from my palm, exploding a pile of cinders on the ground and sending a shower of embers sparking into the sky. I wish I could say it makes me feel better, but it doesn't. The magic draws greedily on my hate and rage, the need to destroy turning more ravenous.

I wonder if this is how magic feels for the others. I glance at my sisters, wishing I'd had more time to train with them and learn about our power. Morgan crouches on the railing to my left, with Glitonea a little way to my right with her arm around Mazoe. The others congregate in groups of two or three with their heads bowed close, while Thiten sits alone with her shoulders hunched.

Morgan moves along the railing towards me, and I have a feeling she's been watching me for a while. 'You know you were once closer to Thiten than anyone,' she whispers.

I raise my eyebrows. 'But she seems so angry with me all the time.'

'Grief is a strange thing. She knows that Merlin is to blame for what happened, but I suspect she harbours some resentment towards you.'

'Why?'

'Thiten has always preferred her own company. She didn't share her secrets easily, but she did with you. She refuses to speak about it, but I think she's angry with you for trusting Merlin, angry at you for dying, even. We've tried to comfort her but she refuses to talk about her feelings. If anything, she's become more withdrawn.'

Thiten scowls out to sea, rain dripping from her hair and down her face. I feel sorry for her. I know what it's like to lose someone you care about.

Morgan adds quietly, 'What she's yet to learn is that vulnerability is not a weakness but a strength.'

I huff, unsure I agree, and Morgan eyes me curiously.

'There is more than one type of courage. There's the kind that requires you to put on armour and charge into battle, and another that asks you to stand naked. Emotional honesty is the greatest gift you can give to a person, for when you're vulnerable with another it allows them to do the same. It gives them permission to be who they truly are.' She touches the locket around my neck, her finger tracing the winged design. 'The caterpillar becomes a butterfly not through struggle, but surrender.'

I nod and look away. Being emotionally vulnerable has never come easy to me and I have a feeling we're going to need the kind of courage that requires kick-ass armour if we're going to defeat Merlin and rescue my mum.

Morgan beats her wings and launches into the sky, her voice loud. 'My dearest sisters, we have been trapped in this world for centuries, barely surviving, a shadow of our former selves – but now we are nine and it is time to go home.' She nods at me approvingly and continues. 'Merlin has a legion of demons at his command, but we have each other. We will fight until our very last breath. We will rescue Ivy's mother and we will reclaim what is rightfully ours – Avalon.'

I smile, surprised and pleased that she used my name. I know

I'll always be Moronoe to them, but it feels like a gesture of acceptance. The witches get to their feet and my nerves rise as I stand with them. They cackle loudly as they fly upwards, the sound a rallying war cry, and I clench my fists. I don't know what's about to happen, but I'm ready to fight.

The wind has dropped for once and as we enter the lantern room the only sounds are the rain and the crash of waves. The silence is like a held breath, too quiet. Spreading along the walkway, we take one another's hands and form a circle around the optic. Mazoe stands to my right, smiling as always, and on the other side is Thiten. She holds my hand firmly, but refuses to meet my gaze.

Morgan glances around the circle and warns: 'Once you follow me into the portal you must be prepared for anything.'

Thiten drops my hand and steps forward. 'No, I will go first. If Merlin's set a trap on the other side then the others will need you to lead them.'

The women shake their heads, each insisting they will take her place, but Thiten is adamant. A memory flashes into my mind – Thiten standing in front of me and shouting at the others. I had tried to do a fire spell, but it had gone badly wrong and I ended up burning the back of my wrist. The others were angry, saying I was foolish to attempt something so difficult. Thiten told them they should be helping me to improve, not telling me off for trying. It didn't matter whether I was right or wrong, she always took my side.

She strides towards the optic, and I touch her arm. 'I know I'm not the sister you remember, but I hope we can be friends one day.'

She sighs and gives me a half-smile. 'Let's see if we survive first.'

I watch her climb onto the raised metal platform, standing in the same spot as my mum before she was taken, and my pulse quickens. What if she really is walking into a trap? I don't want to lose her, or any of them.

Suddenly the red optic darkens as shadows fill the glass and spew out into the room. Within the swirling mass are shifting forms: arms and legs and monstrous faces. Instead of climbing out one by one like before, they issue in a steady stream. There must be hundreds of them. The witches take to the air and I beat my wings and rise with them.

A swirl of darkness rises up and two shadowy arms clutch at Mazoe's legs. She throws bolts of blue energy, but they wrap around her waist, dragging her down. She cries out and Glitonea grabs her and pulls her free.

Morgan releases a huge ball of green light then lands on the walkway and runs at the optic, but she's knocked sideways by a swarm of shadows. Thiten shouts and fires a bolt of black energy that makes the walls of the tower shake, but the shadowy creatures disperse and reform. She tries again, blood streaming from her nose, but she can't push them back.

Beating my wings fast, I rise higher into the sky. Everywhere I look, streams of darkness are wrapping around the witches, entangling their limbs and stopping them from reaching the portal. At least when the demons were physical we could use magic to turn them to ash. Now they simply reform, the flow of shadows never seeming to lessen.

I wait for a gap in the fire then fly down, planning to charge at the portal. My feet have barely landed when a huge snake-like shadow rears up, dozens of monstrous heads snapping and snarling within the twisting mass of darkness. I hurl a ball of black energy but the shadows keep coming, wrapping about my body and turning me around so I can't tell up from down. I cry out and the ground shakes as another bolt of magic lands to my left. Thiten gestures from the air. She's clearing a path for me like she did on the beach.

'Ivy!'

I look over my shoulder and Tom's head appears at the top of the ladder. Panting hard, he snatches a quick breath. 'Please, you have to listen! You can't go through the portal!'

An explosion sounds above and he ducks down, disappearing from sight. I run over to him and his face crumples with relief when he sees me. 'Please, Ivy, you have to be careful. Merlin's cast a spell over the portal. He's enchanted his sceptre so he can enter it – but if any of you go through you'll die.'

Another blast sounds above and I shout, 'How do you know this?'

He rubs his forehead. 'I keep getting snatches of what he's thinking. There's so much cruelty in him, it scares me.'

'OK, I'll tell the others, but you have to go back to the house. It's not safe here.'

'You think?'

My wings beat the air and he does a quick double take, his mouth dropping open.

'Please, Tom, I don't want you to get hurt.'

'If I stay, maybe I can help.'

More explosions boom above us and I'm torn between fighting alongside my sisters and making sure Tom is safe. There's another reason I want him to leave. What if Merlin can see into his mind too? What if he *wanted* Tom to come here? I gaze into Tom's eyes and see only goodness. An overwhelming sense of certainty grips me and I nod, sure I can trust him.

'OK – but stay down here, out of sight.'

He nods and retreats down the ladder. When I turn around, the witches are lined up along the walkway, throwing different-coloured streams of energy in an effort to hold back the shadows. It seems to be working, as Morgan has climbed onto the platform and has her hand on the optic.

'Morgan, wait! Tom says we shouldn't go through.'

She turns and narrows her eyes at me. 'Why, exactly?'

'Merlin has cast a spell over the portal and we'll be killed if we enter it. He's enchanted his sceptre so he can come through unharmed.'

Suddenly, the shadow demons evaporate and Merlin's face appears inside the optic. He stares into the room, his eyes blazing, and I shove my hand to my mouth. Remembering what he did to Moronoe – what he did to *me* – makes my stomach heave.

Morgan jumps down from the platform and drags me behind her. We retreat towards the others and I feel a tug inside my breastbone followed by another and another, like a series of strings snapping taut. It's the connection I feel to my sisters, only this time I'm sharing their emotion, feeling what they feel: fear, along with a desperate need to protect one another.

Merlin's dragon-headed sceptre appears through the optic,

then an arm and leg clad in a long purple robe, followed by the rest of him. He glares down at us and nausea prickles my throat. I swallow a mouthful of thick saliva and step back, my palms clammy.

Morgan drops her gaze, her shoulders slumped, and the others do the same. They look worn out, their hair dishevelled from fighting, some with blood smeared on their faces. It's more than that, though. It's like they've deliberately made themselves seem smaller, weaker.

Merlin's eyes meet mine, and I realise why my sisters can't bear to look at him. There's something rotten behind his stare, something so vile it makes my flesh crawl and my skin shrink on my bones.

Merlin leans over Morgan and I flinch as he grabs her face. 'The years have not treated you kindly, I see.' His voice drips with menace and yet he manages to sound disappointed, bored even. Squashing her cheeks, he turns her face to the other side. 'It's such a tragedy when a woman loses her looks, but then I suppose that's why beauty is so alluring. A flower's first bloom is made more delightful by the knowledge it must fade, and summer's berries taste sweetest the moment they ripen.' He releases her and sneers, 'Whatever beauty you had has withered on the vine.'

Morgan gulps, her eyes filling with tears, but says nothing. It's only when Merlin lowers his sceptre that I notice the line of livid bruises around her neck, as if her throat has been squeezed by an invisible hand.

Stepping down from the platform, he shoulders her aside and turns his gaze on me. 'And *this*, I presume, is what became of

Moronoe. I don't suppose she had many vessels to choose from, but I had hoped for something better. The girl was dim-witted and lacking in talent, but at least she had the good grace to be beautiful.'

I glance in every direction, my insides squirming with a desperate need to escape.

He leans close, his breath hot on my neck. 'Moronoe, Moronoe, Moronoe.' He speaks like he's admonishing a child and the name is a stick to punish me with.

Looking at him brings the taste of vomit to my mouth, but somehow I lift my gaze.

'My name is Ivy.'

'Ah yes, poor little Ivy, all alone in the world. No parents to love her, no home to call her own. She found her mother and then lost her.'

I clench my fists. 'Don't you dare hurt –'

He raises his sceptre and my words cleave in two and fall back down my throat. My eyes water as unseen fingers tighten around my neck and pressure builds in my head.

Morgan cries out. 'Merlin, that's enough. Leave her –'

He lifts his hand without turning around and she drops to the ground, her body convulsing. At the same time, the other witches rise up and hang above the walkway, their wings folded by their sides as if frozen into place, their faces white with fear.

Merlin sees my horrified expression and laughs. 'Return to Avalon as my queen and you may have your mother back. Or stay here with your sisters and your mother will die.'

Tears fill my eyes. How can I choose between them? I can't.

He strokes my hair and whispers, 'I told you I would have you, and I will.'

I recoil, realising that he wants Moronoe not out of love or lust, but because of some twisted need to possess her. He could simply force me to go with him, but he wants to make it harder for me. He wants the decision to be mine, to punish me for escaping him – for dying.

Rage surges through my body and into my hands and I act without thinking. I elbow him in the throat then throw out my arms and hurl a bolt of black energy that pushes him back. Taken by surprise, he lowers his sceptre and my sisters are released from his hold.

Merlin groans. I hope he's injured, but then I realise I've made a terrible mistake. He's drawing the blackness into himself, absorbing my hate and rage and using it to grow stronger.

28

He climbs onto the metal platform then swings his sceptre, and I shield my face as the optic shatters, glass flying everywhere. When I look again the room is dark and the lens has gone, replaced by a swirling red whirlpool. Intense heat radiates from it, the smell of sulphur and ash so strong it stings my nostrils and burns the back of my throat. The dark outline of a figure stands over us: not a man but a hulking beast.

Morgan clutches my arm, her chest heaving. She points a trembling finger at the platform and a shiny transparent film flicks across her eyes. 'What have you become?' she gasps. I glance at my sisters and their eyes are moving in the same way, their expression one of horrified disgust. And then something slides across my vision and my breath stops. On the platform is a creature from hell: its body covered with thick hair, its head a horned skull, its empty eye sockets blazing with red light. I blink and the image changes to a man and back again. I must be seeing Merlin as the others are – witnessing him in his true form, or what's left of it.

A demonic voice growls, 'So be it. I will take you with me and your mother and sisters shall die.'

A movement on the other side of the walkway catches my attention. Tom is climbing up the ladder, his face flushed. He steps into the room and fear reaches into my chest like a hand squeezing my heart.

'Leave her alone!' he yells.

He rushes towards me and I want to shout at him to turn and run, but I can't. Not because there's an invisible hand gripping my throat, but because I'm too shocked to speak. There's nothing he can do; he must know it's hopeless.

The creature on the platform turns its fiery gaze on Tom and he collapses to the ground and slides away from me, his body thumping into the railing.

'No!' I run to him and throw myself on my knees. A ragged howl fills my ears, the kind a wounded animal makes, and it takes me a moment to realise it came from me. I gather up his limp body and blood oozes from the back of his head, wetting my fingers.

I cry out to my sisters for help, but they don't hear me. Tom's diversion has given them a chance to regroup and they beat their wings and dive fearlessly at Merlin. He swings his sceptre, throwing some of them to the ground and sending others hurtling through the sky.

Tom stares up at me, his eyes wide with panic, and my heart breaks. I want to tell him that he'll be OK, that help is on the way, but I can't. No one is coming to save us. Only three witches remain in the sky: Morgan, Thiten and Glitonea. The rest lie crumpled on the ground, their limbs sprawled and their tattered wings heaped over them.

Cradling Tom on my lap, I hold his head with one hand and

hold up my other. A dome of golden light appears above our heads, shielding us.

He tries to speak and I lean closer, but all I hear is a rasping sound.

'Come on, out with it,' I plead. 'You know you always have the last word.'

I stroke his hair and the bubble of light around us intensifies. Glancing at my outstretched palm, I realise that my energy isn't black like it was before when I was drawing on my hate and rage. Understanding washes over me like morning sunshine. I've locked my emotions away for so long, afraid to get close to anyone in case I get hurt, afraid to admit my feelings even to myself. It's only now when it's too late that I realise.

I care about him so much. I want to be more than just his friend. I want to be with him.

Holding my locket, I think about my mum and how good it felt to be held in her arms, to know she loves me and never wanted to give me up. And then I think about my sisters who never stopped searching for me and who shared my pain as their own and helped me to birth my wings. A tidal wave of love builds inside me and I have no choice; I have to release it. Gently placing Tom's head on the floor, I turn over my hands, letting the energy flood out from me. Still the magic pulls at me, hungry for release.

I get to my feet and throw open my arms. My hair blows back from my face as a stream of golden light rushes towards the platform. It crashes into Merlin and he glares at me, his eyes burning with rage. I draw upon all the love I have in me: for my mum, for my sisters, for Tom, for Katie. Light floods from every pore of my being, sending wave after wave into the room.

The witches on the ground raise their heads and my spirits lift to see them revive. Morgan, Thiten and Glitonea help them to their feet and we spread out along the platform, standing around Merlin in a circle. Together, we each hurl a stream of magic towards him. Our energy meets in the centre, hitting his body and exploding into brilliant white light. A deafening explosion shakes the ground and I tremble as the power of nine surges through me.

Merlin raises his sceptre above his head, and his rage slams into my body like a fist. A few of my sisters cry out, but somehow we hold firm. I set my jaw, my head pounding, as blood streams from my nose. My arms ache and tremble with fatigue. Just when I think I can't go on, I feel my sisters' energy rush into me, our magic stronger for being shared. Acting as one, we each keep our right arm extended towards the platform and turn the other outwards, towards the woman next to us. Our love for one another flows between us, growing stronger as it surges around the circle – a primal, unstoppable force.

Merlin redoubles his efforts and cracks appear in the metal walkway beneath our feet. He throws back his head and snarls as if he *wants* to bring the tower crashing down. He'd rather die buried in rubble than see us win. The thought fills me with despondency and before I can stop myself, I feel my hopelessness wash around the circle like cold water, sapping my sisters of resolve.

Merlin stares down at us and barks his disdain. 'You think

that sharing your emotions makes you stronger? It makes you weak. You women have always been weak.'

Outrage stabs at my chest and I gasp as Morgan flies up, her huge black wings opening like an avenging angel. She kicks the sceptre from Merlin's hand and it clatters onto the walkway. Beating her wings furiously, she screams a death-defying war cry, louder than any sound should be.

As if a signal has been given, we hurl every last bit of energy we have at the platform. Rage burns inside me and I scream with my sisters – a single voice carrying the hurt of all wronged women, those whose bodies have been stolen from, those who've been silenced. The noise is impossibly loud – powerful enough to strip leaf from stem and flesh from bone, to shake the roots of history and fell armies of men.

Merlin reaches for his sceptre, but our magic holds him back. We grit our teeth, our eyes welling with tears, as nine streams of coloured light shoot from our palms, the energy crackling and pulsating. Desperate hope fills me and I know that my sisters feel it too.

Merlin draws himself up and lunges for his sceptre. Keeping our arms outstretched, we step forward and our magic merges and forms a shield, immobilising him. He glares at us, his eyes smouldering with hatred drawn from the depths of hell, his fingers just centimetres from the sceptre but unable to move. A strange look passes across his face, as if he's calculating what to do. Refusing to admit defeat, he gives a terrifying growl then throws himself backwards. He falls into the swirling red whirlpool and is gone.

29

While my sisters comfort one another, Morgan runs to me and crouches next to Tom's body.

I kneel beside her and she places my palm on his chest and then lays her own hand on top. She starts to chant and her hair lifts and swirls above her head, her blue eyes luminescent.

Tom's face is deathly grey, his eyes closed. I watch him, desperately hoping for some sign of life, but there's nothing. Morgan chants louder and I join her, our voices stronger as one. She presses her hand into mine and her power surges through my veins like wildfire.

My throat is dry and sore, yet still we chant. Morgan touches Tom's cheek and glances at me, her eyes full of pity, and I shake my head. We *have* to keep trying. Taking a deep breath, I call upon all the magic I have in me. I draw the energy up from the depths of my being, imagining it flowing out of my body and into his chest.

Tom draws a breath, and my shoulders sag with relief. Clutching his arm, I wipe away my tears and smile at him, too overcome to speak. His chest gently rises and falls and my heart swells with gratitude, thankful he's alive, and for the magic that brought him back.

Morgan pats my shoulder and I turn and hug her. 'You saved him, Morgan.'

'It was your energy that revived him. I simply showed it the way.' She smiles and I see a girl reflected in her black pupils – a girl whose eyes are blazing with witch-light. Me.

While Morgan goes to my sisters, I take Tom's hand. He opens his eyes and tries to speak, but only manages to cough.

'Just lie there a minute, it's OK.'

He gives a tiny nod and closes his eyes. After a few moments, he raises his head and looks around anxiously. 'What happened? Where's Merlin?'

I squeeze his hand. 'Morgan managed to take his sceptre. He tried to grab it, but our magic held him back and he fell into the portal.' I remember the strange look on his face before he threw himself into the swirling vapour, and a shiver of unease runs through me. Something tells me Merlin isn't that easy to defeat. Maybe he wasn't killed, but taken somewhere else.

Tom smiles weakly and then pushes himself up to sitting. He looks utterly exhausted, as if he could crumple at any moment. Kneeling next to him, I check the back of his head but I can't see any sign of a wound.

'Are you OK? Does it hurt?'

'I'm fine.' He tries to stand then slumps back down.

'Hey, it's me you're talking to. You don't have to pretend.'

Covering his face with his hands, he leans forward and takes a shaky breath. I rub his back and can almost feel the fear and adrenaline seeping out of him. He glances at me, his eyes heavy with sorrow. 'I'm glad you're all right. I don't think I could take it if you'd died.'

I laugh off his concern. 'I'm sure you'd be OK.'

'I don't know,' he answers quietly.

I rest my head on his shoulder. He was so brave trying to save me, even though he must have known it was hopeless. What was it Morgan said? There is more than one type of courage. I hold my locket and think about how the caterpillar becomes a butterfly not through struggle but surrender. I've spent so long fighting my emotions and trying to keep them hidden; maybe it's time I gave in to them for once.

Steeling myself, I turn and face him. 'Tom, you know how we're friends.'

His body tenses, his voice unsure. 'Yes.'

'Well, the thing is . . .' I pause, wishing I'd spent some time figuring out what I was going to say. He smiles and excitement flutters in my chest. 'Well, I was hoping that . . .'

His face drops and my hope plummets with it.

'You're not going to ask me to go through the portal with you, are you? I mean, driving you to Wales and coming to the island was one thing, but –'

'No, it's not that. You said something to me before, and I wanted to let you know that I *do* have feelings –'

'When I called you a breeze block? I wasn't suggesting you didn't have feelings, just that –'

'Please shut up, Tom.'

He scratches his head. 'OK.'

I take his hand in mine and his eyes widen. 'I hope you're

not going to proposition me when I've just had a near-death experience. Only I'd hate to think you're taking advantage of me when I'm in a vulnerable state.' He laughs and then stops when he sees my face. 'Oh.' Judging by his pained expression, he finds the conversation as excruciating as I do.

I force myself to smile. 'It's OK. I know what you're going to say.'

He rubs his stubbly jaw, his voice serious. 'Look, the truth is I've been hurt by girls before. I wore my heart on my sleeve and it turned out they didn't feel the same way. I couldn't bear to go through that again, not with you. I might come across as this tough, macho guy . . .'

I pull a face and he stops short. 'Well, anyway, my point is –'

'I understand, we're just friends,' I say.

He looks at me incredulously. 'Come on, you must know I've liked you for ages!'

My heart somersaults, hardly daring to believe it's true.

'Why do you think I kept playing practical jokes on you? Why do you think I was always inviting you out for drinks after work? Why was I so keen to give you a lift?'

'But you said we're just mates.'

'When we were in the car, you mean?'

I nod and he sighs. 'Think about it, Ivy. You practically leapt away from me because you thought I was going to kiss you. I wasn't, as it happens, but it wasn't nice knowing that's how you felt about me.'

'I'm sorry. I don't know why I did that.' Part of me does know, though. The way Tom leaned over me reminded me of how Merlin tried to kiss Moronoe in the glass tower. I was

279

remembering my previous life without realising it. If I'm honest, I'm not sure how I would have reacted if Tom *had* tried to kiss me. I wasn't ready then, and perhaps deep down he knew that.

'Tom, you know I'm not the best at talking about my feelings, but I want you to know you mean a lot to me. I'm not sure what happened with those other girls, but I'm not going to change my mind.' I pause, wishing this was easier. 'Sorry, I'm rubbish at this.'

He smiles gently, his voice reassuring. 'You're doing fine.'

'I don't really have crushes, it's not my thing. I just know that you make me laugh and I feel good when I'm with you. When you're around everything feels better. I want to be with you all the time and . . .'

'Steady on, Shorty, you'll give me a big head.' He pushes himself up to his feet with a smile and it feels like an invitation. I stand close to him, my neck craning upwards. His eyes look into mine and I hear his voice, despite his lips not moving.

I'm a terrible kisser. You won't like it.

A tiny laugh escapes me. 'There's only one way to find out.'

He steps back, a look of confused alarm on his face. I expect him to ask me what just happened, but he shakes his head as if he's imagining things. Placing his hands on my shoulders, he gives me an awkward smile. After everything we've been through, maybe now isn't the time to be thinking about kissing me anyway.

A flash of light makes me turn my head. Morgan is standing on the metal platform, holding Merlin's sceptre. She thrusts it into the portal and the red vapour turns white and pulls apart to reveal a forest of treetops. In the centre is a gleaming glass palace with a tower at one end. The witches cackle with joy and an unfamiliar emotion tugs at my breastbone. A sense of belonging blooms inside me and I know that I'm feeling what my sisters feel – their relief and happiness is so strong, my heart could burst. This is how it feels to be going home.

Morgan gestures for me to join her. I squeeze Tom's hand, then climb up onto the platform. She moves the sceptre to one side and I find myself looking directly into the glass tower. My mother stands inside a cage. She's alive – and so close, I could almost reach out and touch her.

Morgan lets out a shaky breath and wipes away a tear, as if she's sharing my emotion. She smiles at me and I see a world of love in her eyes that goes beyond time itself. She nods, then dives head first into the portal. I lean forward and watch in wonder as her magnificent wings open wide. She soars above the treetops for a moment and then disappears from sight.

Several of the others climb up, each of them hugging me before they go through, and then Glitonea clasps me to her, followed by Mazoe. Thiten climbs up last. She kisses me on the cheek and jumps before I can say a word. I watch her fly, thankful that she's my sister. Once they've all gone through, Tom comes over.

Standing on the platform, I find that I'm higher than him for once. I rest my arm on his head and smile. 'You know, I quite like being taller than you.'

'Don't get any ideas, Shorty.' He steps close and holds me around my waist. 'I guess you have to go.'

I nod and he smiles shyly. 'I feel like this is the part where I should kiss you. I didn't imagine you'd be taller than me when it happened, or have wings, but . . .'

I lower my head and kiss him gently on the mouth, liking it more than he can know.

He grins at me. 'Anything to shut me up, eh? And for the record, I want to be with you all the time too. Wait – you are coming back, aren't you?'

I thump him on the arm. 'Of course, you idiot.' I don't know what the future holds, but I can't imagine it not including him.

He flicks his hair and grins. 'OK. I'll save you some cake.'

'Please don't.'

He laughs and starts to say something else, but I plant another kiss on his mouth. I don't want our conversation to end. I don't want this to be goodbye.

'Tell me when I return, OK?' I whisper.

He glances nervously at the portal then nods, his eyes full of hope.

'I'll be back soon, I promise.'

With that, I hold my breath and jump. The wind rushes through my hair and a smile spreads across my face as I open my wings and fly.

THE END

Acknowledgements

Firstly, a big thank you to the fantastic team at Hot Key Books, especially Georgia Murray – I couldn't have asked for a better editor. Thanks also to my agent, Amber Caraveo, for giving me feedback on my many story ideas and always pushing me to do better.

I owe a huge debt of gratitude to the many beta readers who read early versions of this book. There are too many to name here, but each one gave me incredibly helpful feedback that helped to shape the finished story. Thanks also to the lovely team at Write Magic for the writing sprints and various author friends and groups (with a special shout-out to Paul B. in Brighton, whose quick wit inspired a number of conversations in the story).

Thanks to my mum, Leoni, who has read countless drafts of my work over the years and who has shown me endless encouragement, and to my partner, Andy, and son, Alfie – your love and support mean the world to me.

About the Author

Rachel Burge works as a freelance feature writer and has written for a variety of websites, including BBC Worldwide, Cosmo and MTV. She lives in East Sussex with her partner and son.

@RachelABurge
Rachel.Burge.98
rachelburgewriter
https://rachelburge.co.uk

Also by Rachel Burge

'A creepy and evocative fantasy'
Sunday Times

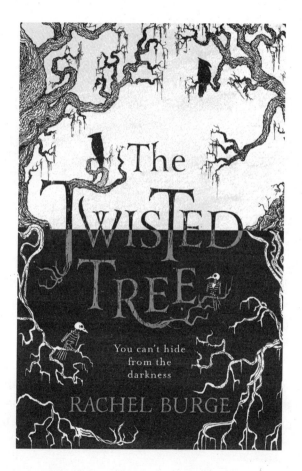

Read on for an extract . . .

MARTHA — 24 JANUARY

*I*t started the day I fell from the tree at Mormor's cabin in Norway. The day I became blind in one eye.

I'm going to write it all down here, no matter how crazy it makes me sound. If I have a daughter one day, she deserves to know the truth –

The truth.

Why couldn't Mum have just told me? The thought is like a knot in my brain, and the more I pick, the tighter it gets. If I had known, I could have done something and no one would have died. If she had told me, the horror of these past few days might never have happened.

THE STAIN OF A SOUL

My stomach shrinks to a hard ball as we pull into Heathrow. The platform is heaving with people. Holding my rucksack in front of me, I grit my teeth and push my way through the crowd. As people brush past me I get flashes of their lives – their memories and emotions – but it happens so fast I can't make sense of it.

My hands are sweaty as I pull my phone from my pocket. I check the time, then wish I hadn't. Last check-in is in fifteen minutes. I *can't* miss this flight.

A train pulls into the platform opposite and dozens of passengers spill out. Worried their clothes will touch me, I veer left and head for the escalator. A man passes me, coming up the other way, and for a horrible moment I think it's Dad, but it's just some other grey businessman.

Inside the departure hall people rush around me, dragging reluctant suitcases and even more reluctant children. The noise is like a swarm of bees, all wanting to sting me. It's not just the hubbub of conversation. The air sparks and crackles – it's like their clothes *know* I'm here, walking among them.

A wet-faced toddler wobbles in my direction, hands outstretched, closely followed by a tired-looking woman. I swerve but not quickly enough to avoid her brushing my arm. The woman had five miscarriages before she had her daughter. She's pregnant again but lies awake at night, terrified she might lose this baby too. My chest aches with emptiness, her loss so sharp it makes me catch my breath. I walk away, then glance back at her red coat. I've been through Mum's wardrobe enough times in the past few months to know it must be at least fifty-per-cent cashmere. Wool holds a person's emotions but cashmere is different – it makes you feel them.

Spotting the familiar sign for Scandinavian Airlines, I head towards the check-in desk, then stumble over a suitcase and nearly go flying.

'Hey! Watch it!' a man snaps.

'Sorry. I didn't see. Sorry,' I mumble.

'It might help if you took off your sunglasses!'

I join the back of the queue, my face burning with embarrassment. Being blind in one eye messes with your depth perception. I can't work out distances; when

4

I focus on something in the foreground it makes stuff in the distance go blurry. It wasn't a problem at home because I know where everything is, but now . . . if I can't even make it across the airport without falling over, how am I going to make it to Norway?

I hold the silver charm around my neck and tell myself to get it together. I've done the journey with Mum lots of times, and I had no problem travelling around London by myself before the accident. I just need to focus.

There are two families ahead of me; if they're quick maybe I can still make my flight. I rummage through my bag and pull out my printed e-ticket and ferry pass to Skjebne. You pronounce it *Sheb-na* – heavy on the Shh, which is kind of fitting, as it turns out. We used to spend every summer there – Dad too before he left us – but since the accident Mum refuses to talk about the island or Mormor, my grandma.

'Next customer, please.'

I step forward and lay my passport and e-ticket on the desk.

'Where are you travelling to today, miss?'

'Bodø. Well, Skjebne, actually. But I have to change flights at Oslo and then get the ferry from Bodø. And it's Martha Hopkins. My name, that is.' My face reddens. I sound like such an idiot.

As I put my rucksack on the scales, the woman behind the desk leans over and whispers to her colleague before turning back to me. I stare at my feet, convinced she can tell I'm a runaway just by looking at me.

5

'Can you remove your sunglasses, please?'

My voice is as shaky as my legs. 'Why? Is there a problem?'

'I need to verify you're the person shown in the passport photo.' She glances behind me. 'Travelling alone? No parent or guardian?'

'No, but I'm seventeen and your website said –'

'The picture in this passport shows a much younger child.'

I bite my thumbnail as she slides my passport across the desk, open at the page with my photo, as if I don't already know what it looks like. I glance at the image of the pale-faced girl with long blonde hair and quickly look away. I hate seeing pictures of me from before.

'I've always been small for my age,' I blurt, then instantly feel stupid.

She studies the photo and I clutch my necklace. Most of the jewellery I made after the accident was rubbish, yet this piece came out perfectly. The feel of its cool edges always calms me. I love metal; it tells me nothing.

I take a deep breath. 'Look, I'm actually late. So if you could –'

'Take off your glasses, miss.'

Somebody behind me tuts. I snatch off my shades and stare at the woman, or rather my right eye does. My left eye is looking who knows where. Her eyes widen, then flick down to my passport. 'Thank you. A last call was put out for your flight five minutes ago. You'll have to be quick. Gate 33 – up the escalator and to your left.'

I shove my glasses back on with a trembling hand and turn away, but not quick enough to avoid seeing her pity smile. I don't have to touch her clothes to know what she's thinking. Her thoughts are written all over her face: poor girl, how terrible, she would be pretty too, if it weren't for that. A patronising look and then she moves on, anxious to lay eyes on someone who doesn't look like a freak.

At the top of the escalator I go through security, where I have to take off my sunglasses and necklace again. Thankfully people are too busy patting their pockets for loose change that isn't there to notice my face. Once I'm through the metal detector, I snatch my stuff from the plastic tray, replace my shades and hurry to my boarding gate.

An air stewardess wearing a jaunty blue hat looks at my pass and shakes her head.

My heart lurches. 'Please. I *really* need to get this flight.'

She takes in my trainers. 'You can run?' I grin and she ushers me onto the connecting air bridge and we rush to the end. When we get to the plane I put my necklace on, grateful to feel its cool silence against my skin.

Everyone is seated, ready for take-off. I walk along the aisle, searching for my place. Boarding the plane was always the most exciting part of the journey when I was little. Now the thought of being crammed in a box with strangers makes me feel sick. I look at the people around me: a white fur coat bristling with outrage; a chunky knit heavy with sorrow. I can't tell what secrets they hold just by looking at them, but it's hard to stop my imagination sometimes.

I find my row and my heart sinks. There's a huge man next to the aisle, and my seat is by the window. Brian – according to the stretched name on his rugby shirt – is wearing earphones, and his eyes are closed.

'Excuse me, I need to get in.'

No response.

A flight attendant is heading this way, folding up tray tables and opening blinds with the determination of a trained assassin. I raise my voice, but Brian doesn't hear. The normal thing would be to touch his shoulder, but I don't want his rugby shirt to speak to me. Maybe I should prod his hand. In the end I pull down his tray table, bashing it against his knees. He jumps awake and grumbles, then stands to let me pass.

I smile a thank-you, then stash my coat and try to make myself as small as possible. Luckily my own clothes tell me nothing. I guess it's like the way you can't smell your own scent.

My phone bleeps: a message from Mum asking if I've arrived at Dad's. I text back straight away, then turn my phone to flight mode. My parents have barely spoken since the divorce; as long as I reply, there should be no reason for her to call Dad.

The plane speeds up and I feel myself pushed back into the seat as the ground rumbles beneath me.

Suddenly Brian's elbow nudges mine. An onslaught of facts washes over me – they come so fast and hard I can barely keep up with them. His mother would lock him in a room as a child. Some nights he dreams he's still there, crying for his mummy. My breath catches. Anger, fear, rejection. They come at me in waves.

I flinch, then rub my head and try to make sense of the jumbled impressions in my brain. His rugby top must be made of polyester. Man-made fibres don't breathe; they throw things at you like a sobbing toddler too distraught to come up for air.

The world tips away beneath me and my stomach turns. I close my eyes until I feel the plane level off. When I look out of the window there is nothing but pale empty blue. The light bouncing off the wing of the plane is brilliant white – too pure, almost.

I close my eyes and instantly I'm back in hospital: waking up to blackness. Just remembering the feel of the bandages on my face makes me shudder. Maybe it was the shock, but after I came round, I couldn't stop shivering. Mum draped her jacket around my shoulders and then . . . even now I can't explain. Something wrenched apart inside me, as if a gust of wind had banged a door open. I saw myself under the tree, my blonde hair caked with blood, and then I felt a rush of emotion: fear mixed with guilt and love. Feelings that I knew weren't mine.

At first I was convinced I must have imagined it – until it happened again. After the operation they weren't sure how much of my sight had been saved.

When the doctor unfurled the bandages from my eyes, his jacket sleeve brushed my cheek. As soon as the material touched me, I saw an image of a bearded man in a reflection on a hearse window, his face pale and drawn. The man's father had died and left everything to his new wife. My heart twisted with jealousy. I could almost taste the bitterness he felt. The doctor removed the last of my bandages and I blinked in disbelief – he was the man I had seen.

That night I lay awake, terrified I was losing my mind. I told myself I must have been hallucinating, even though deep down I knew it was real. The hospital psychiatrist came to see me, concerned how I was coping with my disfigured face, but I didn't tell him anything. If he knew I can tell a person's secrets just by touching their clothes, I wouldn't be on a plane right now. I'd be listening to the ramblings of a strait-jacket.

Brian takes out a book and cracks open the spine. Anyone who does that is not a good person as far as I'm concerned. It's up there with cruelty to kittens and nose-picking in public. Yet I can't help feeling sorry for him. If I touched his top again, maybe I could offer him some words of comfort. Something tells me his mother couldn't help the way she was. I'm sure lots of mental illnesses went undetected in previous generations; nowadays she would be given medication. Like Mum.

Thinking about Mum makes my head pound. I turn my shoulder to Brian and snap the blind shut. His life is none of my business, and besides, what can I say that will make a difference? The past will always haunt him. Pain like that stays with you; it seeps out of your pores and into the fibres of your clothes, and nothing can remove the stain of a soul.

HOT KEY BOOKS

Thank you for choosing a Hot Key book.

If you want to know more about our authors and what we publish, you can find us online.

You can start at our website

www.hotkeybooks.com

And you can also find us on:

We hope to see you soon!